The Opening

Susannah Ellis Wilds

Writers Club Press
San Jose · New York · Lincoln · Shanghai

The Opening
Copyright © 2000 by Susannah E. Wilds

This book may not be reproduced or distributed, in whole or in part, in print or by any other means without the written permission of the author.

ISBN: 0-595-09081-8

Published by Writers Club Press, an imprint of iUniverse.com, Inc.

For information address:
iUniverse.com, Inc.
620 North 48th Street
Suite 201
Lincoln, NE 68504-3467
www.iuniverse.com

URL: http://www.writersclub.com

The characters and events in this book are completely fictional. Although the book is partially set in Atlanta and several long established institutions are mentioned, their use and context are fictional and not intended to represent real persons or happenings.

Dedication

To all the loving friends who risk the clumsy feet and rough, well-meaning hands.

Epigraph

If you can keep your head while all about you
Are losing theirs and blaming it on you,
If you can trust yourself when all men doubt you,
But make allowance for their doubting too;
If you can wait and not be tired by waiting,
Or, being lied about, don't deal in lies,
Or being hated, don't give way to hating,
And yet don't look too good, nor talk too wise;

If you can dream—and not make dreams your master;
If you can think—and not make thoughts your aim,
If you can meet with Triumph and Disaster
And treat those two impostors just the same;
If you can bear to hear the truth you've spoken
Twisted by knaves to make a trap for fools,
Or watch the things you gave your life to broken,
And stoop and build them up with worn out tools;

If you can make one heap of all your winnings
And risk it on one turn of pitch-and-toss,
And lose, and start again at your beginnings
And never breathe a word about your loss;

The Opening

If you can force your heart and mind and sinew
To serve your turn long after they are gone,
And so hold on when there is nothing in you
Except the will that says to them: Hold on!

If you can talk with crowds and keep your virtue,
Or walk with Kings—nor lose the common touch,
If neither foes or loving friends can hurt you
And all men count with you, but none too much;
If you can fill the unforgiving minute
With sixty seconds worth of distance run,
Yours is the Earth and everything that's in it,
And—what is more—you'll be a man, my son!
— Rudyard Kipling, If

These clumsy feet, still in the mire,
Go crushing blossoms without end,
These hard, well-meaning hands we thrust
Among the heartstrings of a friend.—Edward Rowland Sill, The Fool's Prayer

Acknowledgements

Thank you to all who shared their memories of the fifties and sixties. And to Tom, who lets me be me.

Part I

Ashbeen

June 22nd 1961, The Prediction

It had rained for six straight days. The sky was nickel gray, bruised with thunderheads, and crying inconsolably. Lucy Jones and Becca McCollough were simply bored to tears. They usually spent every afternoon at the YMCA pool. Lucy's daddy took them and Becca's mama picked them up. But not in this downpour. Some folks said it was all those rockets the government was sending into space that was messing up the weather.

Becca was a tall, slender girl with a natural swimmer's body, sleek without much up top. Lucy was small and wiry, a perfect diver, as at home in the water as a seal. Both girls had short cropped hair, Becca's so black it was almost blue, and Lucy's a dirty blond that in the summer sun bleached to light gold. This summer they were fifteen, waiting on the brink.

"I hate waiting, I hate rain, and I hate my hair," Lucy wailed dramatically and flopped on Becca's bed.

"I hate rain, I hate my height, and I despise waiting," Becca echoed and dropped beside her. "What are we gonna do? I think I'll start screaming if I can't get out soon."

Just outside Becca's door a falsetto chirp mimicked, "I hate my hair, I hate my boobs, I hate my—"

"Go away, Tim," Becca shrieked, flinging a Little Debbie at him. The cake hit Ricky Nelson squarely in the middle of the poster tacked to the back of the door. "Mother! Tim is bothering us again. He's making me crazy."

Becca's mother, a slim, easy-going woman, who let Lucy call her Mary, poked her head in the door. Her hand lifted the arm of the 45 record player and Bobby Vee's *Tell him, he's the w-un-ne* fell out of the air.

"Well, you all are driving me crazy. Can't you think of anything to do but whine. Put on some quiet music, tell stories, read a book, count your blessings—but do it quietly. Please!" Six days of rain in the middle of June were wearing her patience thin.

Lucy picked up a *Seventeen* and thumbed through the same pages she had thumbed through seventy-seven times already. Becca sighed and stared at a full page spread of *Breakfast at Tiffany's* in her *Screen Play*.

"Lucy, do you think I look like Audrey Hepburn? Bobbie Jean says I do."

"She's skinnier and her nose is bigger," Lucy offered in a bored tone. Then she sat up insisting, "Becca, look at this." She shoved her magazine at her best friend pointing to a feature entitled "Cast Your Fate." In gushing prose, the article described the fun of forecasting the future for the gang of smiling, bubbly girls whose photos illustrated the piece.

"Let's do it. We can write it down about everybody and seal it away to be read years and years from now."

Becca made a face that said, "No way."

"Go get some of your mom's good writing paper," Lucy commanded.

Reluctantly, Becca tossed aside her movie magazine and went to find the paper. It didn't sound like so much fun to her. She returned with a pale pink envelope and one very small sheet of stationary that was blank on

June 22nd 1961, The Prediction

one side and printed with a spray of gold roses on the other. Just as she had expected, Lucy said, "You write. I'll dictate."

Sighing audibly and frowning slightly, Becca sank down at her maple student's desk and picked up the lavender pen. Lucy paced the shag carpet between the door and the closet and composed, while Becca scribbled down as much as she could in an abbreviated notation.

"June 22, 1961. The following are the future thoughts of Louisiana Hartness Jones, recorded by Rebecca Marie McCollough. Bobbie Jean Harris—

"Not so fast." Becca complained.

Infinitesimally, Lucy slowed her dictation. She finished the prediction for Bobbie Jean and tossed out one for Becca that included a ladies' man and a modern apartment.

"What! I don't want an apartment or a ladies' man."

"Write, just write!" Lucy ordered and continued dictating. "Millie Sonders will marry a local merchant and have a large family, definitely an older son. She'll have lots of church activities."

"I could have predicted that."

"Well, some things never change."

"Wallace Anne Anderson will be a secretary—

"She'll kill you for saying that," Becca warned.

Lucy waved off the objection, finished Wallee's prediction, and started one for herself.

"How do you spell *correspondent*?" Becca asked.

"How do I know. Just guess," Lucy replied. "Sally Blackwelder marries a doctor or a—"

The beep of a car horn interrupted her thought. "That's my dad. Hurry up, I've gotta go now. Just do the envelope. I'll finish Sally in the car. Just write: Open only in the presence of Lucy Jones and Becca McCollough on June 22, 1976."

"Lucy, your dad's here," Mary called.

Becca scribbled the message on the envelope and added in large capitals: *DO NOT OPEN.*

Stuffing the note paper and the envelope in her *Seventeen*, hugging her friend, and waving to Mary, Lucy dashed out of the house into the pouring rain and climbed into her daddy's Ford woody wagon.

1

Louisiana Hartness Jones, "Lucy"

*"If you can dream...and not make dreams your master;
If you can think...and not make thoughts your aim..."*
The Laurels, Ashbeen High School Annual, Class of '64.

Louisiana was my father's great-aunt's name. Thank God, they didn't name me Tempy or Temperance for his other aunt. It wasn't the name my mother wanted, but I like it. I don't get other people's mail or credit history.

I'm at loose ends these days having retired early two years ago. Mama had a stroke in November, and that's when I found the prediction that Becca and I had written that rainy summer afternoon so long ago. Buried in the mounds of things that mothers keep was that pale pink envelope, its designated date to be opened forgotten for over 20 years. I have not seen Becca in almost 15 years.

Most days I paint a little, play golf, or swim in the lake. Since I started swimming again, I also dream of flying. Wonderful dreams of sailing above the trees and circling over the world below, swimming in the air. I dreamed of flying when I was a kid, and I always wanted to fly for real.

When Walt Disney released *Peter Pan*, my friends and I spent weeks jumping out of trees and off the picnic table in the back yard, dusting ourselves with sand, flower petals, sugar—anything that might be that magic mix of pixie dust. But we never found it.

About the same time I started swimming lessons at Girl Scout camp, I began to fly in my dreams. It wasn't just the point of view, the ability to see down on the world, that made these dreams so amazing. It was the sensation of lifting and the feeling of air moving over my body, my hair floating around me. The almost-sick-but-more-like-giddy reaction deep in the pit of my stomach as my feet left the ground. And maybe, most of all, the safety of being above it all, out of reach.

I had never expected to reclaim those extraordinary sensations of childhood. And when I did, it was over a year before I began to dream of carrying someone else and fighting the extra weight and the fear of crashing, the dizzying swirls to earth at a speed I could not control, the rushing air flattening the skin against my bones and the pressure deafening my ears, while the rocks loomed larger and larger, until we hit and rolled.

Stu thinks it's because of the dog that I'm having these nightmares. Stuart is my husband, and maybe he's right. The dog is Annie, my neighbor's part golden retriever, who thought she lived at my house. She went wherever I went, including into the water. At least she used to. I don't swim with her any more. Last summer I took her too far out, and Annie nearly drowned me.

We had started out as always, playing in the water near the shore with me floating or diving under, and then popping up and calling to her. Me cooing, "Good Annie, come on girl. Swim to me. That's a girl. That's a good girl. Such a good dog she is." Annie smiling her doggy smile and wagging her tail. Woofing and waggling in agreement.

Then we'd both swim over to the dock across the cove. Just a short hundred yards or so. That's where she usually stopped, got out, shook off, and barked at a smaller, fenced dog. Showing off dog style. I'd pull out for

Louisiana Hartness Jones, "Lucy"

the islands where the power lines march across the lake a mile or so out, while she'd run back home the longer way around the cove.

But not this time. This time she followed me. I realized she was still there about a quarter of the way out, but I thought she was doing just fine, paddling along behind me. I thought about how we could stop and rest on one of the islands before starting back. We were fine, just two playmates. Until I felt the scrape of her claws on my back. Even then I just assumed she had accidentally gotten too close to me, and that I'd been hit by her dog-paddle stroke. So I pulled a little to the right and called to her, "Annie? Puppy?"

I had started to turn toward her when I felt both front paws on my shoulders. She was pushing me under. Panic struck both of us. The shore was almost a half a mile away, and I had never pulled a dog to safety. A dog who was holding me under as she tried to climb on. The claws of her right front paw opened a deep scratch on the left side of my face and, almost simultaneously, her hind legs hit me in the stomach. Involuntarily I swallowed and exhaled. The breath escaped me and water filled my throat and nose. The terror mainlined the adrenaline as I fought for the surface.

A convulsion of water and spittle and mucus exploded from my nose and mouth, and I gagged and nearly vomited before I could finally take in a breath of air. The funky scent of wet dog came with it. I couldn't see her, just smell her. I turned in a close, frantic circle. She was circling too, looking for me. And her eyes. Oh God, her eyes. Those deep brown, doggy eyes were rimmed with white and searching crazily. She saw me. I reached out and tried to touch her, pat her, calm her down.

"It's okay Annie, okay baby, okay." A mistake. Her foreleg hit my arm, her claws ripped my suit. She was beyond calming, she was desperate, and I was losing it too.

Her heavy, wet fur reminded me of the lifeguard drills I used to hate. Jump in fully clothed. Disrobe and make flotation devices by trapping air in the arms of your shirt and the legs of your jeans. Unless your jeans entangled your legs so you couldn't kick, couldn't get your head above the choking water. Water that burned. Enflaming your throat when you swallowed it instead of the coveted, precious, life-giving air. Annie couldn't disrobe. Her long fur was saturated and pulling her down. She forgot she loved me. She forgot I fed her, played with her, bathed and brushed her. I was nothing but a support, a means of keeping her head above water, a device. She was going to drown me.

I plunged deeper, escaping her flailing legs, then rose to the surface and gasped. My cheek burned when the air hit the cut. I could hear her labored pants. Annie's warm dog breath was on my neck. My pounding heart seized in my chest as her claws scraped my back again. But this time I knew what I had to do. I took the deepest breath I could and dove as far below the surface as I could. Then, still under the water, I headed for shore never looking back. It was the longest swim I ever made, and Annie made it too. But it's never been the same between us. Something died that day.

The second rule of lifesaving: *Don't let the victim drown you.*
So, Stuart's theory is that Annie is responsible for the dreams. Maybe. But the extra passenger who sends me crashing to the ground isn't a dog. It's a person. I just don't know who. Anyway, it's time to open the prediction. I need to call Becca. I wonder where she is.

2
Lucy

There is a bond that lies
As lightly on the spirit as gossamer.
It floats unfettered in the air,
And yet, when plucked,
Draws us in to bind the goblin
With silk from our own souls.
                    Lucy Jones

Becca and I didn't meet until high school, but Bobbie Jean, Sally and I were pals in first grade. The first time I saw Bobbie Jean, she had a broken arm and a ponytail. I was very impressed. Even then you could tell she was going to be beautiful. Her blond hair had a touch of red gold, and her eyes were sea blue-green. She also had golden freckles, like she'd been dusted with pixie dust. She sat behind me in Mrs. Harper's class and was too shy to speak the first week. Sally was in Mrs. Alexander's class.

I think we met because we were all blondes of a sort. As blondes we qualified to be angels in the Christmas play. This, we were told, was a great honor and an occasion of great, solemn dignity, despite the itchy tinsel halos. Sally was already taller than anyone else, and she was to stand behind Mary and Joseph with her arms spread out as if to protect the little family. Bobbie Jean and I were to kneel on either side, our praying hands a little below our bowed heads.

"Mama," I asked when she was tucking me into bed on the night before our big debut, "what do angels do?"

"Well, let me see now. Some are messengers, like the angel God sent to Mary, and some are in the heavenly choir, but most, I guess, are guardian angels." She tucked a loose bit of hair back into the pin curl from which it had escaped. "They just look after us. Now say your prayers and go to sleep, sugar. You've got a big day tomorrow."

"Do I have a guardian angel, Mama?"

"Sure you do, baby," she smiled and kissed my forehead.

"Tell me about the wings. Tell me about how, when the little babies are born, God cuts off their wings."

"God takes their wings off so they can't fly away from their mamas," she answered as she had so many times before, smiling and walking her fingers up my shoulder and over my back to where the pointy little bones of my shoulder blades protruded. "And right here is where they used to be, when you were an angel."

On the morning of the play, I was so excited I forgot to change my red shortie pajama bottoms for panties. As the three of us were getting into our white angel robes, Sally pointed out that my red p.j.'s showed through. Her face told me this altogether ruined the heavenly effect.

"Well, just go without them," Bobbie Jean suggested.

"She can't do that. She's an angel," the horrified Sally declared.

"I bet real angels don't wear underwear." I was beginning to like the idea.

"Of course they do. Else you could see right up their dresses when they fly," reasoned Sally.

"Then how do they fly so nobody sees their panties?"

Lucy

Letting someone see your panties was almost as bad as letting someone see your bare tush. This I knew, because I was often reprimanded for hanging by my knees on the swing set. My metaphysical puzzle stumped Sally long enough for me to step out of my pajama bottoms, the decision made.

"We won't tell," Bobbie Jean whispered to me as we ran out on stage to take our places of adoration. She smiled the most divine smile throughout the thirty minute program, an angel with a secret. Afterward our mamas praised us. How still we had been. How sweet. Such perfect, little angels.

In second grade Bobbie Jean, Sally, and I became Brownie Scouts. Our mothers were the leaders of Troop 47. I still have the photo of us in our Brownie uniforms and beanies. Sally the tallest one in the middle of the back row. Bobbie Jean in pigtails grinning beside me. And me. The skinny waif with scraped knees. We went to camp together that summer. I remember proudly wearing one pair of socks the whole two weeks to save Roxanne on laundry. They stood up all by themselves by the time we went home. I learned to swim that summer, but I don't recall any dreams of flying. Perhaps swimming was still too much of an effort then.

As we grew older, Bobbie Jean's hair became more golden red. Sally's stayed blond but fine and wispy. Mine just got mousy. I knew that blond was better. There was Marilyn Monroe and Grace Kelley. Didn't Mama like Grace Kelley better than anyone else in the movies? And Daddy had that calendar of Marilyn Monroe. Of course, she wasn't worried about anyone seeing up her dress. Obviously, I had done something very bad to be turning mousy brown. When I was small and blond, I was Mama's little doll. She dressed me up in fancy dresses, shiny shoes. By third grade, I was convinced she didn't love me any more, and that nobody else thought I'd make a very good angel either.

In third grade Bobbie Jean, Sally, and I were in Miss McGrady's class. Up until then our teachers had been gentle, motherly women. Miss McGrady thought it was her duty to introduce us to the real world.

We had money making projects. We made candles out of wax and the nubs of our crayons. These were sold at the Fall Fair to make money for new art supplies, but the main project involved saving newspapers to be purchased by the local florist for a penny a pound. Each Monday we brought in a week's worth of papers and rolled them into big logs tied up with string or rubber bands. On the afternoon of the last Tuesday in the month, we loaded the rolls into two wagons and took turns pulling them the three blocks to the florist. Until then the logs were stacked at the back of the classroom beneath the windows. Under no circumstance were we children to fool around with the newspapers.

One afternoon the temptation became too great. Little Mary Fowler lifted one of the rolls from the pile while Miss McGrady was out of the room. Much to her surprise she couldn't get it back. The whole pile was in danger of collapsing around her. Sally and I answered her call for help without a thought. After all, Sally was tall enough to reach the top, and we had been taught to help those in need. We each took one end and lifted the roll back onto the top of the pile just as Miss McGrady came back into the room. Sally and I were caught red handed. Mary was just standing there looking at us. As Miss McGrady's wrath descended, Mary denied everything.

"Sally Blackwelder, I'm surprised at you. What were you girls up to?"

"Miss McGrady, we're just trying to help Mary get the roll back on the pile," Sally said, her voice already tearing up.

"I didn't do anything, Miss McGrady," Mary smiled sweetly. "Lucy knocked the roll down and Sally came to help her put it back. I saw the whole thing."

"That's not true!" I cried. "Mary took it down. We just came to help."

Mary backed away from me like I'd been possessed by the devil himself and said sadly, "Lucy, I forgive you. I hope God will."

Lucy

Miss McGrady grabbed Sally and me by the shoulders and pushed us into the hall. Then with our backs against the wall she half whispered, half hissed, "Mary Fowler is the Reverend Fowler's child, and I know in my heart she wouldn't lie to me. You girls always stick up for each other. Well, this time you can both just sit out here and ask the Good Lord to forgive you. When you're ready to tell the truth, you can come in and apologize to Mary and me and the whole class."

With that she pushed us down to sit on the floor and went back in the classroom shutting the door behind her. Sally started to sob. She never got in trouble, never caused a fuss. I was stunned. What about fair? What about *One good turn deserves another*? What about *Do unto others…*? What about *Innocent until proven guilty*?

"Don't cry Sally. She's just plain mean. God knows we didn't do it."

Sally sobbed louder, hanging her head. I patted her hand awkwardly. Just then the door opened a crack, and Bobbie Jean joined us on the floor.

"I told Miss McGrady that Mary lied," Bobbie Jean whispered. She put her arm around Sally and tried to smile at me. "I don't think she believes us, and nobody else saw what happened or will say they saw." We spent the rest of the afternoon sitting on the floor in the hall. Sally sobbing, Bobbie Jean comforting, and me pondering the mysteries of adult justice.

"Do you think Miss McGrady will burn in hell for not being fair?" I asked. Sally hiccupped, shook her head in agreement, and gave a great, wet gulp. Bobbie Jean patted her arm and shot me a look that said, "Shut up."

"Do you think Mary Fowler's tongue will swell up and turn black and choke her, because she lied?" Bobbie Jean tried to suppress a grin, but Sally looked appalled, so I shut up. After everyone else had gone home, Miss McGrady lined us up in front of her.

She put her hand under Sally's chin and raised her sinking head. Then she said as sweetly as Miss McGrady could, "Sally Blackwelder, you are a good child and I know you were just trying to help your friend, Lucy. But it's wrong to tell a lie, even for a friend." She patted Sally's shoulder. "Get your things and go. I won't say anymore to you this time."

Then she turned to me. With the fire of the righteous in her eyes and voice, she chided me. "Lucy Jones, you know this is all your fault. I hope you feel very bad getting your friends into trouble like this. You will sit alone in the back of the class for a week. You are not to talk to anyone in class or on the playground until next Monday. Do you understand?" I nodded, miserable and confused.

Finally it was Bobbie Jean's turn and, while the tone was still firm, it was more reasoning. "Bobbie Jean Harris, I hope you reconsider who your friends are. Lying is never right and telling lies for friends will only get you in trouble. You will not talk to Lucy this week or play with her or sit near her at lunch. Do you understand?" Bobbie Jean nodded. But she waited for me just beyond the playground steps, and we walked home together.

I served my time in the back of the class talking to no one. I read a book alone under a tree at recess. The book was *Les Miserables*. I selected it because I thought the title was *Less Miserable*. It was in the sixth grade section, however Mrs. Isenhower, the librarian, liked me and had been giving me harder books since second grade. At lunch time, I went home to eat in the kitchen with Roxanne, our maid.

"Roxanne, do you think Miss McGrady will ever know we didn't do it?" I asked over my peanut butter and banana sandwich.

"No, honey, I don't reckon that's very likely."

The clean smell of new laundry mixed with peanut butter and bananas was sort of warm and comforting. Roxanne hung up one of my daddy's shirts and bent down to pull out yet another from the pile of clothes. Her old stockings were rolled at her knees, and her blue flowered housedress was pressed and neat. Her children were all grown. Except for Alfred, her youngest. He'd been killed in a liquor store holdup when he was seventeen.

"But that's not fair, Roxanne, is it?"

"Not fair at all, I'd say."

"Then the world is not really a fair place, is it, Roxanne?"

She put her iron down and looked at me. "No honey, it sure ain't. And the sooner you knows and accepts that the better off you gonna be. Don't expect too much from this old world, or you be mighty disappointed."

Bobbie Jean and Sally abided by Miss Grady's rule and didn't talk to me at school that week, yet every afternoon they were there to meet me on the steps from the playground, just as usual. We never talked about it again. We had learned that the world was not fair. And we had learned that there was something better than fair, there were friends.

My trials with Miss McGrady were not over. She sent notes home to my mother telling her I smelled bad. Maybe I did. I was a tomboy, a bully, and generally not a lady, she said. I bit my nails and pulled at my hair. I had opinions on everything and wasn't afraid to voice them. I had the effrontery to ask her questions about where babies came from in front of the whole class. My parents bought me two hens and a rooster and hoped I'd figure it out. I was definitely not angel material.

On the last day of school in Miss McGrady's class, we were all going to walk to the drug store a few blocks away for an end of the year party. Anywhere we went outside the school grounds, we went in two lines of buddies. Bobbie Jean and Sally were buddies right behind me and Douglas Jennings. In a long, double line we started out up Wilton Avenue and over to Falcon.

Tommy Lowder was walking in front of me. Every few feet he turned around and said, "Have a drink. Have a drink." He'd raise his arm in a toast as he said this. Bobbie Jean and Sally giggled. Douglas Jennings stumbled and looked at his feet.

"Watch where you're going, Tommy," I ordered after nearly running into him.

"Have a drink, have a drink," he replied, very pleased with himself.

I stopped and Sally ran into me. "Tommy, cut it out!" I commanded.

"Have a drink," he saluted with a grin. I kicked him. Someone told. Miss McGrady was on my case, but this time there were lots of witnesses.

"Tommy," Miss McGrady said, "apologize to Lucy, please."

"Why? She kicked me!"

"Tommy, men must always apologize to women, even if it isn't their fault," Miss McGrady explained. Later I learned from my husband that every well brought up man in America was trained in third grade to accept that everything is his fault. According to him, the sooner they accept this the better they can get along with the opposite sex.

When we became Brownie Scouts, we went through a whimsical little ceremony that involved closing our eyes, spinning around three times, and peering in a mirror decorated with leaves and flowers while reciting:

Twist me and turn me and show me an elf,
I look in the water and see myself.

And, presto, we were Brownies. But when we became full fledged Girl Scouts, the ceremony was much more serious. It was called the Brownie Scout fly-up because this was the time when a Brownie Scout earned her Brownie wings, the simple gold patch worn by Girl Scouts one inch below the troop crest. Once we reached this status, we could use the three-fingered salute, recite the Girl Scout Promise and Laws, and earn badges.

That summer at camp I began to dream of flying. By day I swam in the cool, green water of the lake at Camp Russell. At night I climbed into the upper bunk above Sally and toe to toe with Bobbie Jean and dreamed. I can still remember that first flight. I can run the memory like an old reel of film.

She is standing on a gentle rise. A skinny little thing in a white cotton gown. It is night, but the night of a dream world, suffused with a glow like moonlight heated over a flame until it is more gold than silver and slightly tarnished at the edges. She lifts her arms and her feet rise off the ground. It is not an unfamiliar sensation, rather like pushing off the bottom of the lake and rising slowly, slowly to the surface. Her arms move in something between a breaststroke and a flap. And when they do, she rises still higher.

Lucy

In those early dreams I needed to flap a little to gain altitude or move about. I think the stroke-flapping gave me the security of having physical control over the flight. Later it was only necessary to spread out my arms and I'd soar.

Over a wall she lifts. Pausing for a moment to catch an excited breath, she's drifting slowly upward. Then she flaps again and rises above the tree tops. She moves her arms as if she's parting a curtain, and she's no longer drifting upward. She's floating, suspended in the air, her body inclined more in parallel with the earth. The tops of trees brush her toes, and she can hear the air they breathe sighing in their leaves. It stirs the fabric of her gown and runs in little whiffs over her legs tickling the backs of her knees. The cool night sky is slightly damp on her face. She strokes upward and goes higher. The lights from the town below are larger than the house lights or streetlights seen from an airplane. They glow warmly and are hallooed by a paler, ghostly aura. They cast no shadows. She isn't afraid. She's enchanted.

She tries a turn, pulling harder with the right arm than the left. It works. But now she is also in a more upright position. She kicks a flutter kick and her feet rise. Then, without thinking, she dives, and just before touching the trees, with one strong stroke, she reverses course, body and spirit flying like a dancer cut free from the bounds earth. As she rolls onto her back the stars come into view. Like the lights below they are larger than waking stars, dancing slightly, silvery, beckoning.

She floats there between the stars above and the tree tops below. How high can she go? A shiver passed over her. These gesturing stars look exotic, slightly menacing and dangerous, as if they could lure her too far out. She can almost hear them call, promising something she doesn't understand. Then, like a startled fish, that's come too close to the surface, she shoots away from this enticement and moves closer to the earth seeking the shelter of the shade.

Could I fly among the trees? Did I have that much control, that much agility, to weave in and out, over and between the branches? Could I swoop right down and touch a flower?

She pulls her arms to her sides and lets herself drop feet first. Just above the trees she flutter kicks. There, beyond her, is a gap in the tree tops, and she heads for it. Stroke-flapping slowly, she does a shallow dive into the gap. The ground rises toward her. The smells of night flowers—evening primrose and dames rocket—hang there. The air is closer. The sky is darker. She dodges a tall stand of purple martin houses, but one foot bumps a gourd and sets it swinging. The startled, nesting birds fly out in a whorl of beating wings. One passes beside her before veering away.

How did he see me, this unexpected and unwelcome nighttime visitor to this land of fantasies and figments. Did I appear like a spirit in his twilight world or something of more substance? If I could inhabit his realm, could he visit mine?

She is heading for a group of tall holly hawks when she hits the spider's web, and flailing against it, she tumbles. Going down, her bottom hits the ground in a dream bounce.

It didn't hurt but I woke up. For a moment I lay there. Was I still floating over the garden or was I lying on the ground? I brushed again at the offending threads of web, as if to brush away any bits of dream still clinging to me. Then I recognized the cabin and my bunk and the common moonlight on the pine trees beyond the window screen, and Bobbie Jean sleeping just beyond my toes. Kicking off the sheet, I climbed over the foot rails of our bunks.

"Bobbie Jean," I whispered, shaking her foot. "Bobbie Jean."

She half opened her eyes and smiled her slow, no-teeth smile at me.

"Bobbie Jean, I can fly!"

"I know you can," she whispered dreamily.

"Can you do it too?"

"No, just you. But I always knew you could."

"You knew? How could you know?" But she was already back in sleep.

The next summer she was with me when I fell out the tree and broke my arm. Bobbie Jean, I wonder how you are.

3

Sally Blackwelder, "Sally"

"If you can wait and not be tired by waiting, Or being lied about don't deal in lies,
Or being hated don't give way to hating, And yet don't look too good, nor talk too wise."
The Laurels, Ashbeen High School Annual, Class of '64

Sally was my grandmother's name. I wish they'd named me for my other grandmother, Jamame, whom everyone called "Mamie." She was a great beauty like Mama.

Lucy called today. She was looking for Becca. She mentioned getting us all together. This time it didn't sound like just something you say. Perhaps she really means it. I gave her email addresses for Bobbie Jean and myself. We've talked on the phone but not seen each other face to face in 30 years. Just what do you say to someone you spent 15 years growing up with but haven't seen for twice as long. Especially if most of your real growing up happened after you parted. What does Brownie Scouts have to do with nearly dying of cancer? Or playing with dolls to do with living with step-children? We're spread out all over the country now, if not all over the world, and probably have nothing in common.

I wonder if Lucy is as bossy as she used to be. Probably. And is Bobbie Jean as lovely? "Sally" reminds me of Sally Lunn Bread—not quite bread, not quite cake. That's me all right. Not quite pretty, not quite plain. And Becca. All I've heard about Becca are rumors of a glamorous life.

Lucy mentioned renting a place for a weekend. A lake or a spa. Any place except Ashbeen.

We grew up in Ashbeen and, as soon as we could, we left. Haven't been back, except to visit, or tie up the loose ends when our parents died.

Ashbeen was like so many small towns. There was a right side and a wrong side and something in the middle. We were in the middle. There were four big churches—Methodist, Baptist, Presbyterian, and Lutheran—and a modest synagogue and Catholic church. There were four elementary schools and one big high school. And when we were twelve, they built a new YMCA. Lucy and Bobbie Jean and I had known each other since first grade. Our mothers had shepherded us through Girl Scouts, ordered us to choir practice, and driven us to dancing school.

Our mothers were the leaders of Troop 47. My mama taught us the social graces—how to set a table, write a thank you note, make a proper introduction. Bobbie Jean's mama taught the homemaking skills—how to bake a cake, sew a hemstitch, make a bed with hospital corners. Mrs. Jones was in charge of the outdoor skills—the names of flowers and trees, the way to cut and arrange roses, how to identify the North Star and the constellations. Each in her own way was very Southern.

Ashbeen was also Southern. There was a statue of an angel holding a Confederate soldier in the middle of Main Street. Every year there was a campaign to move it, because the fire trucks had to slow down to get around it. Every year it stayed right where it was. There was a wonderful green place that was a military cemetery. It had been filled with the bodies of dead Yankee soldiers from the nearby Confederate prison. The prison had been a horrible place, where thousands died of starvation, dysentery, and typhoid, but the cemetery was cool, serene, and tranquil. It was a favorite picnic place for our Girl Scout troop. There was a lazy river flowing just north of town and a large golf course rolling out on the west.

Like most small Southern towns, Ashbeen was historic. When I was five, Ashbeen celebrated its bicentennial. For weeks the local newspaper printed a stream of rhetoric filled with civic pride and articles about how Ashbeen could have been the city that Atlanta was becoming. Ashbeen was older and, before The War, had had more railroads and more people. Of course, all that being older and bigger meant to Ashbeen was that there was more for Sherman to burn. Why, there are as many bodies lying out there in the cemetery as there are folks in Ashbeen today. And any fool can see that is nothing to be proud of.

But unlike most small towns, Ashbeen was twice an All America city. Before the 60's, it had been like a big green mother, softly wrapping her children in her leafy, warm embrace. We napped there, nurtured and groggy, not quite ready to face the real world. Lucy's mother had a colored maid, but none of us played or went to school with Negro children. Our mothers didn't work and Lucy's mother didn't even drive. Her daddy or my mama took her everywhere she couldn't walk. We didn't have after school or summer jobs, because our daddies could take care of us, as my father fondly reminded me. It wasn't so much that nothing bad ever happened then, we simply couldn't see it for the trees.

Oh, we felt small injustices. The ones I remember best are the ones I suffered, but my girl friends had their share too. Lucy wasn't allowed to enter the soapbox derby—boys only. I never got invited to a single dance. Becca's dad wouldn't buy her WeeJun's; he wasn't paying thirty dollars for a pair of loafers.

I was the poster child for the Good Girls, doing everything the way I was supposed to, whatever my mama said, threading my way carefully through an unwritten, moral etiquette. Unlike Lucy, who never seemed to believe anything any adult said. Or Bobbie Jean, who was so charming she didn't have to behave. The last time I remember being bad was the last time I remember feeling really pretty. It must have been in second grade. The Little Miss Sunbeam contest. Miss Sunbeam was the little girl pictured on the Sunbeam bread bag. She had blond curls, blue eyes, and rosy cheeks. She was smiling and eating a piece of bread. My mama said I looked just like Little Miss Sunbeam, and to prove it, she entered me in the look-alike contest.

Lucy and Bobbie Jean were entered too. So, there we were in identical blue and white checked dresses with white lace collars, white socks, and patent leather Mary Janes. Lucy's straight-as-a-stick blond hair was frizzed and crimped but not really curling. Bobbie Jean's was curling but too red for Miss Sunbeam. Kay Kittrell, who was in my first grade class, was also there, but at first I didn't recognize her. Her mama, who owned the Ashbeen Beauty School, had dyed her beautiful black hair blond for this contest. I was a shoo-in.

As we stood in line with twenty or so other little girls waiting to have our pictures made at Woolworth's Five and Ten, our mamas filled out the application forms. Name. Age. Height. Weight. Favorite Song.

"What's your favorite song, honey?" my mama asked. I thought a minute. I knew I should say "Jesus Loves Me," but I really liked "The Tennessee Waltz" best. I hesitated just another minute then I lied.

The cameraman gave us each a piece of bread to hold and brushed our cheeks with rogue. He set me up on a stool covered with a blue rug. I smiled when he told me to. "Smile, sugar. Say 'Whiskey'," he suggested.

I said, "Peanut." Everyone told me how pretty I was. Just like Little Miss Sunbeam. I won the local contest, but we never heard anything from the regionals. My picture was in the paper. Daddy called me his Miss Sunbeam for a week or two. But my conscience hurt so bad it was a long, long time before I told another lie. Lucy's favorite song was "Goodnight Irene," and Bobbie Jean's was "Do Your Ears Hang Low?" They both knew I loved "The Tennessee Waltz."

Sally Blackwelder, "Sally"

After we had our pictures made, our mamas took us to get ice cream. We loved the stools at the counter in Woolworth's. You could spin around and around until you were too dizzy to sit up. We sat at the counter in our Little Miss Sunbeam dresses and our extra pink cheeks licking our ice cream cones, while our mamas drank ice tea and ate chicken salad.

"Sally," Lucy whispered to me. "I've got to go to the bathroom. Come with me."

"Oh, Lucy, why didn't you go at home? I hate the bathroom here."

"I did, but I gotta go again. Bobbie Jean will come with us. Won't you, Bobbie Jean?" She nodded taking a last lick from her cone and dropping the rest in her mama's plate.

"Come on," Lucy said. We slid off our stools and head for the back of the store.

"Don't get lost girls," my mama called.

"We're just going to the bathroom, Mama."

Bobbie Jean took my hand. We walked decorously down the aisle paved with huge black and white tiles, while, ahead of us, Lucy hopped and skipped and ricocheted from counter to counter through this magic kingdom of glitz. Bright, gaudy scarves, cheap jewelry, too red lipsticks, plastic flowers, shiny kitchen spoons, goldfish in pink and blue bowls. Everything caught her eye.

"Hurry up, Lucy. I thought you had to go," I admonished, impatient to get this over with.

"All right, all right. I'm just looking. I'm not touching anything." She sighed and straightened out her route.

While we were waiting for her, Bobbie Jean slipped over to one of the water fountains and started to drink.

"Don't drink out of that one Bobbie Jean," I said in alarm.

"Why not?"

"That's the colored water."

"It doesn't look colored to me." She said with a puzzled face. "What color is it suppose to be?"

"It's for colored people," I explained pointing to the sign above the fountain.

"Oh, that's all right," she smiled. She drank anyway and so did I.

When Lucy came out of the bathroom, she was singing to herself, "…take a great notion just jump in a river and drown."

"Lucy," I said huffily, "that's an awful song."

Being raised Southern certainly had some strange charms.

4

Sally

I saw a swooping swallow and wished to fly away,
I saw a lazing loon and wished to drift all day,
I saw a sunning turtle and wished to sit and dream,
I saw a puff of cloud and wished to be more than I seem.
             Sally Blackwelder, 1958

When you grew up in a small town in the 50's and early 60's, you were pretty sheltered. Most of the four letter words in the movies today we had never heard. By the end of seventh grade, we knew we'd be leaving the elementary school we'd attended and be going to the high school. Bobbie Jean and Lucy were excited about meeting new people and going to dances. I wasn't so sure. We'd heard there were "gang" showers in the gym, showers with no doors. We'd be naked in front of every other girl.

Since we couldn't walk to school anymore, our parents were planning to car pool. One week for my mama, one for Bobbie Jean's mama, and one for Lucy's dad. Her mother didn't drive. We all thought this was pretty strange. We couldn't wait to drive. Lucy's mama was strange in other ways too. She didn't grocery shop like all the other mamas, or sew like Bobbie

Jean's, or play bridge like mine. Lucy's mama had a maid who cleaned the house and washed the clothes, but Lucy always looked kind of neglected. She spent a lot of time at Bobbie Jean's house or mine.

Our houses were a few blocks apart. Bobbie Jean lived close to the elementary school in a one-story white clapboard bungalow. Her grandmother lived with them, but Bobbie Jean had her own room between her parents' room and her grandmother's. It was a very girlish room, as lovingly bedecked with ribbons and ruffles as Bobbie Jean herself. In one corner there was a wonderful dressing table with a large round mirror that I thought was the most glamorous thing I'd ever seen. I can see them now posing and posturing in front of that mirror. Lucy vamping with lips pouting, hip shot, and her flat chest pushed out as far as it would go. Bobbie Jean batting her lashes and cooing in a Marilyn-like whisper, "Oo, Piggy, I just don't think a girl can have too many diamonds, do you?"

But we weren't confined to just Bobbie Jean's room when we played there. We would lie on the floor in her living room, watching the big black and white TV or playing endless games of Monopoly. Bobbie Jean's mama had very fair skin and hair, and she spoke with softly, slurring vowels in a very regional accent. I loved to hear her talk. She baked wonderful desserts and never did seem to mind having us around.

Lucy's house was behind Bobbie Jean's. It was red brick, and it had a brick wall on one side and an iron fence in front. The yard was densely crowded with plants and flowers, almost jungle-like, but the house was smaller than Bobbie Jean's with just two bedrooms, Lucy's and her parents'. Like the rest of the house, Lucy's room was full of antiques. There were two tall spool beds that required a stool to get in and a deep velvet Victorian couch covered with dolls. Madame Alexander dolls, bride dolls, a Shirley Temple doll, china dolls, and baby dolls. But Lucy really didn't like dolls. I don't remember spending much time in Lucy's room. Mrs. Jones seemed to like for us to stay outside on the porch and play with Lucy's baby dolls and not mess up her things. Like my mama, she had a lot of antiques and glass and china about. Mama said Lucy's mama was "used to being done for." That must have been true because we couldn't figure out much what she did all day. She was a small woman with beautiful, black hair and a tight smile.

Not only were four letter words prohibited at Lucy's house, conversational topics in general were deemed either appropriate or not appropriate for company or the dinner table. I have always tried to keep my sons from discussing their bodily functions at dinner, but Lucy's mama also prohibited many other topics such as politics, non-Christian religions, money, sex, race, tragic events, and nearly any criticism of anybody or anything. In spite of this, or maybe because of it, Lucy always seemed to have plenty to say on all these subjects. And her mama was always pursing her lips, raising her eyebrows, and suggesting, "Let's not talk about that now."

I have often thought that maybe Lucy's mama didn't so much neglect her, as simply give up on her. Poor woman, it wasn't an easy job. Rather like Blanche DuBois trying to raise Calamity Jane. A complete stranger could tell that Bobbie Jean was her mama's daughter. And most folks would pair up Mama and me, too. But no one could ever figure out how Lucy and her mama could be so different.

When we weren't at Bobbie Jean's, we were usually at my house, two blocks down and one over from Lucy's. Also white clapboard, it had two stories with the bedrooms upstairs. Mine had blue flowered walls, to match my eyes, my mama said. Although there was a formal living room and dining room, we spent most of our time in the smaller, cozier kitchen and den at the back of the house, because my mama wasn't the best of housekeepers.

She was, however, a talkative, friendly woman, who swept along everyone in her path. And since Lucy, Bobbie Jean, and I were frequently in her path, we were usually pulled along wherever she was going, and she was going all the time. She had very definite opinions about how things should be, and I was pulled along that path, too. She adored Bobbie Jean but always seemed worried about Lucy. Lucy was too thin, too bossy, too big a tomboy, and too smart for her own good.

Mama had a big, tan Packard. The three of us piled in the back seat, and Mama and Mrs. Jones rode up front. There was a small hole in the floor under the mats in the back. We loved to pull up the mats and watch the road stream by, occasionally dropping little things, like a penny or a peanut, through the hole just to see what would happen. On one particular afternoon, we were huddled on the floor of the back seat, supposedly watching the road, but actually whispering about Warren Gibson.

"Warren Gibson said the S-word in class today," Bobbie Jean confided.

"What word?" I asked.

"THE S-word," Bobbie Jean whispered.

"What's that?" Lucy and I said in unison.

"You know. The S-word. The really bad word. I can't believe he said it in class. I thought Mrs. Hamilton would die. I'm sure she heard him and just pretended not to."

"What S-word?" Lucy said. "Spell it."

"No way," Bobbie Jean said primly.

"Then what does it rhyme with?" Lucy demanded.

Bobbie Jean thought a minute and replied. " *Hit*. It rhymes with *hit*."

"S...hit, sh...it, " Lucy sounded. "Shit."

We froze. My mama was still talking away a mile a minute.

"Lucy," I whispered through my teeth. "You should never, never say that word. Whatever it means."

"What does it mean?" she wanted to know. Bobbie Jean grinned her no-teeth grin and shook her head. I shrugged my shoulders in "Beats me."

"Come on Bobbie Jean. You know. Tell us." Lucy pleaded.

"No. It's too awful."

"You know I'll make you tell sooner or later," Lucy threatened.

"No way."

"I bet there's a bug in here someplace," Lucy menaced, knowing Bobbie Jean's fear of bugs.

Sally

"Lucy, you wouldn't."

"Yes, I would. Now tell."

Bobbie Jean leaned in very close to Lucy's ear and whispered, "Do-do."

Lucy let out a shriek of laughter that couldn't help attracting my mama's attention. "Lucy Jones, what is so funny?"

"Nothing, Mrs. Blackwelder. Bobbie Jean is tickling me."

"Well, stop it this minute. And get back on the seat. Well behaved young ladies don't ride on the floor."

"Yes, ma'am," I replied.

For many years I thought that if I just did everything my mama said to do, that I'd be just what she wanted me to be. It took a lot of years to discover that that wasn't enough for either of us. I still cringe when one of my children says "shit." I think that's part of why they do it. Yesterday I heard the word on National Public Radio. Still, maybe our parents sheltered us too much. Lucy told me on her wedding night that she was fucking long before she knew what the word meant.

5

Roberta Jean Harris, "Bobbie Jean"

"If you can talk with crowds and keep your virtue,
Or walk with Kings – nor loose the common touch.
If neither foes nor loving friends can hurt you."
The Laurels, Ashbeen High School Class of '64

I was named for my daddy, Robert, and my mama, Jean. I've never really thought about whether I liked my name or not. It's just me.

Today I got an email from Lucy. She wants to catch up with everybody and maybe try to get us all together some weekend this summer. She didn't say anything to make me suspicious, but I wonder if I really want to see her again. Maybe I'd just like to remember her the way she was twenty years ago. Over the years we've exchanged Christmas cards with one line messages and pictures of her daughter. Sometimes she'd call from the airport when she was changing planes in our city. After my mother died, we lost track completely. I spend a lot of time out of the city, and

Lucy was never standing still. She said she's retired now. I wonder. Can a bird ever stop flying?

My grandmother, Gran Ma'am, lived with us when I was a child. She used to call Lucy "that little sparrow." That's what Lucy was—a nervous, scruffy, little bird. She liked Lucy. Lucy's trials with Miss McGrady, her stream of artless questions and endless curiosity, and her constant bumps and tumbles amused Gran Ma'am. My grandmother was very kind. She taught me a lot about seeing people as they are and as they could be.

When I was seven she told me, "Watch that little sparrow. One day she'll take off and fly." I took her literally. So when Lucy told me she could fly, I wasn't at all surprised. The last time I saw Lucy was at my grandmother's funeral. She seemed to have found herself. She was married, had a child and some job like teaching. Later, I heard her life had really sped up.

Sally and Lucy and I were best friends in grade school, but when we moved on to high school our little group came unglued. Each of us stuck to someone new. Then we all kind of came back together. Lucy found Becca. Sally met Millie. And I discovered Wallee. It seemed as the times got tougher, the more friends we needed to get through. Lucy and Sally and I had all had rather different temperaments. Lucy was daring, Sally was timid, and I was somewhere in between. Our new friends were more like each of us.

Lucy probably met Becca in the high school's swimming pool. Gran Ma'am had said that swimming was the perfect thing for Lucy because it was ladylike, she couldn't get dirty, and it kept her out of her mama's house. Too bad neither Sally nor I liked to swim. Sally hated to get her face wet, and I was just bored. But Becca loved to swim. She and Lucy lived at the pool all summer long.

I don't know how Sally met Millie. Probably in Home Economics, they were both Future Homemakers. Wallee and I met while working on the school paper. We made a good team. While we both wanted to be writers, I was fanciful and she was down to earth. I wrote stories. She wanted just the facts. But we both loved to read and spent hours together never talking just lost in some book. Wallee also looked at people and saw beyond the face. Gran Ma'am was very pleased when Wallee and I became friends. Wallee understood what it was like to be judged on looks alone. I had been told how pretty I was for as long as I could remember, but it wasn't until seventh grade that I felt the envy of other girls and even my teacher. I wish I'd known Wallee then. That was the year of the petticoat prohibition.

In the late 50's, fashion dictated that the mandatory dress in Ashbeen was Capezio ballet slippers, ribboned ponytails, gold charm bracelets, and cotton dresses with tight bodices and very full skirts. To make those skirts stick out, girls wore as many stiff crinoline petticoats as they could. White ruffled petticoats were preferred, but pastels were okay as long as they didn't clash with the skirt. We looked like so many waltzing flowers, we great, great, granddaughters of Scarlett and Melanie.

But if this was pretty, it wasn't very practical. Hooped shirts and pantaloons would have made as much sense. It was nearly impossible to stuff all that crinoline between the tiny chair and desktop of a grade school student's desk. To keep from crushing this foaming concoction, some of the braver girls simply lifted the top layer of their skirts over the backrest of their chairs rather than sitting on them. The skirts were long enough to hang down and keep their panties from showing, but just barely, and plenty of ruffles and crinoline stuck out. Nonetheless, there was a constant rivalry that year to see who could have the most petticoats and the fullest skirts. My mama sewed, and she made me beautiful dresses and petticoats with lots of ruffles and ribbons. I wore as many as five or six some days.

I was out of town at my Uncle Howard's wedding on the day Mrs. Hamilton ruled on petticoats. Later, Lucy told me that she had announced that petticoats had become disruptive. They knocked books and pencils off the desks as the girls moved down the narrow aisles. They made too much noise whenever a girl shifted in her seat. They were distracting the boys. And they were simply overflowing her classroom.

Back then no one mentioned that you could smuggle a small arsenal into school under one skirt. Henceforth, Mrs. Hamilton decreed, no young lady was to come to school in more than three petticoats. Lucy was relieved. She'd never liked petticoats anyway, she declared, and, in truth, always looked rather like a wilted flower on a skinny stem around the rest of us.

When I returned to school, unaware of the dictate, I was wearing six of the fullest crinolines I owned.

"Miss Harris," Mrs. Hamilton called from the front of the room.

"Yes ma'am," I replied as a rose to my feet.

"How many petticoats are you wearing today, Miss Harris?" Confused, I didn't reply right away. What business of Mrs. Hamilton's was it to know how many undergarments I had on? "Roberta Jean, answer me, please."

"Six," I whispered.

"How many?"

"Six," I said louder.

"Come to the front of the class please," she ordered.

I got that sinking feeling of knowing I was about to be made an example, but why I didn't know. The room fell stony quiet in anticipation. Every eye was watching as I walked up the aisle. Dread was stealing in like a prowling cat and creeping up my spine, toying with my heart, that, like a cornered bird, beat and fluttered against its cage but could not escape. I took the last few steps not daring to look left or right.

"You will please remove three of those crinolines. No one in this class is allowed more than three."

"Right here?" I pleaded in a whisper only Mrs. Hamilton could hear.

"Right here, right now," she insisted raising her eyebrows and smiling.

I hesitated just a moment and then leaned over and caught the edge of the top petticoat. As I gave a little jerk, I realized that if I pulled at this top one, I would most likely pull down all my petticoats and, maybe, my underpants as well. I looked up at my teacher's face. I had never seen such a look directed at me. It was the ugly face of a child about to pull the wings off a butterfly. A face intent on injury and harm. The teeth were parted. She was breathing through her mouth, and the tip of her tongue was pressed against one canine. The slight stink of her breath spoiled the air, and the sagging skin under her chin quivered. The tears that had been welling up behind my eyes froze. Tears would do me no good now. I lifted my skirts higher and struggled to find the bottom of the six petticoats. As the first one came off, Mrs. Hamilton grabbed it out of my hand.

"Well, isn't this pretty. All these little bows and ribbons," she sneered at me, holding up for everyone to see the errant garment Mama had hand stitched with such love.

My eyes swept the class. Sally's head was bowed. Lucy was glowering like she wanted to hit somebody. But the other girls were smirking and the boys were laughing. I was determined not to cry. Somebody let out a low, wolf whistle. Mrs. Hamilton pretended not to hear. "Two more, Miss Harris," she demanded. As quickly as I could, I finished the task in naked humiliation.

"Roberta Jean Harris, you will take these home now, and don't come back unless you are suitably dressed."

Grabbing my offending underwear, I ran out of the room. By the time I reached the stairs, anger was thawing out the tears, and they were running down my face. Fired by the heat of my emotions, the concrete steps at my feet seemed to cant dangerously and appeared to slither. They dropped in six, steep coils below me. My trembling knees told me I'd never make it to the bottom. Quietly backing up, I turned into the girls' restroom. Locked in the far stall, I sank down on the toilet and fought the urge to pound the metal walls. I had been there for less than five minutes when I heard the door to the hall open. Two women's voices reached me. One was Mrs. Hamilton's and the other, more anxious voice, belonged to Miss Stein, the art teacher.

"Hazel, really, don't you think you should have just sent her home?"

"And ruin a perfectly good opportunity to take her down a peg or two? No, Annie, that girl is entirely too stuck on herself. Walking around all the time with that dreamy smile on her face. She needed a good comeuppance, and I gave it to her."

"But Hazel, in front of the whole class."

"Believe me, the other girls all hate her. I hear them whispering about her. All but Sally Blackwelder and that Lucy."

"Well, it must be hard to be so beautiful."

"Beautiful. Hah! She's just stuck up, that's all."

I waited, trembling with anger and the fear that they'd discover me, while they used the toilets, washed their hands, and left the room. Then I sneaked out of the building and went home to dump my damaged pride in Gran Ma'am's lap. She never told my mama. And I made Lucy and Sally promise not to tell as well. I couldn't bear to hurt her like that. But she must have known, because she never made me any more petticoats.

I wove a sort of shield out of those memories with a woof of disgrace crisscrossing a warp of pride. I wore it like a magic cloak for the rest of that year. And maybe, for the rest of my life. Lucy would have fought, and Sally would have just taken it, but I wanted to become invisible.

6

Bobbie Jean

Take me with you,
Take my kiss upon your lips,
Hold my words within your mind,
Keep my face inside your memory,
And my love within your heart.

Take me with you,
Take my touch upon your cheek,
Hold my laughter in your spirit,
Keep my passion at your beck and call.
And I will take and hold and keep you with me
until you are.

Roberta Jean Harris

It was in seventh grade, the last year of grade school, when I feel in love for the first time. It was puppy love, and he moved away at the end of the school year, so I never saw him again. But I still remember his name, Danny Taylor. We had a dance that year at the end of school, and I went with Danny. I was twelve and he was almost fourteen. I think he'd gotten behind a year in school because his parents moved around so much.

Sally and Lucy and I had taken ballroom dancing lessons that year from Mrs. Mary Jo Huneywell. She was the first woman I ever met who used eye make-up, and I thought she looked breathtaking and romantic with her huge, blue-shadowed eyes and penciled brows. One morning I saw her without her make-up when I went over to her house to deliver her order of Girl Scout cookies. I was very surprised to find that she was really pretty ordinary. "She not any different from you, Mama, without her make-up," I assured my mama.

I'd never danced with a boy, other than in Mrs. Huneywell's basement where the dancing classes were held. This dance was to be in the school cafeteria. There were only two boys in our dancing class. One was Mrs. Huneywell's son, and the other was one of the girls' brothers. They held you like you had fleas—or something worse. And they both had sweaty hands. I'm sure we must have learned more than one dance, but all I can ever remember doing was the box step. Most of the girls had to dance with other girls in the class, and Lucy declared, much later, that that was the reason she always wanted to lead.

Sally was more than a head taller than all the boys. No one asked her to the dance. She put up a brave front, and I don't think that either Lucy or I realized just how disappointed she really was. Her mama said that girls of twelve and thirteen didn't go to dances.

"I'm not sure why we're taking lessons if we can't go to dances," Lucy retorted.

"Because all young ladies should know how to dance," Sally replied quoting her mama. "It's one of the social graces."

"Well, I'm going and I'm going to wear lipstick," Lucy said flatly. The lipstick was something called "Tangee," an awful, waxy, pinkish-orange gloss that everyone was allowed to wear, but only to Sunday school and dances.

"Sally, you don't have to go with a boy," I reasoned. "Just come anyway."

"That would be worse than not going at all," she sighed.
"And who are you going with?" Lucy asked me.
"Danny. He asked me last Sunday."
"Danny and Bobbie Jean sitting in a tree, K-I-S-S-I-N-G." Lucy teased.
"Please, Lucy, that's so juvenile," Sally declared.
"Lucy's not going with anyone. Are you, Lucy?" I said, more stating the obvious than asking a question.
"Well, as a matter of fact—"

Sally and I stared at her, and for the first time, I realized that my friend was almost pretty. Her mousy blond hair had been cut off very short and was beginning to get the first highlights of summer. She had gained weight that winter and no longer looked like a refugee. The braces had come off. Her large, dark eyes that had seemed too huge and solemn in her long, skinny face, now seemed quite beautiful. Her brows and lashes were dark and thick, and her skin glowed from the early summer sun. Her nails were still a mess, bit to the quick, and her elbows were rough from leaning on them. But, all in all, she really was a pretty girl.

We were sitting on Lucy's front porch around the wrought iron porch set. Sally and I almost climbed over the table. "Who are you going with?" Sally demanded, half rising from her chair and leaning toward Lucy. She was so excited and smiling so big, we almost forgot that she hadn't been invited yet.

"Tommy Lowder!" I guessed. Tommy had teased Lucy so much all through grade school that we were sure he was in love with her.

"Nope, guess again,"

"David Miller," Sally suggested. David sat beside Lucy, and they argued constantly.

Lucy shook her head and her face said, "Not a chance!"

"Tell us then. Who?" I pleaded.

"Tony Overcash." Lucy grinned. Tony was the smartest boy in our class, but he also came from the wrong side of town. He was sweet and well mannered, polite to teachers, and nice to girls. We all liked him.

"Lucy,—" I started to say. We were interrupted by Roxanne and Lucy's mother. Roxanne was bringing us lemonade in tall, green glasses and thin, golden cookies on green glass plates. Lucy's mother was fluttering about sticking fancy, little napkins under our glasses and brushing away a few dead flower petals that had fallen from the large arrangement in the middle of the glass top table.

"Are you girls excited about the dance?" she asked. "Sit up straight, dear," she added as she passed Lucy's chair, giving her a little pat on the back. Lucy momentarily straightened up from her customary slouch.

"Oh, Mrs. Jones, how nice and pretty this looks," Sally said. She was used to these elaborate snacks at Lucy's house. Then she added politely, "Thank you, Roxanne."

"Thank you," I echoed and took a small bite from a delicate cookie. A handful of oatmeal cookies passed out the backdoor or a slice of cake on a paper napkin in the middle of the living room floor was more my style.

"Lucy, did you show Sally and Bobbie Jean your dress for the dance?" Lucy's mother asked.

"Not yet," Lucy mumbled into her plate.

"I took Lucy right down to Rich's last Saturday, the second she got invited. I think it's just grand you all are having a dance to mark the end of grade school this year." We all knew that Lucy's mama couldn't take her anywhere, since she didn't drive, and that Rich's was over a hundred miles away in Atlanta. Lucy's daddy must have been called away from work for that shopping trip. This must be some dress, I thought.

"Show us the dress," Sally asked brightly, brushing her crumbs carefully into her napkin. She was trying to be a good sport about this dance.

With a shy pride that was not at all like her, Lucy lead us into her room. Lying on one of her tall, spool beds was a fancy, taffeta party dress. It had a wide, white skirt with big, black polka dots. The fitted bodice was black and sleeveless. The enormous, stiff, white collar was almost a small cape. It was a lovely dress. A sophisticated dress. A dress that was way too old for a thirteen-year-old girl. It looked like something Audrey Hepburn would wear in the movies. And there were black patent shoes with medium high heels as well.

Lucy was fingering the skirt and smiling. I looked at Sally and she looked at me. Neither of us knew what to say. Sally's mother would know just the right words, but Lucy would be crushed if she heard them. "It's a great dress, Lucy," I managed. "Let's go over to my house and play Monopoly. I'm sure Sally's tired of hearing about this dance stuff."

There was nothing remarkable about the dance. It was just a sweet, seventh grade dance in early June. The chairs and tables had been pushed against the walls of the cafeteria. There was red fruit punch and cookies. We danced a rather stiff and awkward box step to Johnny Mathis crooning what we'd later call "make-out music" and Pat Boone singing the much more innocent "April Love." If any couple should get too close, a chaperone would tap them on the shoulder and motion them apart. Only hands were supposed to touch. I have a vague memory of some chaperone actually carrying a ruler, to make sure we stayed at least two inches apart, but that's probably just something I imagined, some myth from childhood, like the one about saltpeter in our school lunches.

Everyone was cleaner, shyer, and sweeter smelling than usual. The boys were more polite and the girls were more gracious. Every sentence was punctuated with "Please, ma'am" and "I'd love to."

Most of the girls were dressed like me in pastel, cotton shirtwaists with wide belts and full skirts and a hint of lace. Lucy wore her dress, and I heard some whispers about it that night. But over the summer everyone forgot. The next fall was going to see us all split up. I didn't know it then, but I was saying goodbye to more than Danny and grade school. He kissed me on the cheek when he walked me home, and I cried a little when he moved away.

The week after the dance Lucy left for summer camp, and I didn't see her again until the Fall. It was the first summer since second grade that I hadn't been to Girl Scout camp with Sally and Lucy. We wouldn't be eating up mounds of stale, unsold Girl Scout cookies or gritty, campfire-charred marshmallow S'mores. We wouldn't play Strut Miss Lizzie or Red Rover or Jack's Alive. We wouldn't sing "Do Your Ears Hang Low?" and "Kookaburra" and "In the Pines" or any of the other silly, campfire songs. We wouldn't harmonize on any of the beautiful, old songs like "Tell Me Why" or "There's a Long, Long Trail A-winding." Or whisper ghost stories under a blanket by flashlight beam or short-sheet each other's bed. Or ride on the floor of Sally's mama's car. We were officially young ladies now, even if we didn't always act that way. I have never done any of those things again, but Lucy and Becca have daughters, so maybe they have.

By the end of summer, I had to look at Danny's picture to remember what he looked like. It bothered me that love could simply fade away, that feelings could change like that. Mama and I spent more time together getting me ready for high school. She was teaching me to cook and sew and fix my hair. I could see the changes happening to me. Mama gave me a little diary, and I started writing down my thoughts and feelings. But when I read it over, it made me a little scared, and guilty too, to think that I could be so fickle. That what I thought was so cool one week, was so stupid the next. So, I quit writing anything in it for a while. When I saw Lucy again, I knew she had changed, too. And not just her appearance. Something happened to her that summer, and she was never quite the same again.

7

Lucy

False spring, born in winter
Making promises that cannot be kept,
Breaching faith and kindling hope soon extinguished,
Coaxing blooms too soon,
Too tender to stand the freeze
    that's sure to come again.

No garden can protect us from false spring.
No will can hold back the love
    that rises to such warmth.
The flower will die.
The plant will be hurt.
But Spring will come.
               Lucy Jones

That summer of 1959, between seventh and eighth grades, I went alone to a camp for girls in the mountains of Virginia. The lake was cold as ice, and

I got to swim three times a day instead of the usual hour in the morning and hour in the afternoon. The extra hour was for lifeguard training.

That summer the dreams began to change. I was conscious of fleeing from some threatening, but mysterious, something. It was also then that I became aware of how the flapping really had nothing to do with keeping me air borne, and although I had never been able to bid a flying dream to come—and this did not change—that summer I had the dreams more often.

One of the two lifeguards, our instructor for lifesaving, was a guy. All the other counselors were college girls. Two of them were in my training class. We met in the late afternoon, the hour before dinner. There were six of us, three girls of twelve to fifteen, the two counselors, and Matt. The first day was just long distance swimming tests. Since I had gained weight over the winter, swimming was easier than ever. I needed to stroke only to move through the water. To float I just needed to get in. We did two laps across the lake and back with Matt paddling along beside in a canoe. One of the campers began to tire near the end, and Matt let her hang on to the canoe for the last twenty yards, but nothing unusual happened.

On the second day we made the same swim but with our heads above water at all times, watching the imaginary drowning victim. The head-above-water position was both tiring and a pain in the neck, but again nothing happened until we were back on shore. I was sitting cross legged on the end of the dock rubbing my aching neck when Matt walked up. He dropped down in front me, and his hand reached behind my head and massaged my neck. I closed my eyes and rolled my head.

"Ah, Lucy," he said, "you are a beautiful swimmer."

My eyes flew open. He was looking at me and smiling. I had no idea what to say, and he gave me no chance to say anything. He got up quickly, slapping his thighs, and turned to face the other girls who were coming out of the water. "Well girls, tomorrow we begin the real work. Do any of you bruise easily?" he laughed.

Lucy

I was aware of my cold, tight nipples pushing against my suit. And I felt a funny feeling deep in my gut that I'd never felt before. The other girls were giggling and crowding around Matt to get the printed handouts he was passing around. The basic rules of lifesaving, he said. Homework for tomorrow. As I got my copy, his hand grazed mine, and I felt it again, that tug in my groin. My stomach turned over. My God, what was happening to me? Was I going to be sick? I ran for the bathhouse. As the hot water poured down over me, I touched my left breast. It felt so tender. I grabbed the soap and suds up all over. Then turned the cold on and stood there until everything had washed away.

I felt amazingly tired. Slowly I dressed, made my way to the dining hall, ate and returned to my cabin. That night the dream came. It seemed to start in the middle.

She is already in flight and fleeing from something on the ground. The lights below burn harsher and brighter than the usual soft golden glow. They seem to shift their shapes and cast shadows that wave and ripple. The trees are blacker and the air is hotter.

"Faster, faster. Pull harder! Stroke faster!" something seems to be frantically urging her. She does, but she isn't moving any faster. Whatever she is fleeing is catching up. The harder she flaps the slower she flies, the closer the ground rise up to meet her. She can smell something burning.

Then, suddenly, it comes to her. It is her desire to fly that propels her not the flapping. She grows calmer, lets her arms simply drift beside her, and she lifts up and away from whatever danger threatens from below. She leaves the dark trees behind and rises to the cooler air and the silvery light of the stars. They shine so brightly but so far out. She floats for a moment considering whether to go on. They are singing, beckoning, calling her name without words so that she more feels their call than hears it. It touches her. She can go there. She knows she can.

Higher she rises, and her stomach seems to rise and press tight against her abdomen. She has a strange sensation of not knowing which way is up and which is down. Is she soaring toward the heavens or plunging into a lake of reflected stars? Does it even matter? Then the stars are all around her. The ground has disappeared. Her body feels as though it is melting into an entirely different element, not air, not fire, not water, and definitely not earth. All that is left is hot core, rushing to some pentacle. And when she reaches it, there she hangs for one glorious moment, while the stars pulsate and burn. Then, slowly, she rolls and begins a long descent. Down she spirals, a small tight knot, into a warm dark sea.

I awoke with a start. I was wet. My body was covered in sweat. The cool night air raised chill bumps. And there was a strange, warm wet between my legs. Had my period started? I reached for the flashlight beside the bunk and shone its beam under the sheet. I had had only four periods and still wasn't sure what to expect, but this was not it. What was happening to me? I turned out the light and curled up on my side looking out at the night. Slowly I drifted back to sleep to dream no more that night.

The next day we began the training exercises for the first of Matt's basic rules of lifesaving: *Don't go in the water unless you have to*. These consisted of shore-based rescues—like reaching for a victim with a paddle or a tree branch—and throwing rescues—like tossing a rope, throwing a life ring, or pitching a beach ball.

"Keep your eyes on her eyes," Matt instructed. "And keep talking. Calmly, soothingly. Don't drop the end of the rope, and don't let her pull you in."

We didn't go in the water except to play victim. Although we did this with great theatrics, we all swam too well to be really convincing at drowning. Besides, we laughed too much. I didn't dream of flying for several nights.

By the second week I had a routine going. In the mornings I swam with Hillary, my water buddy. She was fifteen and more interested in working on her tan than swimming. Camp rules said you had to keep close to your buddy, and every once in a while, the lifeguard's whistle would blow, and she'd call, "Buddy check. Find your buddy." So every morning Hillary and I would swim out to the dock in the middle of the lake. She'd stretch out to sun, and I'd practice diving. In the afternoons we played with other girls in the shallow water near the shore until it was time for lifeguard training. Then Hillary and the other girls would leave the lake to the five of us in training and Matt.

In the second week we started in-the-water rescues. We began with the exercise I learned to hate—making your own personal flotation device. We went in the water fully clothed over our swimsuits, tennis shoes and all. Well over our heads off the far end of the dock, we treaded water until our clothes were completely soaked. Then we removed our shoes and socks and threw them on the dock, never touching it. Matt said if this were the real thing, we were just to drop them. Next we removed our jeans. Taking a deep breath, we unzipped and started working them off.

With both hands and feet engaged in disrobing, it was impossible to tread water, and I went under. Our jeans weren't so tight in the 50's, or we probably would never have gotten them off. When my feet became entangled in the pant legs, I couldn't kick at all. Real panic crept in, as I couldn't get my head above water. Desperately I struggled to free my feet. With one foot finally released and one still trapped, I made it to the surface dragging my jeans behind. Once the pants were off, I tied a knot in the end of each leg.

The next part was the worst. We were to sling the heavy, wet jeans over our heads from back to front to capture and trap air in the legs. To do this, the jeans needed to be flung high and hard. Each time I tried my head went under and the waist of my pants went below the surface. No trapped air. Over and over I tried until I was worn out.

Matt stood on the dock shaking his head. "You just drowned, girls. Better luck tomorrow. Rest up."

I looked at my fellow trainees. We were gasping. No one was laughing. I never have discovered if this exercise was really meant to teach us how to make a floating device or to give us a taste of what it's like to drown. I dreamed no dreams that night in my exhausted sleep.

The following day Matt gave us some pointers. We might want to start with the shirt rather than the pants. It was smaller and lighter and could give some support while doing the heavier jeans.

"Find a rhythm," he said. "Pretend you're stripping for an audience." And he hummed a few bars of "The Stripper." We laughed for the first and only time that day.

"Go slower, easier. Float on your back."

By the end of the day I could do it, but I never liked it. One of the campers dropped out of the class. "Guess you girls are starting to take this seriously," Matt said.

That evening one of the counselors stopped by my bunk. "Lucy, when is your next period?" she asked quietly. My face flushed and my eyes dropped. I was mortified. No one had ever talked directly to me about this. We'd seen a film at school in fifth grade, and my mama had left the necessary things and a pamphlet on my bed when I turned eleven. She saw how embarrassed I was.

"Just stay out of the cold water when it comes. Cold water makes the cramps worse," she advised with a pat on my hand. "No one will ask you why you aren't going in." The next day I realized she was sitting on the dock while the rest of us started practicing carrying positions.

The second rule of lifesaving according to Matt was: *Don't let the victim drown you*. Toward this end we began to practice defenses and escapes in the third week of camp. These varied from simply going deeper and depriving the drowning person of the use of your body as a flotation device, to breaking his hold, or cold cocking him as a last resort. This last one we didn't practice on each other. We spent one day going through the drills on dry land, then we repeated them in deep water.

To practice breaking a hold, we were grouped in two pairs of victim and rescuer. I was paired with Matt since one of the girls was sitting out. First

Lucy

I grabbed him from behind while he demonstrated how to slip out of the victim's grip, quickly lifting my arms and pushing away.

"Remember girls, it's better never to let yourself get in this position. Don't let her get behind you. Stay face to face. Your eyes on hers. Keep talking. Keep reassuring her. Tell her what you're going to do, what you need for her to do."

We observed while the other pair went through the drill, each taking a turn as victim. Then I played the rescuer, and he grabbed me. I felt his arms go around my neck and his hands grip my shoulders. I grabbed his elbows and pushed up, slipping easily from his grasp.

"You didn't try hard enough," I laughed.

"Next time," he replied with a grin.

We moved on to the face to face escape. "Push against the chest with one hand and use your other hand to push up on the victim's chin," he instructed. "Use you feet if necessary to push away. If you can, slip around behind and into the carry."

I threw my arms around his neck, and he demonstrated the technique. We watched the other pair practice, and then it was my turn. Face to face, eye to eye, I spoke the litany he had taught us. "Okay now, I'm here and everything's going to be okay. You're all right. Just relax. I going to move behind you and—"

Without warning Matt sprang on me pulling us both beneath the water. Then his mouth was on mine, and he was kissing me. As we broke the surface, he whispered, "That works too sometimes."

"Try again, Lucy," he said loudly. I was startled but couldn't wait to try it again, however, the next time he was all business.

We mixed the escape drills with victim carries, and for the rest of the afternoon I was either in his arms or he was in mine. Several times my head went below the surface of the water in the effort to pull us both to safety. He was larger than anyone I'd practiced with before and, although he didn't feign a struggle, his weight pulled me down. At the end of the day, he smiled at me and told me I'd done a good job.

"You swim so well, so effortlessly. The extra weight was hard for you, but you handled it well. Men don't float as well as women, you know." He gave my shoulder a little shake.

I looked at my feet and mumbled, "Thanks. It was fun." Then I turned and ran away.

That night I dreamed again of fleeing something menacing on the ground, rising to the heavens, and, for one brief moment, joining with the cosmos before falling back into a pool of stars.

The next morning I was diving off the dock with Hillary when we heard the screams. Two young girls of seven or eight had strayed out too far, and now both were in trouble. One wore a red cap, a beginning swimmer, the other a yellow for first class. Only white caps, like Hillary and I, were suppose to be out this far. The struggling pair was about half way between the shore dock and the one where we were, well over a hundred yards away. In her panic, one was trying to hold on to the other, and they both were going down. Matt was already running toward the water. Where was the lifeguard on duty? I took a shallow dive and started toward them. The cries for help stopped. They were under the water. The surface churned for a moment and then smoothed with nothing to disturb it.

Matt reached them first. Disappearing beneath the surface, he rose once and dove again. He got the one with the red cap, and the yellow cap came up a few feet away choking. "Lucy," he cried, "Stay away. You aren't ready for this."

"Yes, I am. I can do it," I shouted back.

I approached the little girl with the yellow cap. She was swimming feebly now, not even dog-paddling, circling like a wounded fish. "Help me. Help me, please," she whispered. She had swallowed a lot of water. Her eyes were red and very frightened. There were bleeding scratches on her face and neck from her little friend's attack, and her right arm hung uselessly by her side.

I spoke my rescuers' litany to her. "It's okay. It's okay now. We're here. You're going to be all right. I'm going to move around behind you and—"

She sank below the surface, one arm raised, clawing at the air. I moved in quickly, too quickly. I'd gotten too close. She grabbed my arm, briefly surfaced, then we both went under. Bubbles streamed from her mouth. She inhaled water, and her fingers bit into my arm. But she was weak, already exhausted, and I easily turned her over and caught her chin in my left hand lifting her face above the water.

"Just relax. Float. Don't struggle. I've got you," I whispered in her ear. We came into the carry position with her on top and me underneath, my left arm supporting her. For a moment I was afraid she was dead, or at least not breathing, then I heard a raspy gurgle, and she convulsed slightly, water coming from her mouth and nose.

"Blow out," I commanded. She did, very weakly. Then she took a breath. "Breathe. Easy now."

I took a long pull with my right arm, and we moved slowly toward the shore. My head went under several times, but I managed to keep hers up, except once. When her face went under, she struggled against me, wanting to turn over, to grab my neck. But I kept talking, kept soothing her. "Don't fight. We're okay. Kick your feet a little if you can. It will help to keep us up."

She managed a little flutter kick, and we did better after that. Matt had passed the little red cap into the waiting arms of one of the counselors and was swimming back toward us now. I don't know how long it took for him to reach us. It seemed like forever. He took the little girl from me.

"Are you okay, Lucy?"

"Yeah, I'm fine," I said and followed them slowly back to shore.

Here was a great commotion. Girls crying and hanging on each other. Counselors shouting. In the heart of the hubbub the little victims lay swathed in towels, surrounded by campers and staff. The camp nurse was bending over them. Standing slightly apart from the rest, Matt was angrily questioning the lifeguard on duty. Why hadn't she seen them leave the roped-in area and stopped them? Why didn't she come to the rescue? The poor girl was crying and trying to explain that she simply hadn't seen them. The sun was in her eyes reflecting off the lake. When she had heard their cries and finally saw them, she froze. She'd never before had to rescue someone for real. And there had been two of them. She couldn't decide whether to swim to them or try to launch a canoe. In confusion, she did neither.

I climbed wearily onto the end of the dock and sat breathing hard. My head felt hot and my temples pounded. My heart was still beating double time. Matt swore loudly at the blubbering girl, "Son of a bitch!" Everyone stopped and turned and looked at him. "Sorry," he said, gesturing toward the crowd of girls and women. Then he shook his head, balled his fist, and walked hurriedly out to me. He leaned over putting a hand on my back.

"Lucy, you should never have tried that." His voice was still angry but quieter.

"Would she have made it if I hadn't?"

"Probably not," he admitted. "But she could have drowned you."

"She didn't," I said and managed a smile.

He looked into my eyes and sighed the deepest sigh I'd ever heard, and then he said, "Oh, Lucy, why couldn't you have been nineteen instead of thirteen?" With that he walked away.

We had no lesson that afternoon. I lay in my bunk and wrote a letter to Mama and Daddy. The red cap went home early. I never even learned the little yellow cap's name. The rest of the session she followed me around the dining hall, her arm in a sling, not daring to get too close, just sitting a few seats away and smiling at me. This lifesaving stuff was heady business.

On Thursday morning, my period started. I sat on the dock and watched the other girls practicing the carries and escapes. At one point Matt pulled himself up on the dock beside me.

Lucy

"Why did you do it, Lucy? What made you jump in?"

"They needed help. You needed help," I said and paused. Then I added, "If I had had to watch her drown, something in me would have drown too. I don't think I could ever swim again."

"It was dangerous. Too dangerous. You could have been killed."

"But I wasn't."

"What happened out there? I want you to tell me everything."

I described the way the little yellow cap had looked, the desperation in her face, how I'd almost lost it when she'd clutched at my arm, and how we'd done okay after that.

"Don't do it again. Promise me. Not until you're sixteen anyway." He put his hand on my head and mused my hair, but he didn't wait for my answer. He just dove back in and rejoined the class. As the session was ending, Matt reminded us that our certification test was the next Wednesday and that we'd start resuscitation exercises the following day.

I went back to my cabin to start a letter to Bobbie Jean. "Dear Bobbie Jean, I think I'm in love..."

For the next few nights there were no dreams.

8

Lucy

I saw a bright and distant star and wished to know it well,
I saw two fish in courtship dance and wished to cast the spell,
I saw your face and then I knew,
That I had seen my wish come true.
                    Lucy Jones

The third and last basic rule of lifesaving according to Matt was: *Stay with the victim.*

"Your job doesn't end when you've gotten the victim out of the water," he told us Friday afternoon. "She may go into shock or require resuscitation. So for the next few days, we'll be learning some first aid. We'll begin with artificial respiration. Who wants to be the victim?"

He chose one of the other campers, and she lay prone on the dock face down, while he demonstrated the steps of checking the mouth and throat, clearing the air ways, and administering the rhythmic pressing on the back and lifting of the arms. Then we tried it. I was paired with one of the counselors. At first we were very solemn and serious, but soon there were giggles and accusations of tickling.

Matt feigned disgust with such silliness, "Come on, girls, knock it off. Get serious." But actually, I believe we were all relieved.

He pointed out that the person administering the aid could sit at the victim's head or straddling her back. We tried both. Then he began to time us. It must be possible to keep this up for at least ten to fifteen minutes. We were worn out after five, and our victims were complaining. For the last exercise of the day, Matt demonstrated how to change the person giving aid without breaking the rhythm.

Then the bad news. This was his weekend off, and because everyone was still spooked by the drama of the past week, the camp administrator had decided to close the lake for the weekend. "But, hey, girls, you can practice these exercises without ever going in the water."

We booed him.

Weekends at camp were usually pretty boring since part of the staff was given time off, but this weekend was worse than usual. Friday was the Fourth of July. More than half the staff was gone by five. The lake was closed. The dining hall was reduced to cold cereal, fruit, and bag lunches. We took hikes, made baskets in the crafts building, and wrote letters home. By Sunday evening, the staff was returning, and we had a giant weenie roast around campfires by the lake. Hot dogs, marshmallows, fireworks. Matt wandered up as they were passing out the sparklers.

"Want me to light yours for you?" he asked.

"Yes, please."

He held one of the sparklers in the flame until it caught sending out a plume of tiny stars. Then he lighted the other from it and handed it to me. "It's so pretty. Kind of reminds me of the stars when I fly," I said.

"When you what? When you fly?" he asked and sat down beside me.

"Yes, when I dream about flying and go toward the stars."

"You dream that you can fly?" A strange look came over his face. He swallowed hard and looked away. I had never told anyone about these dreams. Did he think that I was crazy? Maybe he didn't believe me. The firelight danced over his features and made it hard for me to read his expression.

"Is this like flying in an airplane or a rocket ship?" he asked after a moment.

"No, it's more like swimming in the air," I whispered back.

"Do you dream this every night?"

"Only once in a while. Do you dream it, too?"

"No, but I've read about it." His voice sounded vaguely troubled.

But he believed me and, maybe, he didn't think that I was crazy. Our sparklers burned out, and the head counselor announced that the fireworks display was about to begin, but first we should all stand to sing "American the Beautiful." When we sat back down, I moved a little closer to Matt.

"Lucy," he whispered, "what are these dreams like?"

"Wonderful. Sometimes scary. And lately a little weird."

"Weird?" he asked as a rocket burst overhead.

There was a chorus of "Ooh's" and "Aah's." Then another rocket shot into the air and exploded in a rain of red and gold. Girls were clapping and cheering and begging for more. Fantails of goldfish shimmied down. Blossoms of starry chrysanthemums spread across the sky. Three big bangs sounded one behind the other, and silver, gold, and green showered down. He tried to say more, but I couldn't hear him over the laughing voices of the girls, the shrieks of firecrackers, and booms from the roman candles. The bitter scent of spent gunpowder filled the air, and the show continued to light up the sky for another ten minutes or so. Then we sang "Taps" and started for our cabins.

"Lucy, will you be swimming tomorrow?" Matt asked as I turned to go.

"Yes," I promised.

Monday started out cold and cloudy. There was a promise of rain before lunch. Most of the girls decided to watch a water safety film in the dining hall rather than swim. I gathered up my towel and cap and went to the lake. Matt was sitting in the lifeguard's chair.

"Did they fire her?" I asked.

"She quit. Ann and Jane, the counselors in your class, will be certified by the end of the week. Until then, I work both shifts."

"Can I go in?"

"Go on, but it's cold," he warned.

I put on my cap and dove in. The water was warmer than the air but still cold. When I reached the dock, I practiced a few dives and then came back toward shore. When I pull up onto the dock near Matt's chair, my teeth were chattering. I pulled my knees up to my chest and wrapped the towel around me. Matt climbed down and sat beside me. There was no one else on the lake.

"How long have you been swimming?" he asked.

"Since I was seven."

"And how long have you dreamed of flying?"

"About the same," I replied, toying with the frayed end of the towel, suddenly shy.

"Tell me some more about the dreams."

And so I told him about lifting off and flying over the trees. I told him about the flapping and how I had discovered it wasn't really necessary.

"I love the way the air feels as it moves around me. Like the way the water feels when it's warm and rolls against your skin. Like so many stroking fingers, only lighter, softer. In the dreams up and down aren't quite the same. When I float in the water, I come up to the surface buoyed by the lake, but when I fly in the air, I can hang suspended like a moon between two sources of gravity."

"Why is it scary, Lucy?"

"I don't know. I don't know what it is, but something on the ground is after me sometimes. The stars used to scare me too, but not anymore, not since I met you."

"Why not? Why aren't they scary now?"

"Because they sing. They call me to come further out, not with voices but with light and mind-whispers. I used to be afraid I might not make it back, that they might lure me out beyond my depth into some sort of raptures of the deep. Now I know I can make it."

"What's out there where the stars are?"

I tried to describe it, to describe the way I felt when I reached the stars.

"And how do you feel when you wake up?" he asked, not looking at me.

I looked at my lap and said, "Wet, I feel wet."

Matt dove and swam underwater toward the dock in the middle of the lake. He came up like a great fish emerging from deep down and then stroked slowly out and back. When he reached my feet, he looked up at me and asked quietly, "Lucy, do you know what an orgasm is?"

"No," I replied.

"It's the way you feel with a lover."

"Oh."

"I don't think you should tell this stuff about flying to other people. Okay?"

"Are you my lover?"

He didn't answer right away. Instead he turned his head and stared out across the lake. "Lawrence Durrell says that girls who love to swim will be wonderful lovers."

"Who is Lawrence Durrell?"

"Just some guy who writes books. Books I read last year at college."

We stayed like this for a few moments. Me on the dock. Matt in the water looking at the other shore. The clouds parted for a moment, and a gust of wind tossed a scattering of diamonds over the water. I shivered. Then they closed again, and it began to rain.

"Go on, Lucy. Swimming is over. I'll see you this afternoon." He pushed off and swam away.

That afternoon we did mouth to mouth resuscitation. I was very disappointed when Matt chose one of the counselors for the demonstration victim rather than me. At the end of class he reminded us that we had one more lesson, and then the test for certification. "Study. Read your handouts again tonight. Part of the test is written."

Our last lesson was in-water resuscitation. Matt explained that this was not a required part of the course and was very difficult. But he felt that it was extremely useful, especially for boating accidents, when we might have a nearly lifeless victim far from shore. So, he'd like for us to practice the drill even after the course. He put on a lifejacket and chose me for his victim. We swam out ten or twenty feet from the dock. He began by demonstrating how the victim's unconscious body was supported by a kick board, but this could be any floating debris that would hold up the head and shoulders. He then proceeded to give me mouth to mouth, but between the breaths he pretended to give to me, he was whispering.

"Lucy, keep pretending to be unconscious. Just lie still and listen. I'm falling in love with you—and you're much too young. I'm afraid of what will happen—so, I am leaving. I won't be here for second session. I'm sorry—but, I do love you."

The last feigned breath he gave me was a kiss instead. The hand that had given the impression of pitching my nostrils closed caressed my brow. I ached wanting to put my arms around him, but instead I pretended to be revived. Everyone cheered, and that was the end of the course except for the test.

Matt was a wonderful guy. He wisely chose to stop this courtship in its tracks. For him I was serious jailbait. I think I was very lucky. On Friday he presented us with our certificates, and he also gave me a small wrapped package that, he explained, was a thank-you for helping with the emergency. It was a copy of Lawrence Durrell's Justine hidden in the cover of an American Red Cross lifesaving manual.

"Keep it hidden," he advised.

The second session of camp was lonesome and nothing special. I read the book, took diving lessons, and cried myself to sleep. Sometimes the dream would come. I thought of Matt, but his face was already blurring in my memory.

Lucy

When I got home, my mama had let Roxanne go and was doing the housework herself. I don't remember the reason, but we got into a terrible argument. Daddy got involved and, I guess, he took my side. Later that night she said to me, "Lucy, I know if we were drowning in the ocean, your daddy would save you and leave me to drown."

"But Mama," I replied, "I can save myself. And you, too."

9

Rebecca Marie McCollough, "Becca"

"If you can fill life's unforgiving minute with sixty seconds worth of distance run…"
The Laurels, Ashbeen High School Annual, Class of '64

I couldn't believe my ears. Lucy Jones had actually tracked me down through the Internet. Ain't technology grand? Nobody has called me Becca in years. Rebe or Ms. McCollough or Mrs. Rollins, but not Becca. I don't know how my mama came up with the name Rebecca. Surely not *Rebecca of Sunnybrook Farm*, but the Marie part was to carry on her own name.

Lucy said she'd like to get us all together. Could I make some weekend this summer? Yeah, I'd love to. Better than that, why not use my place? I'd recently bought a house on Amelia Island. No husband. No kids at home. Perfect.

We chatted on a while, exchanged email addresses. I'd never recognize her voice. It was deeper, but the Southern accent was, if anything, stronger. Her words kind of spilled out slowly, like honey. We hadn't exchanged a note, a phone call, nothing…not in fifteen years. We both have daughters, hers a bit older than Shea. There was a second husband, a trophy husband, she joked.

"Becca," she closed, "I really need to see you."

"Yeah, Lucy, I want to see you too."

And I do, but why now? Why this urgency to bring back the past? I gave her Wallee's address. The year before I had gotten an invitation to her daughter's wedding. I hadn't gone, but the address was probably still the same. No one knew where Millie was or how to get in contact with her. I can't wait to tell Shea. She'll love it. My daughter was a model for ten years, and I was her manager. Two years ago she decided she wanted to give it up and go back to school. Now I work from home editing photocopy. I get work from some great guys, independent photographers. Too bad most are gay. Two or three times a month I fly out of Atlanta to New York or LA or wherever the client is. I spend a couple of days wrestling with the ad agency, then back to peace and quite. It's a long way from Ashbeen, but then again, it's not.

The first time I saw Lucy Jones was in eighth grade. She was wearing a red and white summer dress and looking for her assigned seat in our homeroom. We had all just been thrown together from our respective grade schools. None of my old friends were in our class, and I was feeling anxious and lonely. She didn't look lonesome, just pissed.

"Alphabetical order. They want us to sit in alphabetical order?" she said to me. I was sitting in the next row and one seat behind hers. "Talk about impersonal. Are we just so many filing cards?"

I didn't know what to say so I just laughed. On the whole Lucy was pretty outrageous. But could she swim. The pool stayed open until October, and we went there every day. In the winter there were movies and dances and football games, but for us that was hibernating. The second week in May the pool would open, and we were alive again.

Rebecca Marie McCollough, "Becca"

High school has never been a friendly place. There were cliques and gangs and ins and outs. As eighth graders, we were all out. Several years later, Ashbeen would build a junior high school, but in 1959, we were simply appended to the older kids but excluded from almost all their activities. Eighth graders weren't allowed to go to high school dances, join their clubs, or hang around the gym at lunch period. We mostly had our own classes, too. But Lucy, Wallee, and I were in a special English class with upper-class men. It was a period of experimentation, when what you had to say was more important than saying it correctly. We loved it. Our teacher was Miss Jennings. She was an older woman, but we thought she was really cool. We wrote a lot of compositions that were read aloud and discussed in class. I particularly remember one that Lucy did in the spring of 1960.

She began by telling us about the Greeks, and how they didn't believe that females had souls or could think or have meaningful ideas. Then she went on to explain that they also believed there were more than two sexes, and that women who could think and reason weren't female, but *hetairae*. The females were wives and mothers, but the *hetairae* were like muses. They had salons and gave parties called symposiums, where great ideas were discussed and philosophies were born. The *hetairae* were lovers and the mothers of great works of poetry and art. Lucy said she wanted to grow up to be a *hetairae*.

What followed was a rather lively discussion of men and women and their proper places in society. I think Lucy got more than an earful from some of the boys in the class.

"Yeah Lucy, you ought to be one of them *whatevers*," Spencer joked. "You always were awful bossy."

"No woman has every created any great art or music or philosophy," sneered one of the sophomores.

"Of course they have," Wallee jumped in. "There's Emily Dickenson and Mary Cassatt."

"What's that part about them being lovers?" one of the upper-class men wanted to know. Miss Jennings subtly deflected this question by asking the boys if they could love a woman who was smarter than they were.

"Women aren't smarter than men. They just think they are."

"Women should support their men, not compete."

"Then why are we going to school?" Lucy demanded.

"So you can read to our children."

"Having children is more fulfilling than writing poems or painting pictures," said one of the older girls.

"My mother says that children always wind up causing you pain and breaking your heart," I stated. "I'm not sure I want to have any."

"Well, at least writing poetry won't break your heart."

When the bell rang, Miss Jennings thanked Lucy for an interesting discussion and asked her to stay after class. I waited for her, but Miss Jennings said to me, "Becca, I want to talk to Lucy alone. Could you wait for her in the hall?" I left the room, but I didn't pull the door all to way closed.

"Lucy, the hetairae were a lot of the things you said," I heard Miss Jennings tell her. "But they were somewhat more as well. Do you know what a prostitute is?"

"Yes, ma'am," Lucy said.

"Well, Lucy, most people today think of the hetairae as prostitutes. And I don't think you want to tell people that you want to be a prostitute."

"But they weren't, were they, Miss Jennings?" Lucy pleaded.

"I'm not sure, Lucy. They wouldn't be what we'd call good women. Why don't you do some more research?"

"I've tried, but I could only find one chapter in one book about them."

"Oh well, that is a problem. Maybe for now you should drop this subject and let me see if I can find you some other books on the topic of women in society. Have you ever read anything about Eleanor Roosevelt?"

"No, ma'am," Lucy replied somewhat dejectedly.

"Well, I think you would like to read about her life. You may go now. And Lucy, do be careful, dear."

I hope she's not in some kind of trouble. Lucy always seemed to be in trouble. I think that's why I liked her. At least she wasn't dull.

The summer after our freshman year, Wallee's mama took us all to Tybee Island beach for a week. That was the year of *A Summer Place*, and we all thought the beach was the most romantic place on earth. The house on the beach was old, elegantly shabby, weathered gray and comfortable, with ceilings so high our voices seemed to echo in the cavernous rooms. It was built up off the ground with double porches all around upstairs and down.

Sally and Bobbie Jean were very fair skinned and had to stay out of the sun a good part of the day. They took turns spending hours with Wallee reading on the lower porch overlooking the ocean. Crepe myrtles and bay laurels screened one end where a hammock hung. White rockers and wicker tables bunched together in satisfied cliques around the tall windows, while the obligatory porch swing piled with flowered pillows balanced the hammock at the opposite end of the house overlooking the sound. Pink and white oleanders crowded against cabbage palms on this end of the house. A sandy path led from the porch steps through the waving, waist-high sea oats to the white stretch of beach and the rolling gray-green ocean.

Sally slept downstairs with Wallee in one of the bedrooms. Mrs. Anderson took the other, smaller one. Bobbie Jean and Millie and Lucy and I shared beds in the two big rooms upstairs. There was a wide central hall between the rooms. Always-opened, screened doors lead to the upper porches from both bedrooms and the hall. The upper porch was the best. It was deeper that the lower one, occupying half of the upper story. Two rope hammocks hung on the ocean side, and green rockers sat on the street side that was shaded from the afternoon sun by a giant live oak and two palmetto palms. On the sound side, to the south, was a clothesline for our wet suits and the outside stairs leading to the lower porch. The roof was a steeply pitched, tin pyramid pierced by a stone chimney. Although there was no air conditioning, the high ceilings, porches, sea breezes, and green shade were enough to keep us cool, except for our first night.

The trip to the coast from the upstate was four long hours in Wallee's mama's '59 station wagon. The only air conditioning was what blew in from the rolled-down windows. "4 by 45 air conditioning" we called it, four windows down and Mrs. Anderson driving a cautious 45. We started out after two in the afternoon. By six o'clock, we skirted the graceful city of Savannah and rode out over miles of salt marshes and sea islands, until finally, late in the day, we reached Tybee. The August air hung like a damp, suffocating, limp rag. We helped unload but didn't even think of waiting to unpack. Lucy and I dumped our stuff, dug out our suits, and flung ourselves in the ocean just as the sun was going down.

For a few precious moments we were cool, but it seemed even hotter when we crawled out. The sticky salt-spray from the ocean and the brackish, sulfur smelling water from the shower never seemed to get you clean on humid nights. We were sweating again before we could even towel off. Lucy and I tossed and turned in our rumpled bed, our gowns sticking to us, our hair curling in wet tendrils at our necks and temples.

"How can the others sleep?" I whispered. "I'm so hot, I'm dripping."

"Bobbie Jean is cold-natured," Lucy sighed. "She needs a sweater in June, and I guess it's cooler downstairs."

"Let's go out on the porch," I suggested. "Maybe there's a breeze out there."

Climbing into one of the rope hammocks with our pillows, we caught what little air was stirring. Lucy rocked us gently by pushing off against the porch railing with one foot. Out across the ocean, lighting played against the horizon.

"Do you think that's just heat lighting or a real storm coming?" Lucy asked.

"Probably just heat," I answered. "It's way off. I can't hear any thunder."

We lay still except for the gentle swaying of the hammock. The waves rolled to the shore, and the mosquitoes hummed in the bushes. The ropes squeaked softly, protesting against the motion of the hammock. Then, very far away, I heard the rumble of thunder. I was still too hot to sleep.

"Lucy, are you ever afraid of anything?" I whispered.

She didn't answer me exactly. Instead she said, "Bobbie Jean is afraid of bugs. I used to think she was just faking, pretending to be a silly girl. But she's really afraid. I felt awful when I finally realized, because I had been teasing her with a June bug on a string. And I think Sally is afraid of what other people think of her."

"Yeah, I think you're right. I'm afraid of disappointing my parents, too. But that's not what I mean. Are you afraid of things in the night?" I insisted.

"I used to be. When we were in seventh grade and had to read Edgar Allen Poe, I got really scared at night, alone in bed. I liked the *Gold Bug*. I wanted to go to Sullivan's Island and hunt for buried pirate treasure. But I hated *The Black Cat* and *The Tell, Tell Heart*. They were creepy."

"But you're not afraid anymore?" Lighting flashed, and we could see the outline of heavy thunderheads over the ocean. A faint breeze blew over us, and a tiny shiver ran up my back.

"One night last year," she whispered. "I woke up in the middle of the night. Because I needed to pee. I was sure that there was something standing by my bed just beyond my feet, where the streetlight shines in the window. Something like a skeleton. Black. And yellow-green where the light came through its eye holes and its grinning mouth. I was so scared I pulled the covers over my head and curled up in a ball."

The lighting flashed again, and we counted slowly from one thousand one to one thousand eight before we heard the thunder. The clouds glowed, lit from an inner turmoil, and the wind lifted in a little gust to rattle the dry fronds and branches against the railings of the porch.

"I think this may be a real storm." Another breath of air sighed over us. "So what happened? What did you do?"

"I prayed. I prayed not to wet the bed. I had to pee real bad. I thought my bladder was going to bust, but I was too scared to come out from under the covers. I was shaking and biting my lip, I needed to go so bad. I knew I would whenever it got me. And that struck me as funny, but I didn't dare laugh. I'da wet the bed for sure then. When I couldn't stand it anymore, I threw back the covers and said right out loud, '*Come get me. I dare you.*' Then I jumped out of bed and ran for the bathroom. And I haven't been scared since." She grinned and poked me in the ribs. But her smile faded, and she added a soft, sighing, "Still,…"

"Yeah, I'm glad I don't have to share my room with a little sister, but sometimes it would be nice to have someone else there," I agreed, and the lighting danced and flashed. The crash of the waves seemed to increase. "I'm afraid of blood. Of being slashed and watching the blood pour out," I confessed. Then, when Lucy didn't answer, I continued. "My mama gives blood. Sometimes the nurse comes to our house to take it. It's awful. She turns pale as paper and nearly faints. Just like those vampire victims in the movies."

"Vampire victims turn into vampires. Maybe your mama is a vampire," Lucy sniggered.

"Don't say that. I don't even like to joke about it."

"What do you think it will be like to sleep with your husband?" she asked me.

"I don't know. Maybe better than alone. Are you afraid of that, of doing it?" A single bolt split the sky lighting up the whole beach. The gust of wind and rumble of thunder arrived together. I felt chilled for the first time all day.

"No, are you?" she giggled.

Before I could answer, the rain began to tap upon the tin roof, and before I could draw another breath, it hammered down with the den of a military tattoo. The booming thunder and clattering rain woke Bobbie Jean and Millie. We could hear them calling to us from inside. The rain swept under the roof and wet our hair and gowns, pressing them to us.

"Look," Lucy cried excitedly, pointing toward the low, uninhabited island just south over the sound. Dancing over the marsh and spartina grass were the balls of St. Elmo's fire. The house shook as the thunder crashed from a near strike. We grabbed each other and flew to our bed. Shaking with chills and giggles, we covered our heads with the faded quilts and slept soundly the rest of the night.

Lucy and I wanted to swim beyond the breakers but had been warned that anything above shoulder deep was out of bounds. So, we stayed close to shore. We walked the beach in the mornings with Millie and Sally looking for small shells. Colorful scallops and coquina, tiny whelks and spiny sea urchins, delicate angel wings and razor clams, sand dollars and star fish, black devil's purses and brown olives with patterns like some ancient hieroglyphics. We'd pile them on the porch for Wallee and Bobbie Jean to string into necklaces or decorate our table.

In the afternoons we caught Atlantic blue crabs in their tidal pools, where we waded bare footed and squealing in mock terror. Armed with short sticks, Lucy and I would uncover a crab that had hidden himself in the sand at the bottom of a tidal pool. Waving our weapons and poking at his claws, we'd engage the crab in a dual, while risking our toes should he scuttle sideways and attack. I can see us now, holding on to each other, pointing at shadowy attackers real and imagined. Splashing and yelling and nearly knocking each other over in our haste to retreat. Then creeping back and giggling and whispering as though the crabs could overhear our strategies. If one took hold of a stick, we'd fling him onto the beach where Bobbie Jean and Millie would chase him down, corner him, and back him into a box. Female crabs were identified by the distinctive apron on their undersides and released. The males we ate for supper in He-Crab Soup.

One afternoon we buried Millie in the sand. This began innocently enough with Millie our willing victim. After piling on the sand and covering Millie's face with her hat to keep off the sun, we turned on the portable radio, and Lucy began to sculpt. Bobbie Jean and I helped by ferrying water from the surf to keep the sand wet and moldable. The result was a graceful, nude female body encasing the short, plump Millie. Even the pubic hair was delicately coiled in one small spot where the arms that covered the most strategic places had missed.

"Gee, Lucy, I had no idea you were so talented," Bobbie Jean remarked not really in jest. "This looks almost like Venus stepping from the sea."

"Thank you, " Lucy returned and mimed a sweeping bow to an imagined public. "Thank you."

"Yeah," I said. "Leonardo couldn't have done better."

"What? What have y'all done? Let me see." Millie struggled beneath the sand unable to move. Bobbie Jean lifted her hat, but Millie's view was blocked by the mound of sand. Only two hills were in her field of vision.

"This truly is a work of art, Millie," Lucy said. "I don't think we ought to disturb it, do you?" she asked, pretending to seek our opinion.

"But I can't get out," Millie protested.

"Not to worry, kid. The tide will be in soon and wash the sand away," Lucy grinned. "In the meantime, I'm sure you'll have plenty of company. I just need to wash off the sand." Then she took off down the beach and dove into the waves with Bobbie Jean and me following.

I don't know how many beach strollers stopped to look at Millie after we left. The sun was low in the sky so she wasn't in danger of burning. From where we were, she seemed to be enjoying the attention. When the crowd began to thin and the tide was moving in, Sally answered her calls before the first wave licked her toes. But Millie acted like she was mortified, and Sally was angry.

"How could you make that awful sculpture and leave her like that? The poor thing. At least six boys stopped to talk to her, and she had no idea what y'all had done until I told her," Sally confronted us with her hands on her hips. Millie was huddled behind her on the porch swing, pretending to be quite put out with us.

"I am sorry, Millie," Bobbie Jean said sincerely. "I never dreamed you'd mind so much." She quickly moved to Millie's side to comfort her.

"I am sorry too, Millie," Lucy said, much less contritely. Then she whispered to me, "Tomorrow we do you." And we did. Unfortunately, none of the boys was Troy Donahue, just the same guys we saw every evening when we went for ice cream at the Sugar Shack.

On the last night, after all the lights were out, she whispered to me, "Becca, let's go out. Let's go swim out beyond the breakers."

"I don't know Lucy. Mrs. Anderson will be awfully mad if she finds out. And our suits will get wet and maybe won't get dry before we have to pack tomorrow."

"We won't wear suits. Come on, Becca, please."

We tiptoed silently out the screen door to the porch and down the outside stairs. Moonlight poured across the ocean and lit the sand so brightly we could have stopped to read. Hand in hand we raced down the path, dropped our nighties on the sand, and ran in leaps into the surf. Together we dove into the breaking waves and swam under the water until we were in the calmer sea beyond the breakers. The air was warm and the water warmer still. The stars were sparkling, and the phosphorus gleamed upon the water and caught in our hair. We floated on our backs, faces to the moon, shining and glittering.

"We're Sirens," Lucy said.

"Or mermaids," I suggested.

"Or star sisters like the Pleiades, exiled to the sky."

We floated quietly for a few moments, and then she said, "Becca, do you want to know a secret?"

"I didn't think you had any secrets from me, Lucy."

"Just one."

"So, what is it?"

"Becca, I can fly."

I started to laugh thinking this was a joke, but just then a light went on upstairs in the house. We flipped over sinking down deeper in the water until only our noses and the very tops of our heads were above the surface. Scarcely breathing we watched the house. If Millie found us out of bed, she'd tell for sure. Then the light winked out. We scrambled for the shore, grabbed our nightgowns, flew up the stairs and dove back into our bed, our feet still sandy and our hair still wet.

"Lucy, you fool, you don't really expect me to believe that," I whispered in her ear.

"I don't care if you do or not," she yawned.

There were times that I wished I could fly. Just get away, before the life was drained out of me.

10
Becca

Autumn brings the fires of life
That scorch the fields and end the strife,
Of over many shoots that sprung
As from summer's heated kudzu hung.
He wrapped me in his warm embrace
That took my air and left no space
For me to grow or find my place.
                    Becca

I met my husband, Richard, when we were still in high school and far from grown. Lucy and Bobbie Jean and I began dating in our freshman year. Initially, these were just boys our own age who couldn't drive, so one of their parents would pick us up and bring us home from a movie or a party at someone's home or a dance at the Methodist church after a football game. In our sophomore year, Lucy began to date boys in the senior class. I was picking up a restlessness spirit rising in her. When winter set in and we could no longer swim, it became worse. Finally one night in late December, she told us about her dreams.

We were at Wallee's house at a sleepover during Christmas vacation. We had stayed up late playing records and dancing with each other to "The Duke of Earl," "Rock and Roll Will Stand," and "Walk Right In." Someone put on something down and dirty, and Lucy started to shimmy and shine. At first I tried to keep up, but then, it was just all of us watching her.

When the song ended, Millie joked, "So, Lucy, is it true? Are you really doing it?"

"No," she replied, sinking into a pile of folded arms and legs, "I don't have to."

She proceeded to describe the dreams of flying, of rising off the earth and into the night sky. She spun out the words like tentacles, drawing us into a world of whispering night air and calling, pulsating stars, until I could almost feel it too. I often wished that I had looked around to see the faces of the others, to gage their reaction to her story, but I didn't. My eyes never left her face. When she came to the part about answering this star-call, it was so still I was afraid Wallee's mama might come in to see what we were up to. And when she finished, she was almost in a trance—her face washed clean of all the passion and emotions I had seen there.

Wallee broke the spell with a heavy, worried sigh, "Lucy, I hope you haven't told this nonsense to anyone else."

"Only you all, and one other person a long time ago."

"Good, because we don't want anyone to think you're nuts. Or worse." She sounded sensible and a little angry. She wheeled around where she could look each of us in the eye and solemnly instructed, "Everyone promise, Lucy's story doesn't leave this room."

Everyone nodded silently, but with cowed looks and sheepish grins, we passed around a glance that confirmed my thought that Wallee was overreacting and ending the fun too soon. Grudgingly, we rolled out our sleeping bags, turned out the lights, and pretended to go to sleep.

"Becca," Lucy whispered beside me in the dark, "I haven't had this dream since we stopped swimming, and I don't know if I can stand it much longer."

"Please, Lucy," I whispered back, "Don't do anything you're going to regret."

Of course, someone did tell, and stories never are repeated the same way twice. Richard told me that he had heard rumors about my friend. That she was nuts, that she was easy, even that she was dying and having visions of God.

In early Spring, just after we turned sixteen, she called me late one night. She was crying and sounded nothing like her usual self. "I did it," she announced. And before I could say anything, she added, "With Nat. On the golf course."

"Oh, Lucy. How was it?"

"Awful. Messy. It hurt and was nothing like my dream. Becca, there's something wrong with me, isn't there?"

"No, Lucy. I don't think so. I just think we're growing up. I sort of want to do it, too. But I'm afraid. Aren't you afraid of getting pregnant?"

"No, I am just afraid I'll never fly again, never feel what I felt then."

"Well, maybe that's not really how it feels."

"Right now, I'm so heavy and so tired, as though I were turning into clay and mire."

"Don't give up, Lucy. Summer will be here soon, and we can swim again."

"Oh God, Becca, I'm so confused, so tired. There must be a way out of this."

"Out of what, Lucy? Out of what?"

But she just sobbed once more then said good night.

By our junior year, Richard was pressuring me. But I kept thinking about what Lucy had said, and about how crazy my mama would be if she ever found out. We wandered though the wasteland of high school, and then, for two weeks in October, we were electrified by the impending doom of the Cuban Missile Crisis. Boys went from class to class with older portable radios, the size of collegiate dictionaries, and the new transistors, the size of a paperback novel, all tuned to the latest news of the deteriorating situation. Most of them had no headphones. We all listened.

Lucy clutched my arm and we watched excitedly, while the boys argued in the cafeteria, calculating how long it would take a missile bearing an atom bomb to leave Cuba and strike Atlanta, and how long after that before we'd feel the blast. Would we feel anything or just evaporate, skipping the melting and burning stages altogether? How hot would the self-destructing air of Ashbeen get?

"Ah, you all are crazy. There aren't any atom bombs in Cuba. Kennedy has got twenty thousand men and forty ships surrounding that place. It's bottled up, and Khrushchev ain't getting nothing in!" one of the football jocks sneered at the slide rule jockeys.

"How do you know? There's missile sites already there, for sure."

"Them Russkies can't do nothing as good as we can. We'll blow 'em off the map."

"They beat us into space, remember."

Even our usually joking and jovial teachers, like Coach Cainn, looked tired and anxious. Some of them talked quietly to us and tried to calm the agitated boys, who were ready to fight each other in lieu of the unreachable missiles. With each passing day the situation looked more grim. New reconnaissance photos from Cuba showed missiles deployed and ready to launch at the US. Kennedy's advisers were urging him to attack. Khrushchev had ordered his field commanders to unleash the missiles if he did.

Then on the thirteenth day, the Russians shot down a US spy plane. Military readiness reached DEFCON2, the highest alert ever issued. The finger was descending on the button. Nine tactical nuclear missiles stood aimed at US cities. Atlanta was less than a thousand miles away from the one destined for us, well within the range of their missilemen.

We gathered at the Methodist Church for an MYF candlelit, prayer vigil. In the flickering darkness, over a hundred frightened young people, of all faiths, cried and prayed and held each other. From the circle of Richard's arms, where I had always felt so safe, I stared with the fascination of one sitting in the lifeboat watching those unlucky ones outside. Millie and Sally were holding a single candle between them, tears bright on both their faces. Millie's low alto and Sally's sweet soprano blended with the other young voices in a faltering appeal to grace.

The words were: *Rock of Ages, cleft for me, Let me hide myself in thee.*

But the two mightiest nations on earth were playing chicken, and at any minute, we could be blown to kingdom come with no place to hide. I'm sure that more than one girl lost her virginity to the thought of nuclear extinction during those last days. Finally, the Russians backed down.

We were riding a roller coaster that pushed to the brink of disaster, then dropped us back into the boredom of Latin III.

In April Lucy confided, "Becca, I've taken almost every academic class that Ashbeen High has to offer. I'm thinking about applying to Emory and skipping my senior year."

"Can you do that?"

"I can if I take an English and a history class this summer. They may not let me into the main campus, but I'm sure I can get into the old campus at Oxford."

"Oh, Lucy, Oxford is an even smaller town than Ashbeen. You'll go nuts."

"I'll go nuts if I stay here. At least there's a college library there."

She did leave, but I'm not sure she found a haven from whatever she was fleeing.

Two weeks before the junior-senior prom, Lucy's prom date, Brinkley, and Millie's date, Allen, and three other boys were coming home late Sunday night from a weekend trip to Tybee Island. Twenty miles from home the car spun out of control and flipped over. Allen was killed. Brinkley was hospitalized with multiple broken bones and internal injuries, but he survived. The other three boys walked away.

On Monday morning, all of us had heard the news, except Lucy. I had just walked up to her locker, and she had asked me, "Why is everyone so quiet this morning?" when Millie came up to her. Slapping her hard across the face, Millie broke into string of ragged sobs.

Lucy drew back against her locker and raised her books to her chest as if to protect herself.

"What's the matter, Millie? Why did you hit me?" she asked in a startled whisper.

Millie opened her mouth, but nothing came out except a choking, "Your...your...your..." Then she turned and ran down the hall. I pulled Lucy into the restroom, past the staring girls, and into the last stall. I took her books out of her arms and set them down on the floor with mine, and then I told her.

"Lucy honey, Allen is dead. And Brinkley is hurt real bad."

She gasped and sank down on the toilet seat. Putting my arms around her, I knelt down beside her.

"But why does she blame me?"

"Because Brinkley was driving. His car flipped over last night on highway 17."

"Oh, Becca, say that isn't so. Tell me y'all are just joking, please," she begged.

"No, Lucy honey, it's true. I'm sorry, so sorry."

The bell rang for classes, and still we stayed huddled in that stall. Lucy was crying softly, and I was trying to think of anything I could say. I knew she wasn't madly in love with Brinkley, not like I was in love with Richard, but they were friends. Some of the tears had to be for Millie and Allen, too. Then I realized, she was trying to take part of the blame.

"Oh, Becca, I knew he drove too fast sometimes. Why didn't I say something? Why didn't I tell him he should slow down?"

"Lucy, this isn't your fault. Don't you let Millie make you think it is."

"But she does blame me, doesn't she? That's why she hit me."

"Only because there is no one else to blame, honey, no one else to hit."

I torn off another piece of toilet paper and gave it to her to staunch the flow of tears. Finally, Miss Jennings came looking for us. She arranged for Lucy's daddy to come get us and take us home.

Lucy spent Prom night at the hospital with Brinkley. Millie stayed the night with Sally and Wallee. Bobbie Jean and I went to a prom that was a little more somber and less joyous than we had wanted for such a long awaited rite of passage. I danced to "Blue Velvet" and "A Summer Place" under a sea of blue crepe-paper and silver stars, then gave in to Richard under a blanket on top of some Yankee soldier's grave. Life just seemed too short, too uncertain, to wait. What were we waiting for? A bomb to drop? A speeding car?

Lucy was right. At least at first it was pretty awful. Some hurried groping in the Confederate cemetery or in the back seat of a car. But once the gate was down, it was impossible to lock it back again. Richard and I married too soon. Right out of high school we eloped. I wasn't pregnant, but my mama went crazy anyway. We were not ready for marriage, but we hung in for fifteen years trying to become who we were meant to be, while being who we weren't. What I did get from that marriage was Shea. And she will never break my heart.

11

Wallace Ann Anderson, "Wallee"

If you can keep your head while all about you,
Are loosing theirs and blaming it on you,
If you can trust yourself when all men doubt you,
But make allowance for their doubting too;
  The Laurels, Ashbeen High School Annual, Class of '64

I have my mother's maiden name, Wallace, and her sister's name, Ann. My brother gave me the name Wallee. I cursed him with male pattern baldness.

When I got Lucy's letter, I really wasn't very interested in going to any reunion until I realized that Bobbie Jean would be there. I had never been that close to Lucy. She was much too wild and flighty for me. But Bobbie Jean was a different story. I had polio when I was nine, and although I recovered, the muscles in my left leg atrophied and withered. I learned to walk, but only with a heavy, clumsy brace, and so, I preferred to spend my life in a wheel chair instead. Keeping up with the other kids was hard enough. Keeping up with Lucy would have been impossible.

The Opening

My father was a doctor in Ashbeen. I don't know that he ever got over the pain of not being able to give me back what the polio took away. That summer of '55, before the Salk vaccine, before the three shot immunization or the little pink sugar cubes of protection, the epidemic had been terrible. Swimming pools and movie theaters were shut down. Even the Sunday schools and churches closed, and near panic was everywhere. I don't remember actually getting sick, only the terrifying recovery, and my fear and guilt and anger. The words *polio* and *cripple* were never spoken in our home.

We had a large house on the best side of town, and for a long time my mother tried to buy friends for me. In grade school she had to take me everywhere in her Pontiac station wagon. An old high school, with four flights of stairs and a freight elevator that didn't work most of the time, was going to be a challenge. When Bobbie Jean offered her friendship, I could hardly believe it. What did I have to offer to one of the prettiest girls in school? I was to discover that it wasn't so much what I had, as what I wanted from her—nothing that she didn't gladly give.

Bobbie Jean was the other half of life for me. She brought me a world full of laughs and fancies and the unexpected. My mind worked in straight, precise lines. Hers seemed to weave a logic out of hopes and magic. She drew me out and made me want to walk again. Bobbie Jean appeared to have the world wrapped around her little finger. As if she were the mistress of a thousand acres, she simply ordered boys to hoist my chair up flights of stairs. And they did it, amply paid with one of her smiles. When I struggled into a room in that clomping brace, she was my shield. No one looked at me, only at her. And finally, I realized that it wasn't any easier for her than it was for me. She was the target of so much envy, and I of so much pity. In the long run the effect was the same.

Sometime in our freshman year, I broke down and told her how hurt and angry I really was. She had made some innocent comment about my being brave, and in a flash I'd turned on her. My fury surprised me, it must have floored her.

"I think *brave* is the cruelest word in the English language," I spit at her. "My mama says it every day, and every day it cuts a little deeper. I'm not brave. I'm scared shitless."

She sat down on my bed beside my chair and looked first at the floor and then sideways at me. "Do you want to talk about it?"

And I knew I did. I'd been hoarding pain and resentment in the empty places of my life for seven years. It was time to clean house. "No one wants me, not really. And they never will," I said bitterly.

She didn't flinch, didn't say anything. She just listened, while I tossed out all the pent-up fears, the tattered dreams that I had clung to, and the mismatched hopes of girl and reality. The grudgingly given gifts I shoved into the back of my soul. "Sometimes I hate my father. I really hate him," I choked. "He can't even look at me, his own daughter. I don't think he has even said my name in five years...just *she* or *her*."

"Or *princess* or *sugar*," she whispered. A tiny, sympathetic smile encouraged me to go on, to get it all out. And I did. I pulled out every ugly doubt and suspicion that I had been afraid to wear, because they weren't like everyone else's, and that made me look like the freak I knew I was.

"Why me? Why did this happen to me? Wasn't I good enough? Don't I count in the greater scheme of things? If I have to suffer this, why can't I at least understand?" I pounded my fists against the arm of my chair and flung these useless rags of unanswerable questions at her, testing the very bottom of my shabby grief.

At last, there remained there only the little, lingering lint of guilt. "I think I've ruined my parents' marriage. They hardly talk, and we never go anywhere as a family. Just mama and me, and sometimes my brother." I dropped my head in my hands and cried, as much in relief as in despair.

She answered then with her own hidden dread. She drew away my tear-wet hands from my face. And playing with my fingers, seemingly absorbed in their likeness to her own, she said, "I'm so afraid that no one will want me either, Wallee. Not the real me. I'm afraid of being just a pretty thing, and that no one will ever get beyond that. I'm scared that I will fall in love with someone, just to discover that it's only my looks he wants. Something to display, like a trophy or a piece of art.

"I think I could stand the resentment and the envy. But until I met you, I didn't think anyone could understand. They'd just get angry that I could be so ungrateful and unappreciative of such a gift." She said *gift* as if it were the worst of curses, and I did understand. Everyone had told me how grateful I should be to have my life.

She lifted her face to me and continued. "Last summer, when Mama and I were shopping in Atlanta, I tripped and fell…right downtown on Peachtree Street. I scraped both my hands and knees and hurt my pride. Some strange woman helped me up, but she never even asked if I was hurt. She just stared at me and said 'My goodness, aren't you pretty. I'd give anything to look like you.' As if nothing else that ever happened to me, that I would ever do, would matter."

I grabbed her hands and smiled at her, and felt really home for the first time I in a long while.

With Bobbie Jean came Sally and Millie and Lucy and Becca. Sally also became a close friend. Since it was years before the guys ever caught up to her height, she had grown used to sitting at home when the others were dating. We went to movies, watched TV, listened to *South Pacific*, and cooked up awful concoctions together. I can remember the first pizza I ever ate. It came in a box like a cake mix and bore no resemblance whatsoever to the wood-fired delights I get today. We saw *Rome Adventure* five times one rainy weekend, and cried in each other's arms when Kennedy was shot. Sally eventually became an excellent cook and a fine chemist. She could rattle off the elements of some polysyllabic compound as easily as reciting the ingredients in a Devil's Food Cake and was equally as at home in a laboratory as a kitchen.

"Wallee," she asked me one night, "do you ever get the feeling that you are just watching life happen? That someone forgot to write your part?"

"No," I answered, "I just don't like my part. I want to be in another play."

"Oh, of course, so much has happened to you. Forgive me, I wasn't thinking."

Millie was more of a mystery. She was plump when plump was still cute. Her round body and fickle nature reminded me of a bouncing ball. Perky one minute, withdrawn the next. Eager to start something, but bored with it long before getting around to finishing. Prom night following the accident was just plain weird.

Sally and I were prepared for a ten-hanky night. I had turned on all the lights in the rec room and hidden all the romantic records. No "Teen Angel" or "Moody River" that night. I stashed the Kleenex behind my chair and put on my best sympathetic smile. I'd even bought a pack of cigarettes. "You can't smoke and bawl at the same time," I'd reasoned over Sally's objections.

"I don't think she'll be really all *that* upset, just disappointed and low. She'd only gone out with Allen once or twice," Sally informed me.

But Millie was, if anything, near manic. I could tell that Sally was worried as soon as they came in the door. Millie's hair was done, and she was made up like the Prom Queen. She kept laughing and telling a string of wickedly dirty jokes.

"What do you call a virgin who practices oral sex?" she asked the bewildered Sally.

"I have no idea, Millie. What is oral sex?"

"You poor baby, you don't know?" She laughed as if this was the funniest thing she'd ever heard.

"I don't know either," I confessed, not at all sure I wanted to know. "I don't suppose it's just talking dirty?"

Millie hooted. "Not unless just talking dirty is against the law in Georgia, honey. Even if you're married," she said smugly, plainly intent on teasing us.

"Then I don't think I want to hear any more about it," Sally said crossing her arms.

She went right on like Sally had never said a word. "A lot of wives won't do it. Especially our delicate Southern belles," Millie giggled, exaggerating her drawl so that *delicate* came out more like *dell·.eye· kate*. "Men love it, sugar. That's why there are so many whore houses in Georgia."

"There's a movie on channel 3 tonight. Doris Day in *Please, Don't Eat the Daisies*. Let's watch that," Sally suggested, desperately trying to change the subject. This just seemed to crack Millie up. She rolled on the sofa, laughing and holding her sides.

"Do you suppose she's taking some kind of medication?" Sally whispered to me. "This isn't at all like her. She sings in the choir and teaches Sunday school, for Heaven's sake. Surely she hasn't been drinking."

"Maybe if we got her to eat something," I suggested.

While Sally was making sandwiches, I changed the records, slowing down the tempo and the mood. Millie started dancing with her own reflection in the sliding glass doors to the patio. Sort of swaying, not quite doing even a soft shag. Suddenly she stopped and slumped down on the floor one hand still extended to the imaginary partner in her dance.

"You know that dream of Lucy's? The one she told us about last year?" She asked my image in the glass doors.

"Yes. So what?"

"I bet she made it up. I don't think she really dreams that."

"Why not?"

She didn't answer. She just lay down on the floor and started humming to herself. Or maybe she was crying. I don't remember now. I limped over to her, and she reached up and grabbed my hand. "Wallee," she whispered, all the tease gone, "I don't know what oral sex is, either. Really I don't. I was just fooling around."

"It's okay, Millie. Maybe there is no such thing."

"Oh, but there is. I've read about it." She perked up with one last bounce before sliding back to the floor. Before Sally returned with the sandwiches, she was asleep. I took my mama's Wedding Ring quilt off the sofa and spread it over her while lifting a finger to my lips to hush Sally's step.

"She's asleep."

"What on earth do you suppose has gotten into her?"

"People react differently to grief. Sometimes the queerest things are funny. Or maybe she is taking something."

"I suppose…but this doesn't seem like grief to me."

We tuned in the movie, the sound low, and sat silently watching over the deflated little ball.

When Doris Day and David Niven finally kissed, Sally sighed and said, "Wallee, do you realize I've never even been kissed by anyone other than my family?"

"Well, I have. But it was in fourth grade, so I suppose that doesn't count," I confided.

"Okay, what do you think oral sex is?" she asked sheepishly.

"I don't know. I'll have to ask my brother. He seems to know everything." I knew it had to be pretty bad when he wouldn't tell me. All he'd say is, "Trust me. You don't want to know."

By our senior year, I almost never used the wheelchair. Lucy had departed for college. Becca spent most of her time with Richard. Millie and Sally entered the Betty Crocker baking contest, and Sally took second place in the state finals. She also took an honorable mention in the state science fair with an entry on food additives. I'm sure it deserved more, but in the early sixties, rockets were much sexier than chemicals in food. Bobbie Jean and I were coeditors of the high school annual. Bobbie Jean insisted that we put Lucy's picture in with the class of '64 even though she had graduated the summer before.

It was also Bobbie Jean's idea to use the lines from Rudyard Kipling's "If" under our senior pictures. Our US Government class was taught by the high school football coach, a nice enough man but a male chauvinist nonetheless. He had the nerve to stand up in front of the class and tell the girls not to get his football players too hot the night before a game. Sex sapped their energy. As part of our graded material for the class, we all had to memorize and recite this poem. Each line defines a trait of an admirable character. But the last line is, "You'll be a man, my son." It was clear that the coach only wanted the girls to memorize this poem so they could spot good husband material. Yet there was not a single Ashbeen High School graduate who could not recite Kipling's "If."

"We'll put a few lines under only girls' photos," Bobbie Jean suggested. "Won't that be a hoot?"

"But Bobbie Jean, some of this makes no sense," I complained. "What about these lines you've assigned to Sally, '...not be tired by waiting…Or being hated….' What's that supposed to mean? Nobody hates Sally. She never does anything but what she's suppose to. I don't think too many people feel anything about her one way or the other. She doesn't stir people up."

"Sally is a late bloomer. You wait. One day she will start doing things. And anyone who does things gets hated," she reasoned. "She won't be a Good Girl forever."

"I just don't think anybody will get it, Bobbie Jean."

"Sally will."

Well Sally, maybe I want to see what's become of you too.

12
Wallee

Towers in the air,
Tentacles floating in the sea,
Smoke drifting in the wind,
Idle dreams adrift.

Random thoughts bobbing,
On waves of semi-consciousness.

Warmed by the sun,
Kissed by the breeze,
Caressed by the sea,
Seduced by the day.

      Wallace Ann Anderson

I hadn't been swimming in over ten years. I was too afraid to go in the pool at the country club or the YMCA, sure that everyone would be looking at my leg so exposed in a swimsuit. Afraid that someone would bump into me and knock me over, or complain because I wasn't getting out of the way fast enough. The river north of town would have been private, but slowly moving, Southern rivers are not the place that girls want to swim. They crawl with water moccasins, and slightly further east of Ashbeen, with alligators.

In the summer after high school, Lucy came home from college and announced that she knew a place where we could swim. She had been to a small, hidden lake an hour northwest of town just where the hills became the tail of the Appalachian Mountains. This sounded like the kind of place fraternity boys learned about, but I was game. We all were. One hot day in late July, we loaded my brother's car—what had been my mama's old station wagon—with bags of food, piles of towels, and thermos jugs of pink Kool Aid and ice tea. Sally, Millie, Bobbie Jean and I piled in the back, and Becca drove while Lucy navigated.

With the windows rolled down and the radio playing "You Don't Own Me," we rolled up highway 17 singing and shouting to be heard over the den. Lucy nearly lost the map out the window. Bobbie Jean got carsick. But we were having a glorious time. I looked at my girl friends, and for a moment, I thought they looked like something out of time. Wild women. Their hair was long and blowing in the wind. Their arms were bare and waving to some Beach Boys' tune. A fine dew of perspiration silvered the base of their throats and upper lips. They looked ready to throw themselves on life.

When we got there, it was everything Lucy had promised. The lake must have been created from an abandoned quarry. On one side steep, etched granite steps, each five to ten feet tall, rose out of the lake and up into the trees of the ancient mountain. A small, sand and gravel beach had washed up on the near side, and a stream flowed out at the point where the woods met the wall of the mountain. The lake was spring feed, cool and clear. And no one else was there.

We dumped our towels and food supplies on the beach and shed our shorts and shirts, stripping down to our swimsuits. Sally and Bobbie Jean helped me remove my brace, and then, carefully balanced between them,

I moved slowly into the water. Becca and Lucy walked in front testing the bottom for any sudden holes or drop-offs. When we were only six or eight feet from shore, Millie called out to us. She was standing on a little ledge eight to ten feet above the water on the far side of the lake. Her bright yellow suit jumped against the gray stone behind her.

"Look at me ladies. Look at me. Here I go. Waheeee," she cried and dove into the water.

I saw Lucy flinch, the old lifeguard instincts revived. Millie's head bobbed to the surface, and Lucy called out, "Hey, Millie, don't do that. It's dangerous if we don't know how deep the water is, or what's beneath the surface." Millie just waved an arm and headed for the far shore. We continued to slide slowly into the deeper water.

At about waist deep, I began to feel the water take my weight. This body that had been weighted down for so long was beginning to float. The ruffles on Bobbie Jean's pink flowered swim suit drifted out around her waist like a ballerina's tutu. Sally smiled and drew her free hand through the water scooping up a splash for Becca's back. We took another pair of steps, and the water rose to my breasts. Lucy came toward me with her arms outstretched.

"If you link your arms with mine and let me support you, I think you could float, Wallee," she suggested.

"I'll hold up your legs to give you a start," Becca offered.

And so Sally and Bobbie Jean gave up their supporting roles. Lucy and I intertwined our arms, my hands on her shoulders, hers on mine. I leaned toward her. Becca put her arms under my knees, and my feet were off the ground. I was floating. I was floating. Lucy moved in gentle swishes, and I could feel the water roll against my legs and tickle my waist and armpits. I tried a little kick and found that I could keep my legs up without Becca's help. She drifted off and turned over to float on her back, her long black hair fanning out to frame her heart shaped face. Sally and Bobbie Jean were whirling in the waist deep water, plowing the surface with their outstretched fingers and laughing. A thrilling shiver passed over me.

"Look down," Lucy said.

I could see all the way to the bottom. Lucy's toes raised little storms, whorls of silvery sand. Bits of mica gleamed and occasionally flashed back the sun, like tiny searchlights probing the twilight depths. Where the bottom had not yet been disturbed by our feet, the sand rippled and rolled, a miniature desert-scape, dotted with hunks of gravel. There was no vegetation. It was as lonely as the surface of a barren moon. I drifted over this tiny world almost like flying.

"Lucy," I whispered, "do you still have that dream?"

"No," she replied sadly, "not anymore. Not for two years. I don't think I ever will again."

"Oh, Lucy, I'm sorry."

She didn't answer. Instead she asked, "Want to try a little faster?"

We moved in a line parallel to the shore, not quickly, but fast enough for me to get the sensation of gliding over liquid air. The exhilaration and freedom of this gravity defying feat made me close my eyes for just a moment and imagine what it would be like to fly. To cut the anchor that held me to the ground, to drop my brace, my bonds, and just lift off into the sky. I opened my eyes and looked at Lucy's face. Her eyes were closed too, and she was smiling. When she opened them, I laughed and she laughed with me.

Just as we were turning back toward the others, we heard Millie call again. Lucy turned her head to look over her shoulder, and I tried to peer around her. Millie was standing on the same ledge poised for a leap.

"Here I go again," she called and sprang into the air. Her head disappeared beneath the surface, and I felt Lucy stiffen. We waited, barely breathing, for her to reappear. Several seconds past and nothing.

"Becca," Lucy shouted, "Becca, come take Wallee. Hurry."

Becca was already racing toward us. Sally and Bobbie Jean stood in knee deep water, their hands shading their eyes, peering at the spot where Millie had disappeared. When Becca reached us, Lucy past me off and rushed toward that spot. She had only covered part of the distance when Millie's head popped above the water.

"Ha-ha, fooled y'all," she sang out.

Becca breathed a sigh of relief and shouted back, "That's not funny, Millie."

"You almost scared us half to death," Sally said.

Bobbie Jean just shook her head. When Becca and I reached the others, they helped me to sit in the water near the shore. I leaned back against Bobbie Jean's knees. Sally dropped down beside us, and Becca turned toward Lucy as she walked out of the deeper water. Her face was red, and she was breathing hard trying to control her anger.

"What is with her?" she asked between her teeth.

"She's had a hard winter," Sally said quietly. "She was so depressed when Allen died and so listless all Fall term."

"But she was never that close to Allen, was she?" Bobbie Jean asked. "I thought they had only dated once or twice."

"That's what I thought too," Sally confirmed. "Then when spring came, I was relieved to see her so much better."

"Maybe too much better," Becca said.

The conversation turned to movies and plans for the rest of the summer. The water lapped against our feet and legs as if to add its own babble to our gossip. Becca and Lucy swam out and entertained themselves doing handstands and water somersaults. Their hair plumed out behind them when they went beneath the surface, and whipped the air as they sprang forward to dive again toes pointing toward the sky. Their grace and ease amazed me. Their suits were plain and simple, swimmers' suits. Becca's was white and Lucy's black. Millie wandered up, her head wrapped in a pink towel.

"Hey, that's my towel," Bobbie Jean said.

"Well, I forgot mine," Millie replied.

"And what am I supposed to do?" Bobbie Jean asked.

"Oh, Wallee always has extras."

I nodded at Bobbie Jean. I did have an extra in the car.

"I'm hungry. When do we eat?" Millie wanted to know.

"We practically just got here, Millie," Sally said. "Let's enjoy the lake a little longer."

"Well, I think I'll go see what we have," she replied and walked off in the direction of the pile of bags and clothes near the woods.

"What did you bring?" Sally called to her.

"Oh, whatever Mama put in," she answered.

"I don't know how she'll manage on her own at college," Sally sighed. "She doesn't even know how to roll her own hair. Her mother does it for her. Do you know she almost flunked our Sewing and Design class?"

"What, Miss Future Homemaker?" Bobbie Jean said in surprise.

"She just didn't seem to be able to finish her dress. Always some excuse."

"You're worried about her aren't you?" I said.

"Yes, I am," Sally confessed.

"Well, not today," Bobbie Jean ordered. "Today's for fun only." Then she splashed Sally, careful not to get her face wet, and ran out into the water.

I watched them all, occasionally turning to look for Millie. Bobbie Jean's towel lay on the ground, but Millie was nowhere in sight. Sally and Bobbie Jean returned to sit with me, and soon Becca and Lucy dropped down beside us, too. Becca stretched out and lifted her face to the sun, eyes closed. I wonder now what she was thinking, because a week later she was married. We never were all together again. In the Fall, Lucy was going to Emory on the main campus in Atlanta, Sally and I were headed for Converse in South Carolina, and Bobbie Jean was going to Agnes Scott. Becca had planned to go to the University of Georgia with Millie, but her marriage changed all that. She followed Richard to Georgia Tech, where he had a scholarship and she had nothing.

When the sun dipped behind the trees, we pulled on our clothes and went to look for Millie and our food. We found her in the back seat of the car asleep, a half empty container of chicken salad cradled in her lap.

"I was hungry," was all she said.

13

Millicent Jane Sonders, "Millie"

*If you can make one heap of all your winnings,
And risk it on one turn of pitch and toss,
And lose, and start again at your beginnings,
And never breathe a word about your loss;*
   ***The Laurels**, Ashbeen High School Annual, Class of 64*

From   SallyB4420@aol.com
Date   Friday, April 9, 1999 7:48 a.m.
To   LouisanaSavage@ibm.net
Subject Re: Millie

Lucy, I'm not having any luck tracking down Millie. No one seems to know anything more than that she went to school at UGA then went on to Auburn for a Masters. But after that she seems to simply disappear. S. PS The week of July 4th is no good for me.

Part II

Atlanta

14

Lucy

Between the dark and daylight hours,
As I pass from the world of dreams into the ever present,
I pause along the narrow corridor in search of that hidden passage
To another world where we have been.
The scent still lingers.
Take me there.

Lucy Jones

Becca was right. Oxford was smaller than Ashbeen, and I did nearly go crazy. The old campus of Emory, with its soft pink brick and white clapboard buildings, and densely shaded lawns, was as different from the new, sprawling campus of peach marble, glass, and steel as the tiny town was from the Atlanta of the New South. Emory had preserved the old campus for students that it deemed promising, but not yet ready for the bustle and competition of the larger university. Three things probably kept me sane—the library, the lake, and Lawrence.

I was amazed how easy it was to get my parents to let me graduate early and go to Oxford. I had expected a fight, an argument about how I was too young or how I'd be better prepared if I waited another year. I thought Daddy would at least mention that I could probably get a scholarship if I stayed in Ashbeen and joined more clubs, did more volunteer work. But there was no fight, no argument, not even a discussion. My daddy just said, "Yes, Louisiana, you should go." And that was that.

To help with expenses I got a summer job as a lifeguard at the YMCA. I had the first morning watch, and it was really pretty boring. Mainly just calling down kids for running or rough housing. Only once did someone get in trouble. A young girl hit the board while diving and came up screaming and crying. That was easily resolved by tossing out a line to pull her in and putting some first aid cream on her scraped legs. The best part of my summer job was that I could swim alone early in the morning before the pool opened.

I found the lake at Oxford in my first week there. It was only opened until late September, but some evenings after that I'd sneak out and swim for half an hour anyway. I had forgotten how much better it is to swim in a lake rather than a pool. The water not only smells better, it even feels better in a lake. It is possible to get away from the crowds of arms and legs, and just drift undisturbed.

When cold weather set in, there was the library, and I could get books from the main campus of Emory, too. But my supreme salvation at Oxford was Lawrence. I met him in chapel. Attendance at chapel was required at least twice a week. Seating was assigned, and seat occupancy was monitored. We were not required to listen, only to be there, and students often slept or read the school paper. Chapel was held on Tuesday, Thursday, and Saturday. Of course, only the truly devoted attended on Saturdays. On the first Tuesday of the school year I went looking for my seat. He had already found his.

"Is your name really Louisiana Jones?" he asked me, pointing to the nametag on the back of my chair.

"Yes, it is. But everyone calls me Lucy," I smiled and offered my hand to him.

"Lawrence Jones," he said, "everyone calls me Lawrence. A pleasure to meet you, Louisiana." And he shook my hand.

"Alphabetical order?"

"Of course, what else."

"I'm a new freshman, and you are…?" I inquired politely.

"A sophomore, transferring to Atlanta as soon as possible."

With these basic introductions out of the way, he picked up his book and went back to reading. I listened to the speaker drone on for a while, then I got out a book too. As we were filing out, he asked me, "What are you reading?"

"Lawrence Durrell's new book," I replied holding it up. "Have you read anything by him?"

"No, I don't read much other than texts."

I neither wanted nor expected this relationship to be more than the polite consideration of forced seatmates. I had already decided that I was through with fumbling around in the back seats of cars trying to find something that was possibly only a dream. All I wanted from Oxford was a jumping off point to the greater world. From Lawrence Jones I wanted nothing at all.

A week before Thanksgiving I got a letter from home. "Oh, shit," I said rather louder than planned. I was reading my mail in chapel.

"Oh, really," he replied with feigned shock. "Is anything the matter?"

"Daddy writes that he is taking my mama home to Port Gibson in Mississippi to stay with my grandmother. Apparently she isn't well."

"I'm sorry to hear that," he said politely.

"It just means that I can't go home for Thanksgiving like I'd planned."

"Well, I'll be here too. Want to get together?"

"Sure, we can eat turkey in the cafeteria."

"Probably not. I think it will be closed."

"Great. Then what do we do?"

"We'll think of something," he replied.

The next day he called me. "Lucy, have you been out this afternoon?" he asked quietly.

"No, I've been reading. What's up?"

"Then you haven't heard."

"Heard what?" I asked.

"Lucy, Kennedy has been shot."

"President Kennedy?"

"Yes. He was in Dallas. I believe he may be dead."

"Oh," I could think of nothing else to say. I was just sort of numb. The only thought that formed was the idle question: Will they cancel classes?

"Lucy?" Lawrence said.

"Yes."

"Would you like for me to come get you? There is a group of us gathering in the Quad."

"Yes, I'd like that. I'll meet you down stairs in fifteen minutes."

I can remember walking toward the Quad with Lawrence and thinking what a nice autumn day it was. The last of the falling leaves crackled beneath our feet. The sounds of television sets turned up louder than normal drifted from the dorms, but otherwise, it was very quiet. The sun was sinking lower in the overcast sky, and winter would be coming soon.

The rest of that day, and most of the following weekend, are just a blur of crying faces, TV images, and voices of despair. I leaned on Lawrence, and he put his arm around me as we listened to the college president speak to a sea of sorrowful students. At some point I found myself in his car, and he was kissing me. Then he stopped and pulled away. Putting both hands on the wheel he said, "Lucy, I have to tell you something. I'm engaged."

"Engaged?"

"To be married. To a girl back home."

"Then what are we doing here?" I asked both hurt and angry.

"I was asking myself the same thing. I think I need you right now. But I know that's not fair to you."

"No kidding." I didn't know whether to cry or to hit him.

"Just take me back to the dorm. It's late and I'm very tired," I said wearily.

When I saw him again in chapel, he asked, "Are we still on for Thanksgiving? I'd like the company."

"Why aren't you going home to your girl in…?" I didn't know where home was for him.

"New Hampshire. It's too far and costs too much to fly."

I thought a moment. Maybe this would work. I'd never had a male friend, and I really didn't need any entanglements if I wanted to move on as quickly as possible.

"Okay. But we've got to lay some ground rules."

"Anything you say," he agreed.

The campus emptied out by Wednesday afternoon. We had dinner in the cafeteria before it closed for the holiday and actually talked for the first time. He was a pre-law student, who had been bumped from the Atlanta campus to Oxford because his high school in New Hampshire was so small. If Emory were not such a great school for the money, he'd be somewhere else in a heartbeat. He liked to run but had never really liked swimming. He was on the track team, and his hobby was photography.

We mapped out our plans for the long weekend. A football game in Atlanta on Thanksgiving Day and, somewhere, some turkey. A picnic and reading on Friday. A movie on Saturday. The rest of the time, we'd see what developed.

The ground rules: We were friends. He could hold my hand or take my arm, but that was it, nothing romantic. I could accept dates from other guys whenever I wanted to, no questions asked.

By Saturday night we were kissing, and by Sunday we were more than just friends. We argued. What would the world be like if the South had won the war? Did Hauptmann really kidnap the Lindbergh baby? Were the minds of men and women different because our brains were physically different? Were not all guilty murderers insane? What was God? When did life begin? Three weeks later, we both went home for Christmas.

When I got home, I found that Mama was still away. I did some cooking, took Daddy's car shopping and to visit Becca. She and her mother had been fighting, and Becca was very quiet.

She didn't want to talk about it. But then she never did where her mama was concerned. Daddy and I went over my class schedule and discussed majors. He seemed reluctant to tell me about Mama or Grandmama. He just said she was doing better, and we would call on Christmas Day. Becca set me up with a friend of Richard's, and we all went to an Ashbeen High senior class dance.

On Christmas Day Daddy put the call through to Port Gibson. He talked to Mama first, then I got on the line.

"Hi, Mama, Merry Christmas!"

"Merry Christmas, dear. Are you and your father doing okay?"

"Yes, ma'am, we're just fine. How is Grandmama?" I asked.

"She's doing well, I'm sure," Mama answered. "Did you like your presents?"

"Yes, ma'am, I love the sweater. Thank you very much."

"I am glad, dear. Study hard and I'll see you soon," she said. "Put your daddy back on now."

"I love you Mama."

Daddy spoke a few more words, then he hung up the phone. When he did, there were tears in his eyes.

"Is Mama really in Port Gibson, Daddy?"

"Of course she is, sugar. Where else would she be?" I was afraid to answer this. "Don't you worry. She'll be back home soon."

But I did worry. About her and about me. I wanted to talk to someone. I wanted to talk to Lawrence.

When we returned to Oxford, I expected our relationship to be awkward, and it was for the first week. Then we just seemed to pick up where we left off. One night in January I decided to risk going all the way. Instead, I told him about my dream and what Matt had told me long before.

"If what I felt when I dreamt of flying was an orgasm, then I've never experienced anything like it when I am awake, and I really don't want to try again. There's probably something wrong with me."

"Oh Lucy, the only experiences you've had were fast gropings with impatient, frightened boys."

"And what about your bride-to-be? How would she feel about us?"

"I love you, Lucy," he said, but added, "and I love her, too."

"You can't have it both ways, Lawrence. I don't think I should see you anymore."

But of course I did, every Tuesday and Thursday in chapel. I dated other guys, was in the May Queen's court, and was serenaded by Sigma Chi. But every Wednesday night I saw Lawrence. We were friends but in a very special way. I told him about the *hetairae*. And how I wanted to be more than just a female.

"Lucy, the *hetairae* were courtesans in an age when women couldn't get an audience for their own ideas. They used their powerful and famous lovers' names to promote their work. I don't think you'll have to do that today."

"You think women are given an equal opportunity in arts, politics, and business?"

"Well, maybe not equal, but an opportunity anyway. That's better than a hundred years ago."

"Not to do what I want to do. I'd rather be a *hetairae*."

"I don't think so Lucy. I don't think you'll want to share the glory."

He taught me to be comfortable with my waking body, and that perhaps, there was nothing wrong with me. In the early spring when I began to swim again, he took a series of photographs at what I came to think of as Wallee's lake. Traced over the light and peaceful surface of the sunlit water in his photos, is an aura of shadow and mystery cast by the wall of the mountain. A graceful spirit floats between the two worlds like a messenger to men from the gods. He called the picture The *Hetaira*.

We drove to the lake one Sunday in early April. The trees were just beginning to bud. Here and there the dogwoods laid a bloom of snow over the hillsides, and the redbuds answered back with a blush of pink. Lawrence climbed up on one of the ledges overlooking the lake on the far side where the stone had been quarried from the mountainside. I slipped out of my clothes and into the water from the beach and swam out toward him. The cold water almost took my breath away, but I circled several times just below the water's surface before I could stand it no longer.

When I climbed out of the icy water, I stretched out beside him on that granite ledge above the lake. The sun warmed my naked body, and the chill bumps slowly subsided. I closed my eyes and leaned my head back so my hair would not drip down my back. He dipped his fingers into the puddle forming behind me and very slowly let one drop of water fall between my breasts. It trickled down across my stomach and into my navel. I felt it. That dream quality of rising toward the stars. The second drop fell, and I was loosing touch with up and down. The third drop fell and rushed to join the other two, and as one, they spilled over my belly and slipped between my legs. I recognized the star call. He drew his still-wet fingers down my body, across my nipples, over the rising ribcage and into the hollows at my hipbones. I was answering. My pelvis arched, all desire released to drive us onward closer to the stars. He spread my knees and buried his head between my legs. I reached that pentacle, hanging there for one short moment and then falling back in a long, deep spiral.

He rolled away and lay quietly beside me for several minutes. I opened my eyes and smiled at him. Then he said quietly and almost sadly, "Lucy, there is no fiancee in New Hampshire. The truth is, I'm a homosexual. You were so lovely and cared so passionately, I thought that I could change. But your Greeks were right, there are more than two sexes. And you and I are neither completely male nor female."

The following year we both transferred to Emory's Atlanta campus. He introduced me to my future husband in October of that year. He was a graduate student in French literature. I was a philosophy major. We were married the next Christmas and had some good years. He taught at Columbia, and I got my Masters. Our daughter, Clea, was born. We spent a year in France during his sabbatical. I started to paint. Shortly after that, I realized that he had a serious drinking problem. I tried for several years to save him. Then one day, while we were drying off after our swim, I heard Clea repeat to me Matt's second rule of live saving: "Mama, don't let the victim drown you."

I took my daughter and returned to the South. It was rough for a while, teaching business ethics at small community colleges, speaking at conferences. Then I began to get clients in Atlanta, and a year later in New York and San Francisco. Soon we were not short on money, only time.

15

Becca Rollins

From   Louisiana Savage <LouisianaSavage@ibm.net>
Date   Friday, May 7, 1999 8:18 p.m.
To   Rebecca Rollins <RebeRollins@aol.com>
Subject   Lenox Square

Guess where I was today? Clea has picked out a wedding dress at Rich's, and we went there for the first fitting. Bring back a few memories? The date for our gathering is now firm, June 25. Finally, we agree on something. Can't wait to see you. L.

Lenox Square. Yeah, Lucy, it does bring back a few memories—more than a few—but not of a fitting at Rich's. I never had a wedding dress or a proper wedding. Richard and I were married by the Justice of the Peace in Conyers, Georgia. We'd planned to keep it a secret, but the stupid state of Georgia mailed a letter of congratulations and a family planning brochure to my house in Ashbeen. Mama opened the letter thinking it was from the University of Georgia. Or so she said. There was a cardboard box filled with most of my clothes sitting on the front porch when I got home from shopping that afternoon. And the stupid letter. And a note: "You married him. Let him support you."

Richard was leaving for Georgia Tech the next day, and I went with him. We got a tiny, dirty apartment near the campus, paying the first month's rent with the refund from his dorm fees. I got two jobs waiting tables in nearby restaurants until I could find something better. Something better—practically anything would have been better than serving cheap, fast food to the Ramblin' Wreck from Georgia Tech. My Aunt Jane was a buyer for Rich's, and she told me about the opening there. There was just one hitch, I needed to look the part. Not like some hick teenager from Ashbeen.

Until I-20 was completed, the only way to get from Ashbeen to Atlanta was via secondary roads. We'd drive through endless miles of nothing but pine trees and red dirt until, suddenly, there it was…rising out of the Georgia clay like Atlantis from the sea, and just about as surprising. To a small town girl, Lenox Square was the height of sophistication and style. The first of the giant shopping malls, it stood on the edge of Buckhead on Peachtree Road and West Paces Ferry. Where Atlanta was crass coinage to some, Buckhead was never anything but solid wealth. I'd never wanted anything the way I wanted that job, but for me, Peachtree Road might as well not have been, because it seemed impossible to pass.

I called Lucy as soon as I was alone. She had only been at Emory for a week herself.

"Becca, is that really you? What are doing in Atlanta, honey?"

"I'm married, Lucy."

"You're not. You are? No fooling?" I knew she was bouncing up and down on the other end of the line.

"No fooling. Two weeks ago in Conyers. But my mama's mad as a hornet. She won't even talk to me."

"Where are you?"

"We've got this dinky, little apartment near Tech on Tenth Street."

"Oh, Becca, you must be ecstatic. How romantic!"

"I'd be a lot more ecstatic if I were still in school in Athens. That's what we'd planned. To just get married and keep it a secret." The full load of reality was just starting to settle in on me and suddenly, for the first time, I began to really regret what we'd done.

"We've got to celebrate," she insisted. "I'm calling Bobbie Jean right now. Is that okay?"

"Sure, call her. There's no point in keeping it a secret now. But Lucy, I won't have much time or money. I start waiting tables, lunch and dinner, day after tomorrow." I heard the romance go out of her voice then.

"What about Sunday?"

"Sure, Sunday will be okay."

"Then Sunday it is. Bye for now. And tell Richard hello. I'll call you tonight. What's your number?"

When she hung up, I put my head down and cried.

We meet for lunch on Sunday at a little tearoom near Agnes Scott in Decatur. All around us were the debs who could afford a place like that. Girls in simple, elegant, Jackie-Kennedy-smart, linen sheaths and Chanel suits, their blond hair shining and swinging around their faces that all seemed to have been made with the same cookie cutter, the same blue eyes, straight teeth, and sweet, little noses.

"My God, Bobbie Jean, how did you wind up in a place like this?" I whispered in her ear when she hugged my neck. I knew her parents weren't rich. Her house might have been more charming and historic than the ranch-style, track house I grew up in, but it was just a bungalow. It wouldn't hold a candle to the Victorian pile of bricks across the street.

"My church gave me a small scholarship, and I have a job," she explained. "It's okay. My roommate's not too snooty." She handed me a prettily wrapped package. "For the bride. Don't open it here, unless you're prepared to take some teasing." She winked and grinned.

The waitress showed us to a teacup size table and took our order of ice tea and tiny sandwiches.

"Why didn't you tell us?" Lucy pretended to fuss, squeezing my hand.

"We didn't tell anybody, Lucy. I knew what would happen. Mama's so mad. Richard's folks are okay, but they haven't enough money to even support him through school, much less a wife."

"Then what are you going to do, Becca?" Her voice lost the note of girlish glee and was full of concern edged with doubt. I knew how important she believed an education was. Her daddy must have sold a kidney to send her to Emory.

"Right now I'm waiting tables from 11 a.m. 'til after 10 at night, but I need to find something else. Something so I can go to school at least part-time."

"Where would you go?" Lucy asked. "Does Tech even take women?"

"Yeah, but not too many want to go there, less than fifty this year. Too much math and science. There aren't even any women's dorms. But, I figure I can read all Richard's texts this semester, then in the Spring, I can take the same courses, and it won't be so hard."

The waitress arrived with a silver tray of tiny sandwiches, ham and turkey between slices of homemade bread cut in the shapes of diamonds, moons, and stars. There was fruit salad in pink gelatin molded into a flower and a basket of radish roses and carrot curls. It was a far cry from the greasy cheeseburgers and fries I'd served up all week. For a moment I was fearful that I might still smell of hot grease and fried chicken.

"What kind of job are you looking for?" Bobbie Jean asked over the rim of her ice tea glass.

"Nights and weekends, so I can go to classes during the day. Rich's has exactly the right thing in better dresses. It's a little store within their store at Lenox Square. My Aunt Jane told me about it. The commissions have got to be better than what I make waiting on students."

"That sounds perfect," Lucy agreed. "Have you applied?"

"No. I can't. To work there you have to have the right image, the right clothes. To even get a job there I need to look like that." I said looking in the direction of the girls at the next table.

"Won't they offer you a store discount?" Lucy argued.

"Sure. And with the discount I could maybe afford some hose and a scarf." I dropped my dainty little sandwich in the fancy little plate and sighed. "I'll be waiting tables forever."

"Don't be discouraged, Becca. My job's not so great either," Bobbie Jean commiserated. "I'm sorting dirty clothes in the campus laundry four nights a week and Saturday mornings."

"Sounds like we're a couple of Cinderella's," I smiled at her, but the smile was only on my lips. At least she was getting to go to college, and a pretty swanky one at that.

"Well, I tried to get a job, too," Lucy announced.

"Yeah, doing what?" I asked.

"Go-Go dancing at a club downtown. But it only lasted two nights, and then the Dean of Women put a stop to it. She said it wasn't the image she wanted for her girls," Lucy sighed.

Bobby Jean and I burst out laughing. "Lucy, are you serious?" Bobbie Jean grinned.

"Of course, I am. I was dancing with another girl in my dorm. We were really good, too."

"What would your mama say?" I kidded her.

She looked at Bobbie Jean, and they both said in a perfect imitation of Lucy's mama, "Let's not talk about that right now!"

Our desserts arrived, mine in the shape of a tiny wedding cake. The girls at the tables around us smiled and mimed a silent applause. I could feel my face flush with embarrassment.

"Congratulations!" Lucy said and kissed my cheek.

"You don't say 'Congratulations' to the bride, Lucy. It's 'Best Wishes,' " Bobbie Jean advised with a good-natured smile.

"Maybe not...maybe not this time," Lucy said excitedly. "Look, I've got an idea." She pushed her chair closer to mine and motioned for Bobbie Jean to do the same. Leaning on her elbows, she whispered, "What kind of things come through your laundry, Bobbie Jean?"

"All kinds. Skirts, sweaters, blouses, sheets, towels...."

"Anything like that?" Lucy said, nodding toward a girl in a light blue suit that probably cost what my daddy made in a month.

"Yes, but dry cleaning is sent off campus."

"Even better. Becca, what size are you? About a six?" she guessed.

"An eight. What kind of scheme are you hatching, Lucy?" I saw the gleam in her eyes. There was no stopping her now.

"I'm with you," Bobbie Jean said with a grin. "These girls don't wait for something to get dirty. They wear it once and send it to the cleaners just to get it pressed. If we borrowed it for a day or two, they'd never miss it."

"And what if you get caught? You could get expelled." I couldn't let her take that chance, not even if this crazy notion of Lucy's just might work.

"How would we get caught? I'll only take things that are very simple navies, grays, or blacks. One navy sheath looks pretty much like every other. You don't want to stand out anyway. Just blend in like you belong. Even if the girl who owns the dress walks in, she'll never know it. You'll wear a pretty scarf and completely change the look."

"Can we do it, do you think? Can we really do it?"

"How are you going to get from downtown to Lenox Square?" Lucy asked.

"The A.T.S. There's a stop right near there." The Atlanta Transit System operated over a hundred bus lines in Atlanta. Mostly designed to move black, domestic help out of the center city and south Atlanta to jobs in the suburbs in the morning and bring them back at night, it also moved a dwindling number of city workers from the white suburbs the other way. Atlanta was soon to be choked with their cars.

"Oh God, Becca be careful." Bobbie Jean breathed. "Aren't you afraid to ride alone at night?"

"Yeah, but I'm more afraid of waiting tables for the rest of my life."

"How will we get the clothes from me to Becca?" Bobbie Jean asked. None of us had a car, and taxis were out of the question. But there had to be way. There had to be.

Lucy sat back, her brow furrowed. She took a forkful of cake and then stopped in mid-bite, started to say something, frowned, and shook her head. Bobbie Jean grimaced and shrugged, empty of ideas.

"I guess I could come by here some how," I suggested.

"No, even if you could get a ride out, you shouldn't be popping up here every other day. Someone would get suspicious," Lucy insisted. "Bobbie Jean, how did you plan to get the clothes out?"

"That part is easy. The laundry is open from ten 'til six. I come in at six and work until ten. Every girl has a laundry bag with her name and room number on it. There's a drop shoot where stuff is left after hours. I open the bags and sort and ticket all the things that have come in during the day and the stuff that is left while I'm there. It usually only takes an hour or two."

"So? How are you going to do it?" Lucy asked impatiently.

"I bring my own stuff in to wash and press. Mama taught me to iron better than any cleaners. I'll just pick out something from the things I sort, press it, and slip it in with my things. And bring it back the same way, in my laundry bag." Her face beamed. She was as pleased with her part as a child playing hide-n-seek who's found the ideal spot. "It will just go out to the cleaners a day late."

"Becca, go on and apply for the job before it gets away. We'll figure out some way to pass the clothes back and forth."

As Lucy walked me to the bus stop on Church Street, I caught her hand and prayed. "Do you really think we can pull this off?"

"I know we can. Have faith," she said as she kissed my cheek before we parted. At the corner she turned, waved, and blew another kiss before she continued walking up Clairmont toward Emory's campus.

I had an interview with the department manager the following Friday. On Thursday, we did a test run of our exchange plan. Every afternoon, Monday through Friday, I was to take the bus to my aunt's house in Druid Hills, just a little west of Decatur. She had agreed to let me change clothes and borrow her car to get from there to work. Every night, except Friday, after I left the store I made a stop in Decatur at Agnes Scott before returning the car and catching the last bus back to town. On Saturday morning, I took the bus to Lenox Square, and Lucy drove her roommate's car to meet me at the mall at ten. She returned Thursday's and Friday's outfits before Bobbie Jean closed up Saturday morning.

"No one will ever see you," Lucy explained. "You can park right beside Rebekah Scott Hall, and Bobbie Jean will simply walk over to say hello on her way back to her dorm."

It might work, it just might, I thought and crossed my fingers while I said another prayer.

Thursday night I borrowed my aunt's car, and Lucy and I went shopping for good shoes. "My wedding present to you," she explained. "Just write a thank-you to Mama gushing over the fabulous place setting I told her we were giving you. What's your pattern?"

"Old Master," I laughed, "what else?" Of course, it was years before I ever owned a piece of that silver or any other.

At nine-thirty, we left the mall as they were closing and waited around until almost ten when I'd ordinarily be leaving. Then we hightailed it over to Agnes Scott. Bobbie Jean was just coming out of the basement of Rebekah Scott Hall. I flicked the car's lights, and she walked right up to the passenger's side.

"Why, Becca, fancy meeting you here." She put the hanging clothes and a small laundry bag down on the seat and leaned in to give me a hug. When she picked them up again, one dress and the laundry bag remained. "Don't be a stranger, now." She grinned and threw me a kiss and went off toward Candler Street.

I was to spend the night with Lucy and be back at my aunt's in time to ride into work with her Friday morning for my interview. Alone in her dorm room, Lucy helped me to try on my borrowed finery. Bobbie Jean had chosen well—a sophisticated, navy dress with three-quarter length sleeves and a small collar that lay softly away from my throat. "For pearls," Lucy said and fastened hers around my neck. "For luck."

I stepped back and looked at her. The label in the dress said "Balenciaga." Lucy's face said, "Lovely."

"It fits. In every way," she smiled. "Oh, sugar, I know you'll get it. I just know you will. You look just like you're going to some sorority rush tea."

From September through January, our scheme worked almost like clockwork. Thank God for my Aunt Jane. She never told my mother she was helping me. She never questioned my story of borrowing clothes from a friend. More than once she came to my rescue when our plan broke down, like the times Lucy's roommate needed to take her car home on weekends or I missed the last bus into town. She suggested a simple hairdo and makeup, cautioned me to just smile and keep quiet around the manager. She coached me on the likes and dislikes of Atlanta matrons. "Watch out for those French and Italian designers whose names they can't pronounce. Stick to Lily, Chanel, and Dior." She prepped me for the preferences and prejudices of Buckhead debutantes. "Think virginal—Grace Kelly, not Natalie Wood. Not since that *West Side Story* thing. And pink, lots of pink."

I used the employee discount to buy a few good scarves and a silver pin that I carefully used to camouflage my borrowed wardrobe. And I learned. I learned to always give these women a choice. Some would go with my suggestions, but others would turn something down just because it was my idea. Soon I could spot them. I'd suggest at least two things but pretend to favor the less expensive one. They would inevitably choose the other.

I continued to wait tables at lunch until November, when my manager asked me to help with the Christmas rush at the midtown Rich's store. I stood behind the cosmetics counter wearing a pink smock, so my clothes didn't matter.

A year or two later Dr. Martin Luther King would be staging sit-ins in the store's famous Magnolia Room, but this year the holiday pace was just a frantic swirl of perfumes and powder, lipsticks and lotions, night creams and foundations. Richard said I smelled like a cathouse whore when I rushed home to shower between jobs. But I managed to save enough for tuition.

In January, I entered Georgia Tech and took four classes before heading to the job at the mall. I was exhausted. I almost never saw Richard. Sunday morning was our only time off, and the day I slept late and studied. But, I was on my way.

Maybe if I hadn't been so busy, I'd have seen it coming. When our grades came in June, I had three B's and a C. Richard had failed all but one course. He lost his scholarship, and by August he'd been drafted.

"Texas!" Lucy wailed. "Oh, Becca, no. Not when you were just getting started."

"I'm going with him. We won't be able to be together long. You know he'll be sent to Vietnam." It might as well be Hell. I couldn't bear the thought of Richard over there. "When he ships out, I'll come back to UGA and finish. They have more of what I'm looking for anyway. The only business courses at Tech are in industrial management."

"But I'll never see you again," she protested.

"Sure you will. We'll visit all the time when I get back. You'll see."

In October, Lucy sent me a handful of clippings from the *Atlanta Journal*. Another new bride, Mary Shotwell Little, had disappeared from the immense parking lot of Lenox Square. Only her blood stained car was ever found.

"Becca, I was so scared for you. I'm so glad you're not riding that bus alone at night any more," she wrote.

It was nearly fifteen years before I saw her again. And by then everything had changed.

16

Bobbie Jean

From   Louisiana Savage <LouisianaSavage@ibm.net>
Date   Friday, May 7, 1999 8:25 p.m.
To   Roberta Jean Morgan <RJHMherbs@mindspring.com>
Subject June 25th Weekend

Okay, it's official. We're going to meet at Becca's place on Amelia Island on the weekend of June 25th. Try to get there by mid-afternoon. Make your reservation and book your tickets now. Can't wait to see you. Gotta go. Clea is getting married in November. I'm running around like a chicken with its head cut off and it's only May!

Clea's getting married? Well, I hope it's less tumultuous than Lucy's wedding. That was a near disaster. 1965. Johnson was President. Vietnam was really heating up and so was the opposition. The Beatles were cool. *A Hard Day's Night* was everywhere. And I was a sophomore at Agnes Scott. Lucy was marrying some grad student right before Christmas, because he was finally finishing up his doctorate and starting a teaching job at a college up North in January, she said.

When she had asked me to be one of her bridesmaids, I had, of course, said yes. What a perfect occasion to get us all back together again! Then I discovered that only Sally and I were to be part of the wedding. Becca and Richard were still in Texas. Richard had made it into fighter pilot training and was shipping out right after Christmas. To Germany, not Vietnam, thank heavens. Becca was coming back to UGA in Athens after the New Year but couldn't afford another trip in December. Millie had disappeared off everyone's radar screen, apparently dropping out of UGA after her freshman year. Her mother was very vague when any of us called about her. But it was Wallee that really upset me.

"Come on, Bobbie Jean, please don't give me a hard time about this," Lucy pleaded. "Mama is driving me crazy. We don't agree on anything, and she's adamant about not having Wallee in the wedding party because of her limp. Wallee probably wouldn't want to do it anyway."

"You could still invite her to the wedding, Lucy." I was so angry my chin was quivering.

"I know. But Mama thinks it's better this way. Oh, Bobbie Jean don't desert me now. I need you to be there, really I do." She looked so forlorn, I couldn't help relenting some. And the bridesmaids' dresses were nearly finished, too. If I backed out now, she would truly be in a fix. We were sitting in my room on the second floor of Inman Hall surrounded by brides' magazines, fabric swatches, shoes, bits of lace and ribbons, and my designs for possible bridesmaids' bouquets. Mama was making my dress, and Lucy and I were trying to get the green velvet swatch she'd sent to match to shoes and ribbon.

"I'll do this, Lucy. But only because I've known you for just about forever, and if you want me to forgive you, you'd better find some way of making it up to Wallee."

"Oh, thank you Bobbie Jean. I knew I could count on you, and I will think of something, really I will," she promised. "I don't think I could make it through this without you. Mama and I don't do anything but fight. We don't agree on anything, and then we compromise and nobody is happy." She looked close to tears. Her shoulders were stooped, her nails were bit to the quick, and her hair looked like she'd been wearing it yanked back it that ponytail for weeks. The tiny diamond engagement ring looked like it was weighing down her shaking hand.

"Honey, do think you're really ready for this marriage?" I asked her softly.

She didn't say anything for a minute. She just sat there flopping the fabric swatch up and down in her lap. And when she did look up to speak, there were tears welling up. "God, I wish I knew. I guess every bride gets cold feet. It's natural, don't you think? I don't know. It's just so…final."

"Do you love him, Lucy?"

"Well, yes, of course I do. I mean, I think so. I'm not sure. I'm not sure I even know what love is."

I didn't say anything, hoping she'd just continue on her own without my prompting her. But she didn't, so I asked, "Have you tried talking to your mama?"

"Are you kidding?" she sort of snorted at me. "Mama, is in the biggest *state* I have ever seen her in. She'd go right into orbit if I even hinted that maybe I wanted to back out."

"Well, do you? Do you want to back out? If you do, now is the time before things go any further."

"No, no I don't." She sniffed up the tears, lifted her chin, and fixed her mouth in a quirky smile that didn't quite make it.

"You're sure?"

"Yeah, I'm sure."

We went on comparing fabric and ribbon samples. I began sketching out some ideas for bouquets at her direction, trying to decide if we liked a single stemmed flower, a simple nosegay, or a cascading bouquet best. No one had yet agreed on what the flowers would be. Lucy wanted red camellias, her mama wanted cream roses. I think they finally compromised on cream camellias and, like Lucy said, nobody was happy.

"Did I tell you what happened to my roommate?" she asked me suddenly.

"No, I don't think you did. Is this the girl who is going to be the maid of honor? She's pre-med? Zoë, is that right?"

"Yeah. Here she is almost ready to start the last semester of her junior year, and Zoë finds out she can't get into medical school. She's changing her major to political science. She'll have to put in an additional semester to catch up since that's in a completely different college. Boy, is she pissed."

"Why can't she get in? Aren't her grades good enough?"

"Her grades would be fine if she were a boy—mostly A's, two or three B's. But not good enough for a girl. They only accept a few, the very best." Was this anger or something else I heard in her voice? "They didn't tell us that in high school, did they?"

"No," I agreed. "That's really too bad. Not fair at all." I went back to sketching out a likeness of Sally in a dress identical to mine carrying a nosegay of roses. But Lucy didn't seem interested. She got up and went over to gaze out at the campus toward Evans Hall.

The leaves were falling, and it was one of those beautiful, sunny days that made me glad I lived in the South. Late autumn days, when it was still warm enough to bare my shoulders or lie in the grass. The kind of day I've often found myself humming "Georgia on My Mind." I stopped sketching and watched the shower of elm leaves, so much like big, golden snowflakes drifting down. The scarlet stars of the sweet gum leaves, the yellow cups of the tulip poplars, and crimson-leafed dogwoods with their bright red button berry clusters. Lucy sighed and turned back to me, continuing a train of thought that she must have been spinning for sometime.

"Mary Ann, a senior down the hall from me, she got a shock this week, too. She signed up for ten job interviews with the recruiters who'll be on campus next week. Only one of them will even talk to her because she's female. The placement office called her and told her to be sure to check the gender requirements before she signs up for any more interviews."

"What was she signing up for…He-man stuff?"

"No, she's an English major with a minor in math. Great grades, perfect. She was just trying to get interviews with banks, insurance companies, and newspapers. You know, Bobby Jean, it's pretty scary when you think about it. Maybe Mama was right. Maybe I should have just majored in early childhood education. Have you thought about what you're going to do once you leave here?"

"With a major in art history, are you kidding?" I laughed, but I could see where she was going, so I gave her a serious answer. "I'd like to get a job in an art gallery. Maybe in New York City. But I'll probably wind up teaching school."

"If you don't get married. I can't believe you've lasted this long, the way you look."

Oh brother, here it was again. And from Lucy of all people.

"Look, friend," I said trying to hold onto my slipping smile. "I plan to do something, too. You aren't the only one who wants to be more than just the property of some man. I may even want it more than you. I'm not the one getting married in six weeks." She looked like I'd just slapped her.

"Geeze, Bobby Jean, I'm sorry. It was a stupid thing to say. I seem to be bumping into your feelings every which way I turn. It's just—"

"Just that you don't know what you're going to do with a major in philosophy either?" I finished for her.

"Yeah. That's one good thing about marrying a college professor. At least I'll be able to stay in school, maybe even go on to grad school. I won't have to decide what to do right away."

"That's not the only reason you're marrying him, is it?" God, I hope not, I thought.

"I'll admit, it has something to do with it. But, no, it's not the only reason," she said. "He's 4F," she added. A 4F draft status would assure her that she wouldn't have to worry about him being sent to Vietnam. Then she whispered with a wicked, little grin that was much more like the Lucy that I knew, "And damn, he's fun in bed."

I wasn't shocked. I'd pretty much suspected this for some time. "So this is a big, white wedding for appearances sake only?"

"You got it. I didn't surprise you, did I? I sort of thought you knew."

"I'm appalled," I teased her. "What would your mama say?"

"That I'd better get married and the sooner the better."

"Then get over here and look at these sketches."

Sally and I met Zoë at a tea for Lucy at the Ashbeen Country Club on the Saturday after Thanksgiving. I don't think any of us had set foot in the country club before, but Lucy's mama had planned this tea, the wedding breakfast, and the reception to all take place there. How she wrangled the use of the place, since they weren't members, I don't know. It was an old structure, not very large, as country clubs go, more like a big, brick, antebellum house with wide porches and tall, white, fluted columns all around. It was all the way across town from where we lived.

Lucy's maid of honor was from Maryland and with her curly, red hair and milky white skin, she was going to look striking in our green velvet dresses. Sally had told me in confidence that Wallee was really very relieved not to have to go through all the hullabaloo of being a bridesmaid, but we were still both put out with Lucy for not standing up to her mama and inviting Wallee anyway. Sally and Zoë hit it off immediately. Zoë's second choice for a replacement major had been chemistry.

"What made you choose political science instead?" Sally asked. Chemistry was her major.

"With chemistry about the only jobs you can get without graduate work are with the government," Zoë told her. "I was an army brat. I don't ever want to work for the government. I got enough of that bureaucracy and regimentation as a kid. With poli sci I hope I can go on to law school or work for a private company that deals in government contracts. Sweet revenge, maybe."

"Now, girls," Lucy's mama interrupted. "Let's not talk all that school and work talk today. I want to hear about Atlanta. Don't you just love being near a big city? It must be so exciting. Bobbie Jean, what do you hear about the plans for that new arts center? I just love art museums, don't you?"

While Lucy, Sally and Zoë were huddled on a camel-backed Chippendale settee with their heads together whispering and nodding, I entertained our mamas with the latest gossip surrounding what would be the Woodruff Center. In 1962, Atlanta's arts community had been very nearly wiped out when their chartered plane crashed on take-off from Orly air field in Paris killing everyone on board except the pilots. The Woodruff Center, named for the founder of Coca-Cola and the largest donor, was to be a tribute to them. In time it would include the High Museum and a college of arts as well as facilities for the performing arts. But in November of 1965, it was still two years away from opening and there was a lot of speculation about who the mysterious major donor was.

"I always say, you can get just as much culture right here in Atlanta as you can anywhere else," Lucy's mama was saying. "I just don't know why Lucy insists on going up North."

"Mama, it's not like I have a choice. That's where my husband's job is going to be."

"Well, you could have married some nice, Southern gentleman, who, I'm sure, would not have insisted on taking you so far away from your family."

"Not now Mama, please."

Sally stepped in to save the day. Gesturing toward the autumnal arrangement on the little Pembroke table beside her, she said, "Mrs. Jones, these roses are so lovely. Such a beautiful, deep red-orange." She leaned over to smell them, closed her eyes and smiled in delight. "Did they come out of your garden?"

"Well, thank you, Sally. Yes, they did. Don't you think Lucy ought to carry roses? Roses are so much more fragrant than camellias, and they don't bruise as easily."

"Both are really nice. I'm sure which ever one Lucy chooses will be just perfect." Sally beamed, the born diplomat. Could she really please everybody? Maybe she ought to be the one changing her major to political science, I thought. She could be a negotiator or something.

"What were y'all whispering about?" I asked her as soon as Mrs. Jones was out of earshot, busily pouring tea and urging the guests to eat more dainty sandwiches and little cakes.

"Bobbie Jean," she said to me in a low voice. "What that girl just told me is frightening. She said that no one she knows has been able to get a job with just a degree in chemistry or biology. They all had to go to technical schools after they graduated and get applied skills. All of the girls anyhow. Then they wound up working in labs with women who never even went to college, doing boring things like testing pond water or cleaning up the equipment. What are we going to college for if we can't get better jobs?"

"Most of the girls I go to school with don't expect to work, honey. They just expect to get married. They're there to get an MRS degree."

"What are we going to do if we don't get married?"

I don't know what I would have told her if I'd had a chance to reply. I didn't get a chance because just then Mrs. Jones caught my arm and said to us in an conspiring whisper, "Now girls, you just must help me convince Lucy that champagne isn't the proper thing to have at the reception. A nice punch is what a good Methodist girl has. I don't know who is putting these ideas in her head. Probably that little Yankee." She was looking straight across the room at Zoë. "She's no where near as pretty as you, Bobbie Jean. All that wild, red hair. I never!"

I have no idea what Zoë thought of Mrs. Jones. She left as soon after the marriage ceremony as she possibly could, and I never had a chance to talk to her alone. I was starting to envy Wallee.

"We'll do our best," Sally promised and rolled her eyes at me over Mrs. Jones' head.

"And while you're at it, dear, could you see if you can't get Lucy to do something about her hair. If she'd just put on some lipstick and curl her hair a little, she'd be right pretty. As it is, she looks like one of those hippies."

I could barely hold in the laughter. Sally pinched my arm, but it didn't help. Oh, dear God in heaven, let me out of here soon, I prayed.

Lucy was coming across the old, faded-to-pink, Aubusson carpet, making her way toward us like a bloodhound who'd picked up the heavy scent of conspiracy. "Mama," she said, "leave Sally and Bobbie Jean alone. I know what your trying to do and it won't do any good. No one is singing at my wedding, especially not Aunt Kathleen."

"Now, Lucy that's not at all what we were discussing, was it girls?"

Sally managed to choke out, "No, Mrs. Jones. Not at all." Then we all ran for the patio on the excuse that we just had to have a cigarette. None of us smoked, except Lucy and Zoë, but all the bridesmaids and the bride spent the rest of the afternoon shivering on the wide, brick patio in a cloud of smoke that we hoped would repel our mamas.

I met Sally again in Atlanta on the Saturday morning a week before the wedding. The shoe store had dyed her shoes to match her dress, but they had come out way too light. I was waiting outside the store when she came running up.

"Oh, thank you for coming with me, Bobbie Jean," she said as she breathed a heavy sigh of relief. "I just can't face that snooty salesman alone."

"What on earth are you talking about, honey?"

"Now, don't you go getting mad at me, too," she whined. "You just don't understand."

"Understand what, Sally? He didn't make a pass at you or something, did he?"

"Of course not," she sniffed.

"Then what is it?"

"Oh, Bobbie Jean, he just acts so high and mighty. Working in this fancy store in Atlanta and all."

I did not believe what I was hearing. "You're afraid of a shoe salesman?"

"Don't jump all over me, please. Mama's already done that. She lectured me but good on how she was paying a fortune for me to get a wonderful college education, and I can't even face down some man who probably didn't even finish high school. And she refused to come with me."

"Well, I hate to be the one to tell you, but she's right. Come on, Sally, get some backbone!"

"Oh, you talk to him, pretty please," she begged as she edged in the shop's entrance and pushed the bag of shoes into my hands.

"I do not believe you!" I half hissed, half whispered. But her face was so pathetic that I laughed in spite of myself and agreed. "Okay, but just this once. You watch and learn. All you've really got to do is smile."

With that and a few sweet words of explanation from me, the young man immediately agreed to send the shoes back to be redone and promised to have them delivered to me by Wednesday afternoon. "See, that wasn't so hard, was it?" I asked her.

"Not for you, maybe."

"And why do you think that is?"

"God, Bobbie Jean, look at you. Men will do anything for you."

"Is that what you think? Do you really think you couldn't handle this situation because of the way you look? There's nothing wrong with your looks. That's not the problem, and you know it."

"You're right," she moaned. "I know. I know."

I don't remember too much about the wedding breakfast a week later. The sun shone. We were all too warm in our winter wools. There were lots of cousins and aunts. I think the colors were Christmas-y, red and green garlands winding around the columns and hanging above the doorways. Arrangements of magnolia leaves, gilded nuts and that Southern symbol of hospitality, pineapples, reflected in the highly polished mahogany tables and sideboards. Lucy was hanging blissfully on the arm of her husband-to-be, a tall, bearded fellow, very academic looking.

All the groom's men were married, so Sally and Zoë and I were pretty much on our own. Neither Zoë nor Mrs. Jones looked like they'd gotten much sleep the night before. Mrs. Jones was probably running on fumes, but very high octane fumes, like she was dangerously close to igniting. Lucy's daddy toasted the glowing bride and groom with the usual well wishes for a long and happy marriage and lots of children. I don't think anyone, including Lucy, had given much thought to how she was supposed to raise a bunch of children and conquer the world at the same time.

There were both hidden and mixed messages in what our teachers and our parents said. On the surface there was one message: You can do anything if you just go to college and get that proof that you've got an education; you can be what we never had the chance to be. But on a deeper level there was another message, usually in our mama's voice: But just in case, you'd better major in education. Not all of us heard that message until it was too late. Maybe we were the lucky ones, the ones who just followed our dreams even when they led us into some pretty perilous places. Or maybe it was just a matter of finding a place to nest and wait until the time was right. In ten to fifteen years, a lot more really was possible.

Sally and Wallee and I had planned to get together over Christmas vacation, but right after Lucy's wedding my Grandfather Harris died and my whole family spent the entire holiday in Cincinnati.

Later Wallee wrote to me:

> BJ,
>
> I'm so sorry about your grandfather. And sorry to have missed you at Christmas, too. Sally told me about L's wedding. Sounds like I missed quite a circus. She also mentioned meeting a girl named Zoë. Sally's really concerned now about what we're going to do after college. I just don't think either of us could stand the thought of going home to Ashbeen and living with our parents, but I don't think our daddies will let us get low-rent jobs in big cities. So I'm thinking about graduate school. Maybe we could all go to Emory or some place together!
>
> See you at Easter. I have a real surprise for you. W.

Writing back to tell her that I wouldn't be in Ashbeen at Easter, because my folks were moving to Cincinnati in March to take over my grandfather's business, was one of the hardest things I ever had to do. Sally and I have seen each other two or three times since Lucy's wedding, but I only saw Lucy one other time, briefly, at Gran Ma'am's funeral. I never saw Becca again after she left for Texas. The paths that Wallee and I were on crossed for a few months in Atlanta without either of us ever realizing the other was there! Oh God, how I wish I'd known it then.

17
Lucy

I want to spend the minutes of each hour,
And the hours of each day,
On one course that,
Like light through the facets of a crystal,
Pulls in different points of view,
But focuses on one common point,
Then breaks into a meridian of color,
And showers rainbow chips.
Lucy Jones

I started out criticizing his business. "Software that can watch people by monitoring their activities is entirely unethical," I flatly declared during a seminar on business ethics and privacy in the work place that Georgia Southern and Georgia State were co-hosting in 1984. He told me later that he was immediately intrigued by the challenge. He had come to the seminar looking for possible customers for his new software company. What he found was this bossy, uppity, sanctimonious, self-righteous bitch. How could he resist?

During a break, when he came up and introduced himself, I knew immediately he had something more than business on his mind. He grinned this mischievous grin that has always reminded me of a little boy who has done something very bad, but knows that rules and love were meant to be tried. He looked down at me, his green eyes dancing with the tease, and accepted my challenge.

"Really unethical or just a little?" he asked.

"Really unethical."

"Stuart Savage," he said and offered me his business card. "Of WatchWord Systems Software," he added with a smirk. I felt my confidence shrink up like a resurrection fern that hadn't been watered for months. Of course, I'd never actually *talked* to anyone who developed monitoring software.

"What do you say to meeting me for a drink after the session today?" he asked. "My partner, Dave, will be there in case you're afraid of being seen alone in the company of such an unscrupulous ne'er-do-well. I think you would be wise to learn more about our company."

I managed a smile and accepted.

"What does she know? She's just some ivory tower academic," I overheard Dave say as I approached their table. It crossed my mind that I should announce my presence. But, on the other hand, just how ethical did I need to be around them?

"Yeah, but think of the possibilities. We need a foot in the door. You said so yourself. Well, she's our foot. We help her publicize her little seminars, jazz up her presentations with some sexy graphics. And while she's bullying corporate America into good citizenship, she plants the need for our software."

"For our immoral and unethical software, you forget."

"Leave that to me. I bet I can change her mind," Stu replied confidently.

"Yeah, I bet you can. But is it worth it?"

"It would be worth it even if I can't get her to work with us."

"Hi, I'm Louisiana Jones." I smiled at Dave and offered my hand. "What did I miss?"

But it really wasn't quite as easy as he'd thought. I actually was dedicated to those ivory tower principles. He took me to dinner on the pretext of wanting to hear more of my concerns about using private data for the public good. He smiled at me while I championed the rights of the individual over corporate greed.

"Corporations are immortal legal entities. They have no souls and, hence, no moral rights."

Do mortal entities have the right to get lucky? I'm sure he was thinking. But he asked, "If it were a question of the rights of one individual over another, would you be more open to discussion?"

"Of course," I smiled, knowing exactly what he was trying to do.

"Well, suppose our software could help a person prove that they had been discriminated against? That they hadn't been given a fair shake." He leaned toward me, his hands resting on the table between us.

"What do you mean?" I asked, avoiding his eyes and pretending not to see where he was leading.

"Lots of oppressed people are afraid to speak up for themselves. If a manager gives a woman a review based on gender rather than merit, she may just keep quiet. If a company is using our software, she won't have to speak up and take the risk of getting fired. The software will discover the injustice," he argued with just enough passion in his voice to make me look up at him.

Did I really seem this naïve? "Couldn't the software be used in just the opposite way to prove that a person with a complaint wasn't being discriminated against?"

"Not unless they really hadn't been," he told me sincerely, probably crossing his fingers under the table.

"You wouldn't be just telling me that, would you?" I smiled at him.

"*Moi?* You think I would try to put the big sell on *you?*" he feigned innocence and grinned at me.

"In a heartbeat," I grinned back.

But slowly he did win me over. And I could see I was touching something in him as well. Our first joint client was Delta in at Atlanta. He could tell I was nervous speaking to so many chief executives and corporate officers at one time. He'd finally gotten me out of those frumpy, academic plaids and tweeds and into a short skirt, navy suit, and feminine blouse. I think he'd rather get me out of the suit and into his bed, but so far I would only tamely flirt.

"You look great. You'll do fine. They're just guys. Smile and they won't notice anything else but your legs," he promised giving my shoulders a quick squeeze.

"Thanks a lot. And I'm promoting sexual equality," I said and rolled my eyes.

"Well, some people are more equal than others."

I did okay. Maybe they even did remember more than my smile. At least he'd taught me that you didn't try to make these men feel guilty. Everything was a matter of enlightened self interest—and the bottom line. I knew the law and the business school buzz words. I'd memorized a pile of data on the company. I knew all their names. I knew everything, but the reality of the business world. About that I knew nothing.

We made the sale to Delta. It was so sweet, I wanted to sing. To shout. To dance. To kiss everybody. I had done it. I had actually done it. I had played in the big leagues and made a hit. It wasn't just words anymore. The wheels of change were starting to grind, and I was making it happen. If I hadn't made the wheel, at least I had greased it a little. And the fun was just beginning.

To celebrate, the tiny startup team of nine went out for dinner at The Abbey. Dave toasted us with the least expensive champagne on the menu, "Today Delta, Tomorrow Coca-Cola, Next Week the World!"

I had at least one drink too many and wound up in the swimming pool at Stu's condo. With all my clothes on. Somewhere that night he kissed me and said, "Lucy, this won't go anywhere you don't want it to go."

And where I went was home. To call Becca.

"Lucy, he's your boss."

"Sort of. It's more like an alliance."

"He's married," she insisted.

"He's separated," I corrected.

"He'll break your heart."

"Probably. But maybe I won't care."

"Then you're a fool."

Being alone for two years had been awful. When I'd returned to Atlanta, I'd re-established contact with Becca, but everything between us was different, because now Richard was between us. And I knew so little about grownup dating. Becca and Richard tried to set me up with a friend of theirs who was newly divorced. He brought a date. The five of us had a very awkward dinner, and I left as soon as possible. I'd tried to meet someone by going to happy hour at a bar. I must have arrived at least an hour too early, because there was no one there, and I was too embarrassed to stay. One of my students offered to sleep with me for a better grade. Did I look that desperate? Stuart was the only good thing to happen to me in a long time.

But for a while, I was content to only work with him. It felt so good just to see my ideas applied. His initial product scanned computerized personnel files hunting for patterns that might indicate supervisors or managers who, wittingly or unwittingly, were discriminating against certain groups, like women or minorities. There were other projects in the works to detect fraud, insider trading, or customer billing abuse. I felt like maybe I was really making a difference.

One day Stu was standing in the back of an executive briefing room while I was doing my thing. The topic was "Don't Kid the Kidders."

The expression referred to management's expectation of naked truth from each other, but the discussion pertained to just how much truth a corporation owed to its employees and customers. I guess I got kind of carried away, because afterward Stuart was pretty quiet. When he did speak, I didn't like it.

"Your voice gets kind of high and squeaky when you get excited. It isn't pretty." I looked over at him. His usually firm jaw was tight and clinched. His nose looked pinched and his eyes were squinty.

"Thanks, I'll remember that," I answered coldly.

"You lose credibility."

Then it hit me. "Did I lose the sell?" I asked, dread creeping into my heart.

He paused, then let me have the truth, "Yes, probably."

"Oh, God. I'm sorry," I said and started to cry.

"God damn it, Lucy, don't cry. It's just business. You don't cry."

I cried harder. He stopped the car and put his arm around me. "You have a good heart," he whispered into my hair. "It just breaks too easily."

We were in New York talking to a large insurance company when I finally decided to sleep with him. The client had canceled our afternoon session, so we went for a long lunch at Cumbio's, a small Northern Italy restaurant on John Street. He plied me with soft shell crabs and a soft white wine, and when we returned to our slender, black monolith hotel, it just seemed like the natural thing to do. Clea and Becca weren't so easy to convince.

"Mom, he's just using you," Clea insisted.

I tried to remember what it was like to be thirteen years old. *Matt and the dream. My mama telling me that Daddy would save me instead of her.* I didn't even know what Clea dreamed. But it was clear from other conversations we had had that no one needed to explain to her what an orgasm was. I gave her a hug.

"Don't worry, honey. You won't have to save me. I can take care of myself."

"You've got a great job, Lucy. Why do you want to put it in jeopardy by sleeping with your boss? What are you going to do when it's over?" Becca reasoned.

"Why does it have to be over?"

"Because this only happens in fairy tales!"

I didn't see the cracks that were opening in her marriage. On the few occasions that I saw them socially, Becca and Richard seemed like the perfect couple. Both of them professionals, both successful. I thought she would tell me if there were problems. I hadn't completely realized what the fifteen years apart had done to our friendship. Her loyalties were to Richard, even if he didn't deserve them. Then it finally dawned on me—whenever we talked, it was always about me or Clea or Shea, never about Becca. One day she called and announced that they were separating. She was taking Shea and moving to New York. No, she didn't want to talk about it.

There was no one point in time when Clea was won over. It happened slowly. But I think she truly wished us well when we were married in 1986. I never met Stuart's boys until after we were married. I sent an announcement to Becca, but it was returned *Address Unknown*.

In the second year of our alliance, I pulled the biggest gaffe of my professional career. We were working with a very difficult group of executives in Atlanta. The company had been recently acquired and downsized, and everyone was very tense. The corporate statement was going slowly. Several of the men were far too hassled to devote any time to something they viewed to be as meaningless as business ethics. And although they didn't say it out loud, it was pretty evident that they felt they'd either been screwed over or had been forced to screw over their employees. Maybe both.

"Ah, shit, Melvin, you can't put that crap about loyalty in that damned thing. Your staff will laugh right in your face," one of the more disgusted men finally declared. "They already think this is just a fucking whitewash." His arms were folded across his chest, and his face was sour, as though everything we had said had left a bad taste in his mouth.

"What the fuck do you know, Ebert?" the executive vice president replied. "Just how long have you worked here—not counting today?"

I had a vision of more than mere words being thrown. Ebert's face flushed red except for a ring of bloodless white encircling his mouth. His hands clinched into fists, then dropped below the table and into his lap. I noticed that almost all of the men had their hands out of sight. How many fists were balled under that table? Just then the CEO walked in. "How's it going, boys?" he drawled, just a good ol' boy come to check on his newly purchased minions and lackeys.

His hair was graying, and he had a solid layer of fat around his middle, but he walked like he should be wearing riding boots and carrying a whip. I wanted to look behind him for the hounds. He was smoking a cigarette, and I noticed that everyone else lit-up in spite of the discreet, No Smoking signs in the briefing room.

"God damn, JC, this sucks. We ain't getting nowhere," a third man fumed, obviously glad to see the ringmaster.

"Well, Miss Jones, I'd have expected you'd be about finished by now," JC said to me in a falsely sweet, sarcastic tone, that reeked of condescension. "Y'all need some help, girlie?" *Help* came out *hep*. But I didn't have any problem understanding it or the *girlie*.

"No sir," I said and shot him the finger.

For a moment everyone was deadly quiet. JC smiled an evil, little smile and wagged his cigarette at me. The men all laughed uneasily, and the CEO left without another word. A few minutes later Stu rushed in and hustled me out of the room and into his car.

"What the hell did you do that for?" he yelled at me.

"Do what? What did I do?"

"You shot the meanest CEO in Atlanta the bird!"

"So—everyone else was saying *shit* and *fuck* and *sucks*. Why can't I express myself?"

"Lucy, you don't tell the CEO to get fucked!"

I gasped. "Is that what it means? I thought it meant something like 'In your face!' or 'Up yours!' " Not that I was real sure what those expressions meant either.

"My God, are you for real. Do you really not know?" He fumed the rest of the way home.

As he slammed into the house, he met Clea in the kitchen. "Tell your mother what it means to shoot somebody the bird."

She did.

"See. Every ten year old knows. Where have you been the last twenty years?"

"I've known at least *that* long. I've known forever," Clea said.

Stu had to grovel to get his apology accepted. I wasn't allowed back. But the corporate statement of business ethics was completed in record time. And Stuart made the software sell. He sent me a big bouquet of yellow roses. The card read: "I love you the way you are. Just learn the rules. Then you can break them all." I did try. I got several women's How-To-Succeed business books—the kind they don't teach in business school. But they didn't all say the same thing. Some recommended that women try to blend in, but avoid drinking and never use profanity or sleep with your boss. Others endorsed the opposite approach: stand out, be different, use your femininity…even tears were okay. How could I know so much and, at the same time, so little? When boys learned all those things in the high school locker room, apparently they also learned when and how to use them. What had we been talking about? Make-up? Clothes? Boys.

By the time Clea was in college at Randolph Macon, most of WatchWord's clients were outside Atlanta. Stu and I were traveling all the time. We were Million Milers in our fifth year. We made the Mile High Club on a nearly empty midnight flight from the West coast in the middle of a raging thunderstorm. The L-1011's wide seats were unoccupied except for us and the stewardesses, who were firmly buckled in at the front and rear of the big plane. I'm sure they'd seen it all, but I didn't want them to see me. Not doing this. Not astride my husband's lap, my feet hooked behind his knees, my shirt hiked up above my hips, and his hands wrapped round my waist while I was holding on to the headrest for dear life. As the plane bucked and rolled, and the storm roared with frenzy outside the darkened cabin, we reenacted its passion on the inside. I thought about that long ago dream of the star-call and just had to laugh because I knew I'd at last found something even better. It was all so much fun then.

In the late eighties, I began seeing some women among the senior executives I worked with. Most of them were reserved and distant. I wondered if we were all playing the same game, because they seemed to each have a different set of rules, unlike any I'd ever read. I finally found myself alone with one of them in the Ladies' Room on the top floor of one of those towering buildings with a vanity address, like One Big Deal Plaza. The Ladies' here was unlike anything on the lower floors. It was the first executive Ladies Room I'd ever seen. Needless to say, I hadn't seen any executive Men's Rooms, so I couldn't compare, but this was better than the Ladies' at any country club or resort I'd ever been to. Nearly anything you might want was discretely available, and not from a vending machine. The lighting was extremely flattering. There was a telephone instead of an attendant. A small sofa occupied one corner. Some very delicate and subtle scent, like oranges, permeated the air. I had discovered a new standard for measuring employee worth, the Ladies Room scale. This one rated at ten. If this woman merited such a place, I had to get her to talk. I cornered her.

"You haven't had much to say," I ventured.

"I don't dare," she replied, drying her hands on an individual, crisp, clean linen towel and trying not to look at me.

"Then just tell me what you think."

She drew a deep breath and hesitated a moment, then she looked me in the eye and said without even a hint of a smile, "I think the women are as responsible for sexual harassment as the men. Walk through our company. Every day I stop at least four or five women. 'This is not a beach,' I tell them. 'Dress more appropriately.' What do they expect?"

She helped herself to the gently scented, bottled lotion, and when she continued her tone was lighter, kidding. "I believe in truth in advertising," she laughed. "Look organized, you probably are organized. Look available, you probably are."

"You don't think women deserve any protection?"

"To be blunt: No. The truth is, business is risky. Very risky. If you can't afford to take chances, you shouldn't play. And you certainly shouldn't expect somebody to come rescue you."

"Don't you think everybody should play by the same rules?"

"Why? We aren't all playing the same game."

We certainly looked like we were. She was dressed in the same uniform-for-success that I was, navy suit, medium heeled, dark pumps, *LA Law* blouse. Serious hair, short or neatly pulled back. What was I missing? Two months later, at an executive retreat a few hours outside Dallas, I met the missing link. She was striking, but not beautiful, big-haired, boisterous, and even foul mouthed on occasion. Her suits shouted with hot pink, lemon yellow, and powder blue. Her heels were dizzyingly high. Not even her jewelry was conservative.

"Who is she?" I whispered to Stu.

"Acquisitions and mergers. A babe with balls," he replied, pushing deeper into the heavily padded, leather chair of the sumptuous conference room at a resort called Opossum Canyon. The conference center sat at the very edge of the steep canyon wall. Used to the lush green of the eastern seaboard, I was unprepared for the almost unnaturally stark beauty of this arid countryside. But the clear night skies were wonderful, and the liquor flowed day and night. Stu grinned at me. "This ought to be fun."

And it was. For one thing, these were line, not staff, executives and even a few board members. Details weren't their thing. That was somebody else's worry. They were mainly computer illiterates, but they didn't care. And they weren't afraid to talk.

"Look, honey, if you look like a flight attendant, then men are going to treat you like one," she bawled at me after a few drinks one night. She was looking pointedly at my little, navy suit, which did, I had to admit, looked pretty much like a stewardess's uniform.

"Nobody asks me to fix the coffee! And they wouldn't dare put a hand on me unless I asked them to, either."

"I bet they don't. And bet you have more fun, too."

"I love it. I just dare the bastards to cross me. It makes my day." She smiled, and I knew she meant every word of it.

Her accent was thick as molasses, and she flirted like crazy. I liked her immediately. Maybe there was a different standard for her level of management, but the message was the same one I'd heard before. Women shouldn't expect to be rescued, not even by other women. Life is dangerous, the stakes are high. And, just maybe, there are no rules, only legerdemain and deception. Some magicians blend into their background, others distract you with dangerous or flamboyant gestures. Most of executive management appeared to be just so much smoke and mirrors, anyway, and like good magicians, no one was really going to tell the secrets.

I noticed her rolling her eyes and squirming in her chair the next day. Several of the men wanted to couch their corporate ethics statement in football terms (*team, coach, take the hand off*) or military terms (*generals, captains, squadron, take the hill*) and the metaphors were getting a bit mixed to say the least. But I'd come to expect this from Texans; after all, this was Cowboys country. Finally she leaned across the table and let us have it, "Assholes. All these analogies to war and sports you men throw out...cause you think the girls won't get it. Well, let me tell you. Business ain't like either one of them. It's much more red of tooth and claw." She waved her crimson-nailed hands to illustrate her point. "It's a jungle. And everybody knows, it's the lioness who hunts in the jungle."

The men laughed uneasily, and she continued, smiling sweetly at me, "I don't mean to hurt your feelings, honey. But there ain't no ethics in the jungle either."

As we moved into the '90's, I traveled alone more often than not, and it had long since ceased to be fun. The seminars became more tense and hostile as downsizing spread throughout corporate America. The job was taking more and more of people's time and often replacing the family. Men and women were looking to work for the validations and celebrations that they used to get at home. And if they didn't get it, they weren't afraid to rage. Domestic violence grew into workplace violence. Sexual harassment could no longer be hidden and tolerated. Companies needed written statements of policy and documented proof of active vigilance and diligent pursuit of offenders. Just what we at WatchWord Software Systems offered. We were very much in demand.

When we were together, the weight of the times was heavy on Stu and me. We watched a copy of a light, delicate Impressionist painting take shape on the side of a Wall Street building for the set of *Die Hard 3*. Two months later we were slammed against the floor of a concourse at Heathrow as militia pursued a suspected terrorist through the crowd. Without the special effects, the real world seemed less so. There were no screams, no protests. It was almost business as usual.

One night Stu sat across from me as we shared a rare dinner together. I had been consulting in New York with the international division of a giant conglomerate, modifying the US company's policy statements on discrimination for international use. Stu was working in New Jersey with the team installing the WatchWord software for the domestic group. It hadn't been going well or he would never have been involved. Tonight was worse than usual. He hardly spoke. His mouth was just a thin slash, and his eyes were fixed on the glass of Scotch that he was twirling slowly in his hand.

"So how is Saddam Maisun?" I asked, referring to the dictatorial Chief Information Officer Stuart compared to the Iraqi leader Hussein. He raised his eyes and stared at me through slits, not amused.

"They fired the whole IT staff today, Lucy. Over three hundred people. They're outsourcing the whole thing to some bunch of Indians with green cards."

"Oh, no," I cried. "What about Jake?" Jake had been working closely with Stu and had earned his seldom given respect.

"Gone. The installation is on indefinite hold. Your work may be, too. It's no great shakes for us, but all those people." He paused, still looking at his twirling Scotch. Then he added softly, "Security took a gun away from a man in the parking lot."

I dropped my fork and gazed out the window overlooking the East River. Rain smeared the glass and fractured the millions of tiny lights burning in the night, blending them into one great haze.

Is it worth it? All those hundreds of written words about loyalty and concern for customers and individual employees. All those declarations about how our people are our greatest asset. Is it just another distracting gesture, another slight of hand? And was I nothing more than the smiling magician's assistant, all part of the shill? The sorcerer's apprentice blundering into a world out of control?

"It's business, Lucy. Just business," he whispered to me in the elevator. But that is not what his lovemaking said. It was personal. It was a jungle. It was kill or be killed. And it didn't stop at that. The winner had to kill all the cubs—cancel all the projects—to bring the lionesses to heat. To start his own kingdom. Savage. Driving. Ruthless. Without pity, without humor. He stared into my face with that same hard knowledge in his eyes as he played out this pent-up passion, this urge to vanquish, to rule, to conquer. Until finally we both cried out, and he rolled away, spent and heavy. I lay there for a few minutes, then slipped out of bed and stood looking out on the wet, shining streets of Manhattan. Becca, I thought, are you out there somewhere? Are you safe?

Shea's picture was on the cover of *Elle*. I saw her staring out from the magazine rack on the plane to Chicago and took the magazine to my seat. I'm sure it was her. She looked so much like Becca at eighteen. The same pale, heart-shaped face capped with blue-black hair. And melting, navy eyes. I thought of Becca in her appropriated ensemble on the night before her interview at Rich's. I gazed out the airplane's window into the night, and her image from the magazine in my lap reflected there brighter than my own. I had an overwhelming urge to put my lips to the glass and kiss her cheek. Where had all the years gone? Was I losing too much of reality pursuing something that was merely a mirage? Where were we leading our daughters—into freedom or into Hell? I picked up the Areophone and called my Clea. After listening to her gripes about graduate school professors and her thesis, I made her listen to my doubts as well.

"Maybe it is just a jungle without any standards, not even the monetary one," I said to her. "People are literally killing each other."

"Don't give up, Mom. We just need some down time."

"And where should we put down?"

"Hawaii. Stu is taking us all there for Christmas. He told me because he wanted to make sure my winter break was long enough. It was supposed to be a surprise, but I think you need it now."

"Oh, boy. Another airplane. I'm excited."

"Mom?"

"Yeah."

"Don't forget, like it or not, I'll be out in that jungle soon."

With the rapid growth in technology, companies emerged with phantom products and illusive shareholder value. Product liability and shareholder lawsuits blossomed. Many of these issues couldn't be addressed with software, but I always tried to include at least some of them. I was determined this wasn't going to just be a sales pitch.

I met her first in Chicago, and then in Dallas and LA. Sometimes she was small and neat and dark, and sometimes tall and blonde and sophisticated. Sometimes she was a vice president over product development. Sometimes a financial officer. Sometimes the business was insurance. Or banking. Or fast food. Or transportation. But she was always worried. Always nervous under her smiling facade. She was responsible for several projects, and at least one—a very worthy one—was in deep trouble. WatchWord's latest software product was designed to find just such projects, those overrunning costs and resources and slipping behind on revenues and schedules. It could even forecast which projects might go that way before they started and suggest what to do about the problem.

But the ability to do that worried her. It reduced the process to just the statistics, just the numbers.

"It's like a Sophie's Choice for her," I told Stuart on the phone one night.

"Like a what's-it?" he asked, obviously only half listening as he did something else on his laptop.

"You know. The movie we saw with Meryl Streep. Where the Nazis forced her to choose one of her children or see them both gassed."

"Yeah, so what?"

"She sees it as just such as dilemma. Is there any way to save her baby and her honor? Can she throw some innocent to the wolves and buy the time to get the other safely away? She'd do just about anything to save it. But what would that make her, a pandering collaborator? A Nazi slut?"

"Why would she feel like that? You're talking drivel." He just didn't get it. Men didn't worry about such things. It was only business after all. A simple mathematical formula of what would maximize profits and minimize risk. There weren't any messy feelings of creativity, just survival. No protective mother urges. No Madonnas or Medusas. He'd never understand.

Lucy

I called Bobbie Jean whenever I was in San Francisco, but only got to talk to her once or twice. The phone was always answered by someone else. Someone who called her Mrs. Morgan. I tried to find Becca when I was in New York. I was often lonely and really wanted to talk to someone friendly. Someone female. Someone who wasn't just another weary road warrior.

Finally in 1997, Stuart and Dave sold the business, and we retired to our house on Lake Lanier. We lazed about enjoying retirement, getting to know each other again, catching up on life. I'd rake leaves or work in the garden or just lie in the hammock as the season and my mood dictated. I watched the great blue herons lift across the sky, screeching like some ancient pterodactyls when the eagles disturbed their wading by the shore. I saw the big land-locked bass come into our cove turning it into a boiling fury as they chased the enormous schools of shiners that wheeled and turned so much in step they appeared to be of one mind. I tracked the path of the old turtle that every year came back to the same spot to lay her eggs, moving with such determination that nothing could deter her or make her deviate from her course.

Such a sweet life. Until the dreams began. Becca, I hope you want to see me as much I want to see you.

Part III

Amelia Island
Day 1

18

Lucy Jones Savage, "Lucy"

Lucy Jones: marries intellectual type, he will be a politician, in research, or a news corespondant (sic), 3 children, may live in a foreign country, occasionally has small groups over to her house.

Pulling this group together was much easier with e-mail. By the first of May we had decided on a weekend in June and Becca's place on Amelia Island. We continued to correspond, exchanging plans and arranging travel schedules, so we were not arriving as total strangers. On Friday afternoon Sally and Bobbie Jean flew into Jacksonville, Sally from Colorado and Bobbie Jean from San Francisco. The rest of us drove down.

The first day we spent catching up, looking at pictures of children, and admiring Becca's view of the Atlantic. The old, gray shingled cottage with wide, wrapping porches welcomed us back to another time. Becca had framed our senior class pictures with Bobbie Jean's quotations from Kipling and hung them by the front door. Every corner of the house said *beach music*, from the bottles and shells in the salt-spray stained windows to the watercolors on the walls. The over-stuffed sofa and chairs were casual and shoes-off comfortable. There was even a hammock on the porch. It was everything I wanted it to be.

Putting my arm around Becca, I whispered, "Do you remember Tybee Island and the last night we were there?"

"Of course I do. Why'd you think I wanted this place so bad? Why I wanted you all here?"

I took Shea's room upstairs with its white wicker furniture and photos of Becca's beautiful daughter. Sally and Bobbie Jean were down the hall. Becca and Wallee were downstairs. We had an early supper on the porch. I brought chicken salad, Southern style except for the almonds. Sally had baked bread from her Savannah Junior League cookbook. Wallee came up with Blenheim's Ginger Ale. Bobbie Jean had wine, from a vineyard near her home she said. Settled in, we stopped for the first time to look into each other's faces.

If I were painting them today, rather than thirty years ago, there would be more purples and grays and fewer pinks and golds. The eyes are more smudged and the lips less full. The edges of our faces are not so sharp, and the lines around the eyes don't go away when we are no longer smiling. Yet the smiles are just the same. Bobbie Jean's no-teeth, lazy grin. Becca's smile that curls up slowly like a cat settling into your lap. I hadn't realized it before, but Sally had the largest smile. Her whole face was more animated, more open than the rest of ours. Wallee's was the smallest, the most cautious smile. In most of these faces I saw more peace less fear, more confidence less hurt. This was the face I saw in my mirror, too, before I began to dream of carrying someone else in my flights and of crashing out of control. This was the face I wanted back not the one from thirty years ago.

We claimed our spots in the living room overlooking the ocean. Becca on the floor, Bobbie Jean and I on the sofa, and Wallee and Sally in the armchairs. Wine was poured all around, then I handed the faded little pink envelope that held our predictions to Becca. She opened it carefully. Her eyes scanned the page and lingered over her handwriting for a moment. Then as Becca read aloud what we had written so many years ago, we each gave the fifty cent tour of our lives since graduation. She started with the lines that cast my fate, so I lead off.

"Well, I guess that describes the first part of my adult life pretty well. My first husband was an intellectual, a professor, and we did lived in France for a year, but I have one child, a daughter Clea, not three, unless you want to count my two stepsons. During my first marriage, we did have small, intense groups over to discuss big, intense things. Those were my *hetaira* years, I guess."

"Oh, God. I remember that," Becca said. "Miss Jennings. Eighth grade. She was so afraid you were telling everybody you wanted to be a whore."

"What?" Sally said, "I don't remember that."

"Lucy did a report about the *hetairae* in Miss Jennings' creative writing class in eighth grade," Wallee explained. "At the end she said she wanted to be one when she grew up. Apparently not everyone romanticizes courtesans like Lucy does, because Ms. Jennings felt the need to persuade her to consider other career opportunities."

"Oh, I think courtesans are romantic too," said Bobbie Jean. "I loved *Camille*. Robert Taylor. Greta Garbo. Heaven."

"Go on Lucy," Wallee coached. "Why did you leave?"

"My husband had a drinking problem that just got worse and worse, and finally I had to go."

"How long were you married?" Sally asked.

"About fifteen years. Clea was almost ten when I left. I've been in or around Atlanta ever since. First I taught at a small liberal arts college, then the school of business at Georgia State."

"What did you teach?" Wallee interrupted.

"Philosophy, business ethics. One day I met Stuart at a seminar the business school was co-hosting, and he got me some corporate clients. Much more lucrative, and I liked the feeling that I was doing something in the real world that might make a difference. I was tired of empty ideas with no application. I wanted to come down from my ivory tower, but I never dreamed how much of a jungle the business world really is. I was still pretty much of an observer, but I was close enough to smell the lions and get a little bloody. Basically, I advised customers on matters of business ethics, helped them formulate a corporate statement, held executive seminars...that sort of thing."

"I know you traveled a lot, you used to call me when you were passing through," Bobbie Jean said.

"Yes, the heavy travel is one of the reasons I decided to retire."

"Tell us about the trophy husband," Sally urged.

"It's a joke—what Stu calls himself, because he's younger."

"Okay, give. How much younger?"

"Six years."

"Way to go Lucy. I'm very impressed," Bobbie Jean cheered.

"So you're not a *hetaira* any more?" Wallee queried, and I saw the little smile.

"I don't know. Maybe I was something worse," I joked, "a corporate *hetaira*."

"And your folks. How are they?" Sally asked, not quite getting what we were talking about.

"Mama died last November. Daddy still lives alone in Ashbeen. Clea and I visit him every other week. Or we did. We're pretty busy now getting ready for Clea's wedding in November."

"What does Stuart do?" Bobbie Jean asked.

"He's retired. He owned a software company, WatchWord, that provides software to corporations for detecting fraud or alerting the company to illegal or unethical behavior, such as insider trading or sexual discrimination."

"So Stuart's used you to do some soft marketing," Becca said. "You did the head work, and he came in with 'Oh, by the way we have software to see that your managers comply with these principles.'"

"Yeah, I guess you could call it that. I've never thought of it that way," I answered defensively. "I saw it more as actually helping women and minorities get a fair break or saving shareholders from value stolen by insider trading."

"Can software do that?" Wallee inquired. I knew she's sensed the bit of friction there and was moving in to ease the strain.

"Sure. Most companies have their accounting and personnel records computerized. The software merely scans the records looking for certain patterns, like managers who consistentl rank female employees lower than males or who have given an employee, or group of employees, a much better or much poorer review than what they received from previous managers."

"Wouldn't the employee just complain?"

"Sometimes, but often they are afraid to. In a way, the software is an advocate for them. It can't fix the problem, only suggest that a possible problem exists. It's still up to the senior management or board members to investigate and take action."

"But surely there are ethical questions and issues surrounding the use of such software, too." Bobbie Jean said.

"Yes, of course there are. Big-Brother-is-watching-you type questions. Who has the right to such information and what are their responsibilities? Questions about who watches the watchers. Most companies monitor their employees more than they know. Every phone call—time on the line and number dialed—every email, every minute of every day. Oh, they'll say it's for billing and accounting purposes, but it's more. To fire someone, they need a documented case of cause. With enough information, they can even predict what you'll do, before you do it. I covered most of these issues in my seminars. As large databases grow, and companies and governments share information, it will get used. For good or for greed, it's inevitable."

"Then I can see why you'd like this better than being a *hetairae*," Wallee smiled.

I passed around a few snap shots of Clea and Stuart and me at Christmas and one of Clea and her boy friend and one of Stu's boy's.

While they moved from hand to hand I said, "I have a confession to make. There is another reason why I wanted to get us all together. But that can wait until tomorrow."

"Oh, come on, Lucy, drop the other shoe," Becca pleaded.

"Not today. Today we have to catch up. There's plenty of time tomorrow. But I do want to know about Millie. Could no one find her? Not even anything about her?"

"The last time I heard from her was in 1969," Sally said. "She sent me an invitation to UGA graduation. There was just a note scribbled at the bottom that said 'I finally made it!'—then not another word."

"Well, I found a Millicent J. Sonders using the People Finder on the Internet," Becca said. "I sent a postcard to her, but I don't know if she's the right person. This one lives in Florida. She never responded. The phone had been disconnected."

"What did you say in your postcard?" Sally asked anxiously.

"Oh, just that we were getting together this weekend and that we'd like for her to come. Please let me know. Phone number. That's all, I think."

"It's probably not the right person," Sally said. "Anyway, she doesn't know where you live."

"Oh, that's easy to find on the Internet," Becca said.

"Okay, Becca, it's your turn. I'll read, you tell all," I said.

"Wait a minute," Bobbie Jean interrupted. "Lucy, I have one more question…well, two actually. Remember the quote under your picture in the annual?"

"Yes. 'If you can dream…and not make dreams your master…' " I quoted.

"Well, have you mastered your dreams yet?"

"I don't know. Why don't we save that for tomorrow, and you can tell me."

"Well, do you still dream about flying?" Wallee asked.

"Yes, I do."

19

Lucy

If I am the lock and you are the key,
What passions do you free from this box that is me?
They should at least crush boulders, part rivers,
Shatter rainbows and reverse time,
For they rush and weave and dance and claw
And tear their way from ancient well springs, mine.
                    Lucy Jones

That night Sally and Bobbie Jean turned in around 1:30. Wallee had been asleep for hours. But Becca and I couldn't give up. We left the house and went for a walk on the beach. The moon was not so bright as that night at Tybee Beach, but there was enough light to see without the flashlight. It was so calm that only the distant waves of low tide disturbed our talk with their soft murmuring. As I slipped my arm around her waist, I realized that under those gracefully draped and flowing silks she wore, she was not the slim girl of yesterday.

"Becca, are you happy?" I asked her, wanting her confidence now more than ever.

"Who knows, Lucy. Life's not exactly what I expected. I know I love my daughter. How about you?"

"I was. I thought I was. Until...," I left the sentence dangling.

"What's really bothering you? Does this have something to do with the real reason you wanted us here? Come on out with it," she ordered.

"Do you remember my dream? My dream about flying?"

"Oh, come on, Lucy, you aren't still trying to find the dream orgasm are you?" Becca joked, but underneath she sounded annoyed and pulled away from me.

"No, no it's not that. Real life hasn't disappointed me there. This is something new. A new dimension to the dream that has just started in the last year."

"Just since you retired?" she asked.

"After I retired, more recently."

She kicked at the sand, then asked, "When did you start to dream about flying again?"

"When I started swimming again a few years ago. Do you still swim?"

"Not any more. Who has the time?" She shrugged and prompted, "Go on. The dream."

"At first I just had the good dreams again. This new dream didn't start until later."

We stopped walking, and she turned to look at me. "So what is this dream? Do I need to sit down?"

"No let's keep walking." And we continued on up the beach. There were fewer houses here. In the dark, it was easier to tell her. It didn't seem so silly or hysterical.

"I dream I'm fleeing something. Flying like before. But the ground is more menacing. Nothing is soft or misty like in the good dreams. The trees are very black. Their edges are sharp, and the shadows they cast are shifting and sinister. On the ground there are no houses that I can see, only fires. Bright red and orange bon fires. They aren't cozy or glowing, but hot—smoldering and dirty. They smoke and I can smell the smoke.

Sometimes I think I hear horses, but I can't see them. The stars are either not shining or very far away. Tiny and never calling to me. Sometimes gray clouds obscure the sky. There is no moon, no other source of light, and yet, I can see as well as we can tonight. There are mountains on three sides. Dark and looming, with huge rocks spilling down their sides and scattered over the open ground below. This plain of rocks and bond fires completely fills the fourth side all the way to the horizon."

"Sounds like Hell to me," Becca said and took my hand.

"At first I am flying alone, and then I'm aware of someone else. I'm carrying them on my right arm. To begin with, small and child-like. Then heavier and heavier until they are riding on my back, and I can't control the flight."

"You don't see them? Can't tell who they are?"

"No, the face is always dark, oversized. Like a hood is over the head, only perfectly round."

"So it could be anyone, anything?"

"Yes. I don't know if I'm trying to escape and, if so, to where. Perhaps over the mountains. We are high enough to make it over, flying just below the clouds at first. Then I'm forced closer and closer to the ground. I can see the bushes growing between the rocks and taste the soot from the fires. I fight to go higher, and instead we go into a sickening spin, and then we're falling fast. The ground looms up. At last the dive levels out, and I think we can land. But we hit the top of a tree and skip off, momentarily gaining a little altitude, only to fall again. This time we're crashing into the rocks. I see them getting larger and larger. We hit, and I roll across the rocky ground. And that's the end. That's when I wake up."

"What does Stuart think about all this? I assume you've told him."

"Yes, he thinks it's the dog's fault."

"The dog?" she almost laughed.

I explained about Annie and how she had almost drowned me the summer before.

"Well, Stuart could be right, but you don't think so, right?"

"No, I don't think it's Annie."

"So, what's this got to do with us?"

"I thought it might be my mama. You all knew me better than anyone ever has. I thought maybe you could tell me."

She stopped and looked at me, and I could see some emotion flit briefly across she face and then it was gone. "Oh, Lucy, too much stuff gets blamed on mamas. And the South is the worst. All that crazy Southern women shit. Yours was different, but I don't remember her being really strange. Maybe someone else does. Sally and Bobbie Jean knew her better than I did."

"That's true. So you don't think that's it?"

"Look, Lucy, my mama said stuff to me that no mother should ever say to their kids, but I don't dream about it."

"Like what? What did she say to you?"

"Oh, stuff about breaking her heart. How I'd never amount to anything and would end up a miserable failure." So this was it.

"Do you think your mama wanted to live through you…for you to be what she wanted to be, but couldn't because she never got the chance?" I was remembering Becca's old fear of the vampire sucking the blood out of her, draining away her spirit, possessing her body. Perhaps, I thought, that old fear was her way of expressing what she couldn't or wouldn't say in words.

"Maybe," she replied. "Maybe she did want my life. Women of her generation didn't have many opportunities. When she was so sick near the end, she started talking about her day as if she were twenty or thirty. I think she thought that I was her sister, my Aunt Jane, who died twenty years ago. I never realized how much the Great Depression deflated her hopes and dreams. She didn't get to college. She didn't even get to finish high school. There wasn't any money to keep it open in 1935."

"It would be hard not to envy the bright futures we seemed to have."

"There was more, Lucy. She lost three babies to still births or miscarriages after I was born. I think her children were breaking her heart even before they were born."

"Did you ever reconcile?"

"We put together some sort of truce when Shea was born, and the only hard parts after that were when she was dying." She paused and then asked, "Have you told Clea about this dream?"

"No, I love my daughter, and we talk about everything but this."

"Well, maybe you should."

"We're lucky to have our daughters, aren't we?"

"The luckiest!" she agreed and raised her chin with a slight jerk to gaze down the beach.

"You were a good daughter, too, you know," I whispered. "You never told me any of this. Never said anything except that y'all were fighting or that she was mad at you. You never said you hated her."

"No, because I never did. I always loved her," she sighed.

We turned to walk back home. Most of the houses were dark or dimly lit by night lights. The surf sighed and the sand squeaked beneath our feet. I lifted my head to the sky. The waxing moon shared the heavens with some high, light clouds that allowed the thousands of sparkling stars to shine through. I wondered what it was about beaches that made them so unfailingly romantic. Was it only the way the rhythm of the waves matched the tempo of our hearts, the cadence of their rise and fall in step with each breath we draw, the pull of the surf like a lover drawing you ever nearer?

"Becca," I whispered. "In all these years, has there never been anyone else but Richard?"

"What do you think?"

"I think there should have been."

She was silent for a minute and then said, in a voice that wavered only slightly, "Oh Lucy, you can't imagine how much it hurt when I found out he was sneaking around, seeing other women."

Somewhere inside me something shut tight, then opened slowly so that I could say, "Yes, I think I can. Secret visits to a bottle aren't a whole lot different. Regardless of what anyone tells you, in your heart, you believe he could stop, if only he really loved you."

"Or if you simply tried harder to be what he wanted."

"Or to save him," I echoed the futility of her hopes and then asked, "What did he want you to be?"

"A bonsai tree," she laughed, and then explained, "Something small and perfect and never changing. He wanted me to give up the agency that I had worked for fifteen years to build, just when I was finally seeing some success. He told Shea that I loved the agency more than her."

"Wow. That must have made you angry."

"I just couldn't get angry for the longest time," Becca said. "Just hurt, really hurt."

"And slowly it eroded away who you were?" I added, filling in from memory.

"Yeah, I remember some marriage counselor we went to telling me that I needed to do something for Becca. And I couldn't think for a minute who Becca was." She laughed when she said this, but I knew it wasn't really funny.

"What did you do?"

"Well, he told me to buy myself some new make-up. Clinique, I think. My make-up came from Kmart. Or I just used Shea's rejects. I was so used to doing without while I supported us through college, that I never got over it. Even when we had plenty of money."

"So did you buy the make-up?"

"No. It seemed like putting paint on a ghost." She was quiet for a minute as we walked on toward her porch light. Then she sighed a deep sigh and steely-voiced, confessed, "I had an affair. Got a divorce. And changed my name to Rebe."

"You had an affair?" I repeated, not really surprised.

"Yeah, I met a man at an advertising and marketing conference in Orlando. He was a great dancer. They were playing 'Hungry Eyes.' You know the song?"

I nodded, "Yes."

"Well, I was pretty damned hungry. Starved was more like it. No amount of counseling did for me what those couple of nights did. I saw myself through his eyes, and I realized that I wasn't Becca anymore. I was tougher, smarter, and better. I knew all about selling things, and I realized it was time to sell myself, my new self."

"Not literally, I hope." We giggled almost like we were thirteen again.

She grinned and said, "I got a new hair cut and make-over even before I left Orlando. But, it didn't do much but make Richard suspicious and anxious. Things were just too far gone. Anyhow, the change I'd finally recognized on the inside was more important than the change on the outside anyway. I just needed room to grow."

"Why didn't you tell me when all of this was happening?" I asked, already knowing the reason.

"It just hurt too much. And you seemed so perfect with Stuart. It made me feel like just what my mama had predicted I be—a miserable failure. I could barely stand to talk to you let alone see how happy you were."

I let my finger tips go to my mouth and chewed at a nail. What could I say? I'd hurt my best friend just by being happy. I remembered the time when I had accidentally poked her in the eye while playing some stupid game of blind-man's bluff. I had thought I'd felt bad then. It was nothing compared to this.

"Did you ever see him again, the man in Orlando?"

"No. But there is someone else." We had reached the steps to the porch, where we hugged and said goodnight.

"Sweet dreams," she said.

20

Rebe Rollins, "Becca"

Becca McCollough: Marries a big town exec, ladies man, one or two children, spacious, modern, penthouse apartment, maybe a summer home, goes out to dinner and dances, very fashion conscious, at least one maid.

"Well, to begin with, nobody calls me *Becca* anymore. I'm Rebe Rollins. *Becca* is just too soft and sweet. And, in this business, I'm nobody's fool," I announced after Lucy read aloud the prediction she had made for me thirty-seven years before. My story is going to be the hardest to tell because I am the only one without a husband, I thought.

"No, I didn't marry a big town executive, as you all know. I married Richard, straight out of high school. But, maybe he did turn out to be a ladies' man. He started seeing other women, that's for sure." There, I'd said it, the rest would be easy.

"And has there never been anyone else for you?" Wallee asked.

"I am not sure you need to know everything."

"There's still time," Lucy insinuated, and the others laughed.

"Anyhow, I have one daughter, Shea. We lived in an ordinary, suburban home on the golf course until Shea was twelve and started modeling big time. I ran an ad agency in Atlanta. Then Shea began getting jobs in New York. I think that's when Richard and I realized it would be better for all of us if Shea and I left. We went to New York, and I was her manager for ten years. I started a small agency for Shea and five other girls from Atlanta. It never grew really big, but we found a niche, the ethnic look. I wouldn't say our apartment there was a penthouse, but it was nice enough. And now I have this sort-of permanent summer home. I learned a lot about the fashion business first hand, and now I edit photocopy and beat up other ad agencies for my clients. No maid, never had one."

"What happened right after you and Richard were married? Did you ever get to college?" Sally asked.

"Yeah, but I worked my way through. My mama was livid when she found out we'd eloped. She cut me off without a cent and declared that I'd broken her heart and ruined all her dreams for me."

"It must have been rough working full time and going to school," Bobbie Jean prompted sympathetically.

"Richard had a scholarship and couldn't take much of a job since he had to keep his grades up. So I worked two jobs. One at night and on weekends, and another at lunch waiting tables," I explained to Sally and Wallee. "We never saw each other."

Then I turned to Lucy and Bobbie Jean and said, "I couldn't have done it without you all. Thank you, Lucy, Bobbie Jean. Y'all are the greatest."

Bobbie Jean grinned and explained to the others how our little slight of hand had worked to keep me employed that first year. "Becca actually went to work in a few Schiaparelli's and a Chanel or two."

"After Richard lost his scholarship and was drafted, it was actually easier. I just worked and went to school all the time."

"Mothers can be very hard to understand sometimes," Lucy commented.

"I guess I've been out to prove that I could fill that '*unforgiving minute with sixty seconds worth of distance run*,' huh?" I smiled at Bobbie Jean as I recited part of the quote she had selected for my senior class picture.

Then I finished, "But I don't blame Mama. It made me strong. Taught me that I could do it. Could take care of myself. I did it because I had to."

"And what's the fashion world like? Is it really so glamorous?" Sally asked.

"It's exciting, back stabbing, cut throat, dirty, petty, beautiful, ugly.... I love it. With my background in advertising, I had the contacts in New York to tap into the ethnic market trend. Everybody was white, blond, and Cheryl Tiegs back then. Two of my Atlanta girls were black and one was a Cherokee Indian. A little later we attracted two Asian beauties. It wasn't easy, but the demand was there. I saw it coming. I loved the fight, still do. But, I love it here, too. I go into New York or LA and rough and tumble for a week, then I come back here and restore my soul. I think I have the best of both worlds now."

"You really have made it on your own, haven't you?" Lucy said. "No man to pave your way or fiend off the lions. To take the blame or the credit."

I looked at her face. I thought I could read just about any emotion the camera could capture, but this one had me stumped. It wasn't envy and it wasn't puzzlement, although they might be in the mix. It certainly wasn't pity. "What is it Lucy?" I asked. "What are you trying to say?"

"Just that I know how hard it must have been. I remember 1969, when I was looking for a job, and almost nobody would even talk to me because I was a woman. You could get a job teaching or nursing, but that was about it. Business...forget it, unless it was typing or answering the phone."

The others seemed to agree. And she continued, "Even ten years ago, I don't think I could have gotten the contacts I needed without Stu's help. I would say that what you've done is quiet an achievement. You've really made something." But the look on her face said she wasn't telling me everything, something was missing. Maybe she didn't know herself what she was really feeling.

"Well, I'd love for it to have been more, but I know my limits," I concluded.

"Do you?" Bobbie Jean asked. "I got the answering machine an awfully lot last month when I called here."

"This is tame compared to what I was doing. In '94 we were on a shoot in Norway just before and during the Winter Olympics. It was a rush job, to get the pictures before the Olympics were passé. The pace was frantic but the backdrops were so fantastic. All those primary colors against the snow and the clear blue sky. Those wonderful Scandinavian costumes and bizarre trolls and wood nymphs. But it was colder than Hell, and the snow was so deep in places that it was higher than the buses. They were urging people who were very old or very young not to come to the games. It was just too frigid. I even broke down and bought a real fur hat and fur lined boots. I haven't worn them since. Just my *Harpoon a Norwegian, Save a Whale* tee shirt.

When we got back to Oslo, we had a message. Could we go to Australia? All of the models they had booked were down with food poisoning, and they wanted Shea and three other girls to fill in. They Delta Dashed us visas and summer clothes, and twenty-eight hours later, we were on the beach outside Sydney, oiled down and roasting."

"But you loved it. Couldn't get enough, right?" Lucy smiled.

"Yeah, I did. I still do. It's like a great roller coaster. When I walk out of a hotel in New York, I can almost hear the clink, clink, clink of the gears and chains pulling toward the top. And as I push through the big glass doors into one of the agencies, I know that any minute now I'll be hurdling through space and silently screaming from the sheer thrill and near terror of it. You know it's coming." I was silent for a minute. I doubt if anyone but Lucy really understood. "Anybody need more wine?" I asked and topped off her glass.

I was just starting to pass around my snap shots when the phone rang, and I stepped over to the table by Wallee's chair and picked it up.

"Hello."

"Hello, Becca? This is Millicent Sonders."

"Millie," I said. "Is that really you?" I spun around to face the others and turned on the speakerphone.

"Yeah, it's me, Becca. Are y'all all having fun?"

"We're having a great time. Where are you?"

"I'm in Miami, but if I drive up early in the morning, I can be there by noon."

"Hey, Millie, it's Wallee. How are you?" Wallee called out.

"Hey, Wallee. Who else is there?"

"All of us. Why didn't you call sooner?"

"Well, I just looked at my mail. Been kind of occupied lately. Is Sally there?"

"Yes, Millie, I'm here," Sally said, her voice strained.

"So, why didn't you tell me about this little get together, Sally?"

"I don't think I knew about it when we talked," Sally said vaguely.

"Well, we all know now, don't we? Is Lucy there?"

"Yeah, Millie I'm here. Come on up."

"Millie, it's Bobbie Jean. You've got to come. We won't be complete without you."

"I'd love to, sweetie, but I was just joking. I can't make it tomorrow. Maybe some other time. Gotta go now." And she hung up.

We all sat there staring at Sally. Finally, Bobbie Jean said, "Okay, Sally, give. What are you hiding?"

"Oh, Becca, I am so sorry. I should have told you. I just didn't think it was necessary for anyone else to know."

"Know what?" I asked. I could hear the clink, clink, clink in the back of my mind and I knew something was coming.

Sally took a deep breath, looked at her hands clasped in her lap, then raised her head and said, "Millie has been in jail for the past six months. And not for the first time."

21

Millicent J. Sonders, "Millie"

Millie Sonders: Marries a local merchant large family (older son), many church activities.

"Jail," Bobbie Jean said in a stunned voice. "Lucy, did you predict this?"

"Not a chance," Lucy replied and read aloud the prediction she and Becca had written for Millie.

"Okay, Sally," Wallee said. "Just what do you know. Spill."

"It's true that I got the invitation to the University of Georgia graduation in '69. But later Millie told me that she had gotten it from another student. She never graduated. And it's not true, of course, that I haven't heard anything more. I did hear from her every couple of years, mainly begging for money. She just never did seem to learn how to take care of herself."

"Like Mama," Lucy mused.

"Like most men," Becca laughed.

"Yes, she did remind me of your mama in some ways, Lucy. Doing the everyday chores the rest of us take for granted just never seemed to occur to her. That was always someone else's worry. Those things would be done for her. But somewhere along the way your mama got married. Then your daddy thought it was his job to take care of her. Millie has never married."

"So what has she done?" Becca demanded.

"Well, about fifteen years ago, when my mama was so sick at Emory's big hospital in Atlanta, I was staying at the Marriott, and one night my husband, Bob, called. He said that Millie had left a message on the answering machine to call her, and the number was in Roswell. So I called. She acted really glad to hear from me and suggested we get together. I wasn't sure I wanted to, but she was talking about a new job and how much she liked Atlanta, and I was all alone at night after visiting Mama at the hospital, so I said yes."

"Come on Sally, get to the point," Becca urged.

"We met a couple of nights a week for dinner or talked on the phone. She seemed pretty much the way she was that last summer. Happy, almost too happy. Then, one night, she showed up with a black eye, and she'd been drinking. I had already ordered a bottle of wine, so she had a few more drinks. And that's when the facade came down. She was crying, and I didn't know what to do, so we went back to my room."

"Sally!" Becca cried waving her arms in a come-on-come-on gesture.

Sally glared at Becca, then stared at her hands again.

"Leave her alone, Becca. Can't you see this is hard for her," Bobbie Jean said, as she left the sofa to sit on the arm of Sally's chair.

"She's been hooking ever since high school," Sally said with her eyes closed.

"*Hooking*, as in selling sex?" Wallee asked in astonishment.

"Of course that's what I mean. What did you think I meant? Hooking a rug?" Sally answered in exasperation. The rest of us burst out laughing.

"It isn't funny. It's pathetic, terrible. She told me more than I ever wanted to know that night. All about how much fun it was at first. How easy it was to make money. The really nice places men took her. All the nice things she had had—a maid, a masseuse, a personal trainer. She'd even done movies, she said. She just went on and on. But, she was old at thirty-five. Nobody wanted her anymore. All she could attract were the weirdoes and the sickies." Sally's voice was getting higher and higher, and she finished on a near shriek.

"What did you do?" Wallee asked.

"I just kept nodding my head. And every once in a while I'd say 'Oh' or 'Really' or something. Just like Mama used to do, when really she had no idea what Daddy was talking about. Millie said that when she'd called me for money, she'd been sick or beaten up. That she'd tried to get other jobs, but they just didn't pay enough. She'd already been in jail a couple of times for prostitution. Finally, I told her I had to be up early, and she'd have to go. I changed hotels the next morning." The tears were running down her cheeks as she finished, and Bobbie Jean was digging a Kleenex out of her bag.

"That was fifteen years ago," Becca reminded us. "What's she been doing since? Surely she's not a fifty-plus hooker?"

"As near as I can tell, she alternated between trying other things and going back on the streets for at least three or four more years. She got real sick at one time. I think she went home and lived with her mother for a while. Then, when her mother died, she got a little money, and I think a, quote-unquote, *boy friend* set her up with her own business."

"What kind of business?" Bobbie Jean asked.

"What do you think," Becca said.

"Sally?"

"Becca's right. It was her own house or brothel or whatever you call it. She rents girls."

"My God," Wallee said in a low voice.

"Wow," Bobbie Jean breathed. "You don't suppose she will really show up tomorrow do you?"

"I doubt it," Becca answered. "She's probably on probation or something."

"Bobbie Jean," Lucy asked turning toward her, "what did those lines from Kipling mean that you selected for Millie's senior picture? The ones about losing everything."

"I'm not sure I remember. Maybe I was thinking of Allen and the wreck."

"But I didn't think she was all that close to Allen," Wallee said.

"She wasn't. But she told me once that her mother had big plans for them." Sally answered. "I think Mrs. Sonders knew even then that Millie couldn't make it on her own. She was the one putting all her chips on Allen."

"Well, we don't know that Millie has lost her winnings, now do we? Maybe her business is doing quite well," Becca speculated.

"Oh Becca, really. How can you say such a thing?" Sally sniffed.

Wallee stood up and stretched. As she poured herself another glass of wine she said, "Let me see if I can summarize. We have a would-be courtesan on her second husband, a needs-no-man businesswoman, and a hooker so far. Bobbie Jean, I'm dying to her about you. And since nobody rented any of Millie's movies, I suggest we move on to you."

22

Roberta Harris Morgan, "Bobbie Jean"

Bobbie Jean Harris: Marries a sporty, Wall Street exec. One child (probably girl), big house, gives and goes to big parties, lots of servants (to order). Close family ties. Wears slacks a lot.

Becca read the prediction, and I thought how close it was to the truth. How dull my life was going to seem, just some young girl's idea of the perfect life, compliments of 1950's movies.

"Well, that about sums it up, except no Wall Street, no girls, and no slacks," I said trying to make my voice as breezy as I could.

"Wait a minute, you're not getting off that easily," Becca jumped in. "I assume there is an executive, so you've at least got to describe him and the house."

"Well, like you Becca, nobody calls me by my childhood name anymore. Now I'm just Roberta. Jeffery was the executive vice president of a big insurance company in San Francisco. We have a house in Pacific Heights and a weekend place near St. Helena about an hour and a half north of San Francisco. It's really beautiful up there. That's where I spend all my free time. We have several acres, but no vineyards. We do entertain a lot, however there's just one housekeeper, usually, and a part-time gardener and caretaker for the place at St. Helena."

Lucy looked at Becca and they exchanged a high-five. "Right on!" Becca said.

"How did you met?" Wallee asked, ignoring their antics.

"I was working in an art gallery in Atlanta. He came in to browse, just wasting time because his flight had been canceled by that freak snowstorm in '76. Remember the one that crippled the east coast from Birmingham to Boston?"

"Yes, I remember. Clea was three. I have a picture of her standing in a path we'd cut through the snow. It was above her head." Lucy said.

She doesn't look old enough to have a daughter who was three in '76, I thought. And then continued, "He pretended to be very interested in a Chagall we had, spending hours looking at it, going over the papers and the history. Finally, he asked me to dinner. Ordinarily I'd have said no, but with the snow and all…I wouldn't have opened the gallery at all that day except I was stuck downtown, and since I was going to be spending another night alone…well, I accepted."

"How romantic," Sally sighed. I could tell she much preferred my story to Millie's.

"Did he buy the painting?" Becca asked.

"Yes. And I delivered it to his house in San Francisco two weeks later. A year later we were married in a quiet ceremony at his mother's home." I took another sip of my wine.

"I know it's personal, but why no children?" Wallee asked, leaning forward slightly.

"Oh, Jeffery was already forty-seven. His daughter had just gotten married. He didn't want to start over." I could see them doing the math. "He's seventy-two."

"And you've never wanted children?"

"I don't think you can have it all. I chose Jeffery and the life he could give me."

"How do you spend your time?" Sally wondered.

"Gardening, art galleries, charities, volunteer work…. You know."

I handed her a small book of pictures of Jeffery and me taken over the years at various vacation spots.

"He's very handsome," she said.

"Yes, he was."

"Let me see." Wallee leaned over Sally's shoulder.

"Anyone for dessert?" Becca asked moving toward the kitchen.

"Of course," said Lucy, "I'll help you."

She knows, I thought. *She knows that this can't be all there is to my life. I wonder if it shows on my face. No one has ever found out, and I see no reason to tell anyone here.* Becca returned with a tall Angel Food cake. Lucy brought in the strawberries and whipped cream and chocolate sauce.

"Coffee's in the kitchen. It's the real thing. No decafe tonight," Lucy ordered.

"You can be as sinful as you like," Becca said, and it took me a minute to realize that she meant the dessert. I helped myself to berries and cream, and took half a cup of black coffee back to my chair.

"So, Bobbie Jean," Lucy asked then corrected herself, "*Roberta*. What volunteer work do you do?"

"I'm on the board of the San Francisco Arts Commission. I've enjoyed that for years. Then in the eighties, when AIDS began to devastate the art community so badly, I began doing volunteer work with those organizations too."

"That was brave," Sally said, as if she knew first hand.

"It was a terrible time. I'd only made one close friend in San Francisco. Most women my age had children, and every conversation centered on them. I felt very left out. So when I found someone else who was childless and loved art, I was ecstatic. But the AIDS thing hit not only the artists, it divided the supporters as well and torn the patrons apart. Old friendships were shattered. A curtain of ice hung invisibly in the air at every social and fund raising event. One day my friend informed me that I had to choose. It was her or my volunteer work. At first I was very hurt, then very angry."

"And Jeffery," Lucy asked, "did he support you?"

"Oh yes, but it cost him too. The insurance industry is very conservative. Fortunately, he was close to retirement. Lately, I'm working more with women's shelters. We get a lot of small time hookers, I'm afraid."

"It must be torture to watch someone die and know you can't save them, especially someone young." Lucy's voice carried a hollow note and I wondered if there wasn't more she wanted to say.

"Yes, and treacherous, too," I agreed. "It's so easy to loose control." And Lucy told us what she called the second rule of lifesaving: *Don't let the victim drown you.*

"That's right, Lucy. I forgot, you used to be a lifeguard," Wallee recalled. "I remember how you went after Millie once."

"Don't we all," I said. "But you couldn't save her then, and you can't now."

"I'm not sure she needed saving, then or now," Lucy countered.

"I edit a lot of work for a gay photographer," Becca said. "He's a dream. Such a waste."

"I've had gay friends too," Lucy added.

"But AIDS is a bigger threat to women today than gays, isn't it?" said Sally.

"Yes, or very nearly," I agreed. "I never felt in peril from the disease, but I was hurt by the reaction of my friend and others that I thought I knew so well."

"You always had an idea of what it was like to be on the outside, didn't you?" Wallee said softly. "You certainly understood me. You and Sally let me talk about how I felt when my parents wouldn't hear how much polio had hurt me. I didn't have to be brave and cheerful with you. I could be discouraged and angry. Maybe what you save is the life that is still left. You let them live in reality. You let them be who they are."

"Thank you, Wallee, I hope so."

"Well, Wallee, since you've started telling us about yourself, why don't you take your turn?" Sally suggested.

23

Wallace Anderson Mason, "Wallee"

Wallace Ann Anderson: will marry in her late 20's. She's a secretary and will marry her boss or a friend of her boss, 2 children (girls), live in south, before and when first married goes out a lot but then slacks off because of family.

We carried our dessert plates back into the kitchen. Becca turned on the lamps, since the night was coming and the light was fading fast. I knew what I wanted to say, but I had no idea what Lucy and Becca had written. So far, they were batting about 700. Becca sank into the sofa beside Lucy, and Bobbie Jean curled up at the other end. And we listened to my prediction.

"That's amazingly close. I wasn't exactly a secretary, more of a glorified administrative assistant, and we just have one daughter, but the rest is true."

"I can't believe that," Becca said. "I always thought you'd be something brainy."

"Wallee, I can't help noticing that you aren't wearing a brace anymore," Bobbie Jean pointed out. "What happened?"

"While Sally and I were at Converse, I learned to swim. That day at the lake made me want to try again, Lucy. Since there were only girls at Converse, I wasn't so embarrassed in the pool, and swimming was wonderful exercise for rebuilding muscle. Between Bobbie Jean's getting me out of the wheelchair and the swimming, I was able to do without the brace most of the time. I was able to dance at my daughter's wedding."

"Whoa, whoa, that's getting ahead," Becca said. "How did you meet your husband?"

"I met Stephen at a support group for polio survivors, while I was taking graduate school classes at Emory. He'd never had the disease himself, but he was doing research work. He interviewed me. I told him about my experiences and about all of you. Two years later, he looked me up through the support group. He had a practice in Savannah counseling survivors and needed an assistant, would I be interested? I typed and filed, answered the phone, did research, gave him my opinions, listened to his, emptied the trash…you name it."

"And you started dating?" Bobbie Jean postulated.

"Not right away, but after the first year. The only problem was he loved to dance, and I was clumsy and afraid I'd trip. The special shoes, you know. But one night he caught me swaying to the radio as I was closing up, and nothing would do except a lesson. It wasn't anything difficult or fast, just slow dancing or some easy shagging—beach music, "Carolina Girls" and "Stay." We started out with the basic steps and pivots, then, before I knew it, he'd added a little sugar footing and some belly rolls. It was six months before I'd try it outside the office, but then we started going out a lot."

"Wallee, I can hardly believe it," Sally said smiling her biggest smile. "I'm so happy for you."

"We had a small wedding a year or so later, and I continued to work for him until Anne was born in '76. I still help out now and then."

"What a wonderful story," Sally said.

"Well, that's not quite the end. One of the things our clinic sees a lot of is PPS, Post Polio Syndrome."

"What is that?" Lucy asked. "I don't think I've ever heard of it."

"Not too many people have, but it affects about a quarter of a million people. Basically, many of those who thought they'd conquered polio years ago begin to feel the symptoms again or new symptoms."

"What does that mean?" Sally asked. I could hear the worry and concern in her voice.

"Pain, fatigue, loss of muscle function."

"Oh, Wallee that hasn't happened to you, has it?" Lucy cried.

"No, not yet. It seems to start thirty to forty years after the initial bout, so maybe I'm past that point and will never have it. But I can't be sure. I do get tired more easily these days."

"But don't we all," Bobbie Jean concluded. "We're all older."

"There is one theory that those who recovered the most tired the muscles too much in their efforts to conquer the disease. And now they are prematurely aging. Perhaps I'm lucky that my recovery was slow."

"Oh, Wallee how unfair," Lucy wailed.

"Is there any way to know for sure if you'll get it?" Becca asked.

"No, sometimes the symptoms come on fast, but more often gradually, moving from just fatigue and loss of strength to atrophy. The odds are about 50/50."

"What's Stephen's take on this?" Becca wanted to know.

"We talk about it. He sees patients every day with PPS. And even though the clinic was started to help polio survivors with lingering emotional problems, he'd heard of PPS even before we married. I don't think he can go into denial the way my father did. Either way, I know he loves me."

"And what about your father? Did he get to see you dance at your daughter's wedding?" Bobbie Jean asked. I knew what the real question was: Did he ever get over it?

"No, Mama and Daddy died not long after Anne was born. But I don't think it would have mattered. You can't acknowledge a victory if you've never admitted a defeat. I used to dream that one day he'd see how far I'd come and tell me he was proud of me, that he'd been wrong to cut me off emotionally when I needed him the most. But, of course, it never happened. He never said the word *polio* in my presence and never even correctly referred to Stephen's work. Mama and Daddy just told people that Stephen was a doctor with a small general practice in Savannah."

"Oh Wallee," Becca said, "I think we all have some version of that dream. The one where we can say one last time, 'Look at me, Mama. Look at me. Didn't I do that well, didn't I turn out wonderful?' And this time she says, 'Yes, baby, I'm mighty proud of you.' "

"There's the other side to that dream, too," Sally suggested to us. "The one where she wants you to hear her say it. Maybe they have said it, but just not with words you understand. You have to believe it yourself before you can hear it sometimes."

I looked at her and realized that this wasn't the same uncertain, people-pleaser I had known. Something had happened to her.

"Well, it's getting late, and we haven't heard from Sally yet. So enough about me."

"Then here's to the rest of our lives," Bobbie Jean said, lifting her still half-full glass. And we all agreed.

24

Sally Blackwelder Matthews, "Sally"

Sally Blackwelder: Marries a doctor or a...

"Well, Sally, I'm afraid that's all there is," Becca said.

"I'm so sorry," Lucy apologized, obviously embarrassed to have left me out. "Please, forgive me. I never finished your prediction. I must have just stuck the sheet in the envelope and forgotten all about it."

"Oh Lucy, how like you," I said. "You were always forgetting about me, but I'm kind of glad you didn't finish it. It's easy to see where you were headed, and I'd like to think that *I've* out smarted *you* for once."

"Hey, ladies, watch out. I think Sally has developed an attitude," Becca teased.

"More like backbone than attitude. Although it was a long time coming, when it came, it came suddenly, and it shook up quite a few people including my husband, Bob," I rejoined. "I bet the next word in that prediction was going to be 'lawyer' and that's just what Bob is. I was thirty-two when we met. I'd been working in a research lab at Proctor and

Gamble for five years. I loved my work, but I hated the politics. I just didn't get the corporate ruse of sowing the winds of aggressive competition amongst your own staff and reaping profit from the whirlwind. I'd been taught to play nice."

"What do you mean?" Lucy asked.

"Oh, I always told the whole truth and nothing but. Wouldn't over commit. I was given small projects that I brought in on time. I watched some of the others make big promises, promises that I knew they couldn't fulfill. But they got the big projects. And even if they were late and over budget, or even out right failures, they got the next big project, too. And, of course, I was always called on to bail them out. The good team player. So I was ready when Bob asked me to quit my job and marry him, even though he had three young children."

"Uh-oh," Wallee said, "instant family."

"Instant nonexistence was more like it. The first year of marriage was the second worst year of my life. The children could have taught corporate America a thing or two about competition. They were supposed to live with their mother, but they spent every weekend, holiday, and all summer at our house. Bob was working sixty or seventy hours a week, and it seemed that any spare time belonged to the kids. As soon as he got home in the evenings, the phone would start ringing, and it would be one of the kids or his ex-wife. At first I tried very hard to be the good, understanding wife, but it wasn't long before I caught myself fantasizing about running away from home."

"And feeling guilty about it too, I'll bet," Lucy guessed. "There's something very undignified about competing with children for your husband's attention."

"Did they treat you like the evil stepmother?" Wallee asked.

"That's just it, they didn't treat me any way at all. They just acted like I wasn't there, or like I was some well trained servant who knew her place was in the background—way in the background. The house was clean. Their favorite foods were always there. They could watch whatever they

Sally Blackwelder Matthews, "Sally"

wanted on TV. Nobody made them clean their rooms, fill the dishwasher, or rake the yard. They did hate my cat. He ran off whenever they showed up, and more and more that's what I wanted to do, too."

"And you were afraid to try to make friends with them because their mother would resent it," Lucy inferred tipping her head to one side and looking at her lap as she spoke.

"Yes, how did you know?"

"I've been there. So what did you do?" She smiled encouragingly.

"There are two boys and a girl. The girl is the baby and the apple of her father's eye. The older boy would do anything to please Bob. But the middle child seemed the most left out and the most desperate for attention. So I decided to pay attention to him, to try to make a friend there, to take his part and call Bob's attention to his accomplishments when I thought the other two were hogging the spotlight. Of course, it backfired and blew up in my face. His mother called and accused me of trying to steal her children. She implied that I'd probably stolen her husband as well, even though they were separated when Bob and I started dating. Bob asked me if, just for the sake of peace, could I please stay out of it. Out of what? Out of their lives which were most of his life outside of his firm? I can feel myself getting angry just thinking about it, but at that time I didn't know how to get angry for myself, just hurt."

"And you said this was the second worst year of your life. What happened in the worst year?" Becca asked.

"I started feeling physically tired, not just emotionally spent, and finally went in for a checkup. That's when I found out I had cancer. I remember thinking how unfair it was. I had always been so good, had done just what I was supposed to do. I even remembered that day, Lucy, when you and Bobbie Jean and I had to sit on the floor in the hall all afternoon, just because we'd tried to help Mary Fowler with the newspaper roll."

"God, I was just thinking about that, too," Bobbie Jean cried. "Poor, Sally, what did you do?"

"I went home to Mama," I said with a laugh. I saw them all draw back a little in surprise. I took the last sip of my coffee, then I continued, "She helped me get through the surgery and the chemotherapy. I had always thought that aimless prattle and constant babble she immersed us in were just her friendly personality. But I discovered that it was a trick she used to just focus her attention at the surface, and never let herself think too deeply."

"Think too deeply about what?" Lucy asked.

"About her life I guess. I knew she had left college after her junior year to get married. She finally told me that she had always wanted to finish, but Daddy wouldn't let her. He said he could take care of her, and it would be a waste of money to send her for that last year. He wouldn't even let her use her own money and commute two days a week to Athens after I left home. I guess he'd never heard about a mind being a terrible thing to waste."

"But the don't-think-prattle-on trick worked for you, too?"

"Yes. For all the days when I couldn't bear to think of withstanding the nausea and pain, and maybe dying anyway, Mama's trick worked. We just babbled to each other about clothes and china patterns and gossip and movies and cleaning products.... But, when the worst of the treatment was over, and I was ready, we had some long overdue, real talks as well. And I learned that being good is usually not enough."

"Yeah," Lucy said. "Being good is sort of like not going in the water unless you have to, that's the first rule; but sometimes you do have to go in. Sometimes you just have to wade in pushing and swinging and grab control."

"And that's what I did," I confirmed. "I never would have thought that I could have endured it if someone attacked me or questioned my motives and morals, but I did. And it wasn't even too hard. I set some ground rules, laid down some like-it-or-lump-its, and let the fur fly."

"Oh, Sally, I knew you could," Bobbie Jean smiled and gave me a hug.

"And did the kids like you?" Lucy asked.

"Not at first. At first, they hated the new me. They told me so to my face. Now—they respect me and I'm part of the family," I said. "Maybe even its heart."

"And the cancer?" Wallee asked.

"That was twenty years ago. It's stayed away this long. I can never have children of my own. But then life isn't fair, is it Lucy?"

"Not always. But sometimes it's better than fair."

"What was really unfair," I laughed, "was that I lost so much weight during the chemotherapy that I only weighed 89 pounds. And I still had saddlebags. And no hair!"

They all enjoyed in my joke, but I could see they felt the pain there, too. So I added, "Now I teach Mama's trick to other women. I do a lot of work for the Cancer Society. And sometimes, I help them help themselves, too." I realized how satisfying it was to say that.

"I hate to be the party-pooper, but I go to bed early these days," Wallee said with a big stretch.

It was ten-thirty. We'd been talking since five. I handed around my pictures of Bob, the children and my daughter-in-law, me, and the cat. Wallee left for bed, and the rest of us helped Becca load the dishwasher and put away the leftovers. Then we had a second cup of coffee or third glass of wine. The moon was rising over the ocean, and Becca opened the doors onto the porch to let the night breeze in. We turned down the lamps and just sat quietly for a few minutes.

"Do you think Wallee is all right?" Becca asked very softly.

"I think she would have told us if she knew more," I said. "But she did seem tired."

"Well, you and I are on West coast time, Sally," Bobbie Jean reminded me. "And Wallee had a long drive from Savannah."

"Not that long," Lucy said.

"I just don't want to think about that PPS happening to her, I guess," I admitted.

"Don't go turtle on us, Sally. If she needs to talk about it some more tomorrow, we're here for her," Bobbie Jean said firmly.

Silence fell again while we sipped our drinks and listened to the waves. Then Becca said, "Stephen sounds like a good guy. I'm glad they found each other."

A sudden stronger breeze blew through the door and lifted the curtains at the window. I caught the scent of salt and marsh grass. Far off some night bird called, and I stifled a yawn. Bobbie Jean's eyes were closed, her wine glass empty in her hand swaying to the distant sounds of the surf.

"Sally, do you think there's any chance that Millie might show up tomorrow?" Lucy asked.

"I wish I knew. She's so unpredictable. I guess that even if she's on probation, she could leave Miami, just not Florida."

"Oh, Lordy, I didn't think of that," Becca laughed.

"If she shows up what do we do?"

"Why do we have to do anything? We're big girls. I don't think she can shock us," Lucy said. "I'd kind of like to see for myself how she's doing. I doubt she'd be looking for recruits."

"Speak for yourself," Becca kidded. "I bet I could still sell it."

"To a certain extent, Becca, you are the only one here who hasn't sold it," Lucy said.

"What are you talking about Lucy Jones?" I huffed in the best imitation I could do of my mama.

"Just that anytime you let a man support you, you are sort of selling it."

"But I give my husband a lot more than just sex." I protested.

"I know that. We all do. Maybe Millie got the best deal," Lucy laughed. "It just has a short term contract."

"There's even something to be said for that," Becca countered. I hoped she was just joking.

"There's a difference between love and sex," Bobbie Jean declared. "I wonder if Millie has ever been in love."

"Sex is just friction," Lucy stated flatly. "I think it would be easy to sell sex if you didn't love anybody, and very difficult to if you did."

"I think it's more than friction—it's friction set to imagination," Bobbie Jean said. Then she asked, "Do you all worry a lot about your kids these days? Everything seems so much more perilous."

"My daughter and I talk so much more than my mama talked to me. Not just about sex but everything." Becca said.

"Yes," Lucy agreed. "And the opportunities today make at least the older girls more careful. They don't just think of marriage as a way out."

"That's what I found really surprising about your predictions, Lucy. They were all about where we'd live and who we'd marry and what *they'd* do. I would have thought you'd predict what great things *we* would all do. You know, stuff like discovering a cure for cancer or winning a Nobel prize," Bobbie Jean suggested with her famous grin. Her make-up was worn away by the long day and the dusting of freckles had reappeared across her nose, but in this light that warmed her fading red-gold hair, she was very nearly as beautiful as ever.

"We've all done so much more than we predicted, than we ever expected." Becca said.

Then Lucy added, "We had such low expectations, but it isn't surprising when you consider when we wrote this, 1961. The Age of Aquarius was barely dawning, especially in the South. We were still influenced more by Doris Day and *Pillow Talk* than the thirty-something Jane Fonda in *A Doll's House* and Sally Field and *Norma Rae*. We were talking careers, but our only models were for marriage and family. I don't think we knew how to do both. I don't think we knew how to do *anything* but get married."

"Oh God, I just remembered Mrs. Whiterspoon's Rules for a Happy Marriage," I laughed.

"Who?" Becca asked.

"Mrs. Whiterspoon taught Home Economics. Her rules were a combination of "Wives Should Always be Lovers" and "You Will Be His."

You remember those songs? Stuff about fixing your hair the way *he* liked it before *he* comes home from work, and having his drink ready and the children fed and quiet so you could hear about his day. Can you believe it? That's what *we* were being taught in high school. My daughter-in-law reads articles for young mothers about how to squeeze an extra fifteen minutes out of the day for herself."

"I can't believe how much things have changed from our mothers' day to our daughters'," Becca summed up what we were all thinking. "We really were women on the cusp. Out there without a compass, without a clue. How did we ever get from high school to here without falling off the edge of the Earth and being consumed by dragons?"

"Well, we must have learned something in school. They weren't still teaching that the earth was flat," Bobbie Jean joked looking at Becca through her empty wine glass.

"Our education didn't teach us much about the real world," Lucy said. "I was over forty before I really began to understand what it took to get something done in the business world. It's like before then I was on stage with a script from Disney while everyone else was doing *Becket*."

"I haven't been very proud of my alma mater," I admitted. "They were in cahoots with The Citadel to stave off the enrollment of female cadets just a few years ago with some phony *leadership* program."

"It wasn't just our education. It was Ashbeen," Becca offered. "How can you think big when everything you see is small?"

Lucy reached up and removed the comb that was holding her long hair away from her face and neck. She shook her head, and a tumble of tarnished silver cascaded around her shoulders. She reached under her loose, black cotton shirt and released the clasp on her bra. She stretched and groaned with the pleasure of relief, and only then continued, "Have you ever thought that maybe there's not that much difference between men and women? Maybe the differences are really only between people of one personality type and another. Women, like Sally, who are good at cooking are just as good as men in techno-detail stuff like lab work."

"Yeah, put Sally back in that Proctor and Gamble lab today, and I'd bet she'd kick some butt, too." Becca interrupted.

"Women who can patiently give detail directions to children or can organize a home are just as good as men at programming or organizing an office. And any woman who can smile, pour on the charm, and weasel donations for some fund-raiser, the way Bobbie Jean does, could easily get a bank to loan her money to start a business. They just need to transfer the skills. I think that's what we did. We transferred the skills. The same way that, for years, men have been transferring the skills they learned on the football fields and basketball courts to the conference rooms and boardrooms. It just took us awhile to figure out that we could do it," Lucy concluded.

"Then what is the female equivalent of the testosterone-driven, male entrepreneur?" Becca asked, and without waiting for a reply, she preceded to answer her own question. "No, Lucy, I don't buy it. There is a difference, a big difference. Women like to create things, to mother and protect those things. Men have a completely different urge. It allows them—no, it *drives* them—to tear things apart, to destroy, to risk it all. And even when they fight to protect what is theirs, they do it for a completely different reason. It's something about having balls."

I yawned, I was tired and this conversation was getting beyond me. "Looks like I'm getting close to following Wallee. I think I'll go get ready for bed and read just a little. It helps to put me off to sleep."

"Me, too," Bobbie Jean agreed.

We said our good nights, and I left them. Of all of us, I think I've changed the most.

Part IV

Amelia Island
Day 2

25

Lucy

Your touch collapses city-states,
That rise again as legions,
Sweeping over civilization,
Leaving only smoke and mirrors and
Eyes that glow with passions.
                    Lucy Jones

"I had the dream again last night," I whispered to Becca when I found her in the kitchen the next morning. She looked into my unmade-up face, and her finger traced the faint scar on the left side.

"Annie. The dog." I replied to her unasked question.

She frowned and said, "You need to tell the others."

The doors to the porch were open, and they were seated around the table there drinking in the day. The smell of their coffee mixed with that of oranges and cinnamon, sea salt and marsh, and wafted in upon the breeze. It would be hard to describe a dark and dangerous dream world on such a morning. But, perhaps, Becca had already prepared them, because

Bobbie Jean said as soon as I appeared in the doorway, "Okay, Lucy. Why are we really here? Becca says you're having nightmares."

Becca and I sat down with the others and filled our cups. Then I repeated what I had told Becca the night before on the beach. I described the landscape, the sound of unseen horses, and the smell of smoke. I told them about the unrecognized passenger in the cape and hood, who gets heavier and heavier until we crash into the ground. In this light it seemed silly and insubstantial, and I felt foolish to be involving them. But Wallee reached over and laid her hand on mine and said, "This is really bothering you. I can see it in your face. What do *you* think it means?"

"I thought it might be my mama. Becca doesn't really remember her that well, but I was hoping maybe Sally or Bobbie Jean did."

"Don't you remember anything about your wedding, Lucy?" Sally asked and then amended, "Your *first* wedding."

"No, I was pretty stoned most of the time."

"You were?" Bobbie Jean sounded surprised. "You stinker. I wish you'd shared with the rest of us. Some of it was pretty hard to take."

"Bobbie Jean and I were bridesmaids at Lucy's wedding," Sally explained to Becca and Wallee. "Becca, I guess you weren't there because you and Richard had been sent to Texas when Richard lost his scholarship and was drafted. But, Wallee, I don't know why you weren't there."

"I know," I said. "Mama wouldn't have Wallee in the wedding party because of her limp. I'm sorry Wallee, but we had fought over so many things, I was just beyond caring."

"Wow, looks like I missed some fireworks." Becca tried to sound careless and light.

"Don't worry about it, Lucy," Wallee instructed, with a dismissive wave. "It was a long time ago." Suddenly I remembered that I'd promised Bobbie Jean to do something to make it up to Wallee, and I never had.

"I was thinking about the wedding because your mama worn a dark garnet-red cape with a hood that night. Like the figure in your dream," Sally went on. "Of course, the hood wasn't pulled up over her head during the ceremony, but when we arrived at the church, it was sleeting, and she had it up then, protecting her hair."

"It was a beautiful, December wedding," Bobbie Jean added. "Right before Christmas. Everything your mama wanted, I'll bet."

"Everything except the bride," I replied.

"The church was all ivory, white, green, and gold," Sally continued, ignoring my remark. "Lucy's dress was ivory lace."

"My great-aunt Louisiana's dress."

"Sally and I had dark green velvet dresses and cream camellias with green bows," Bobbie Jean remembered. "Two of your Port Gibson cousins were the flower girls. And your roommate…Zoë, is that right…the girl with the wonderful red hair? It was really pretty, and your daddy looked real proud when he walked you down the aisle."

"But your mama cried through the whole thing," Sally said. "Not like most mamas do, but like she was terribly upset. I don't think too many people noticed because mamas are expected to cry some at weddings."

"After the church ceremony, most of the guests had gone on to the reception, and we were staying behind to have our pictures made," Bobbie Jean picked up. "Your mama got very angry with your daddy about something being messed up. He tried to calm her down, but she just wouldn't let it go. She dragged him off in a corner, but we could still hear her voice even though I couldn't hear what she was saying. Finally, it was like she just wore herself out. He got someone to take her home and made some excuse for her at the reception."

"About midnight we went back to your house with you, Lucy, to help you get dressed," Sally continued, speaking right to me, but her eyes were looking at something that happened a long time ago. "Everything was laid out on your beds waiting for you. Your suit and corsage. The luggage. We were helping you get out of your dress, joking and laughing about wedding nights and honeymoons, when your mama came in. Her hair was all messed up, and she had on this old, torn and stained nightgown. She didn't look anything like your mama, who was always so elegant and genteel."

"She started to apologize to us for leaving, for ruining everything," Bobbie Jean said.

"Oh, dear God," Becca breathed. "What did you do then?"

"Sally and I didn't do anything. Lucy, you put your arms around her and took her back to her bedroom," Bobbie Jean said. "I can still see you in your lacy bridal underwear, walking that poor, unhappy woman back to bed and whispering about how everything was going to be all right because you were there."

"And you don't remember any of this?" Sally asked.

"No," I said, "not a bit. Is that some form of denial?"

"Yes!" they all said at once.

"What happened to your mama?" Becca asked.

"Not a lot. She just never was very happy. There never seemed to be much joy in her life. She always reminded me of an impotent, caged animal endlessly fussing over some tedious little thing when he should be out roaming in some wide open space. Except the cage was of her own choosing. When she died last year, her world just seemed to be too small. I've always suspected that she was hospitalized with depression at least once or twice, but Daddy wouldn't tell me."

"Lucy, I think it tormented you that you couldn't save her from herself. It still bothers you. But I don't think that this is what is causing the dream," Wallee said. She paused a moment and then suggested, "Have you considered that the passenger just might be yourself—your inner self?"

"How so?"

"Well, do you worry about having inherited some of your mother's disposition?"

"That's ridiculous," Sally interjected. "Lucy is nothing like her mama."

"Except in passion," Bobbie Jean said. "Lucy, you could get worked up over things just as ardently as she would. But the *things* were at the same time more abstract and more substantial. I can remember her getting really put out with Roxanne when the flowers weren't just so. And I've seen the same fire in your eyes when you felt someone's rights had been stepped on."

"Yeah," Becca said. "I saw you light up yesterday when you started talking about workers' rights."

We were all silent for a moment, sipping our coffee, enjoying the rich mix of Sally's cinnamon nut bread and Bobbie Jean's orange butter. I was beginning to believe that this had been a futile notion—this hope that maybe some how they could help me solve this puzzle.

Then Wallee asked, "What feelings do you have during this dream? Is it all fear for your own safety or are you trying to save someone else?"

"I don't think I am afraid at all, at first. The ground is menacing but not terrifying, and I can easily stay above it. It's only after the weight becomes too great that I can't escape the ground and fear enters in. Even then, I think I'd welcome a controlled landing, but instead, we are out of control and we crash. I don't know if I am worried about this stowaway or afraid for me. How could I be trying to save them if I don't know who they are?"

"Could it be your daughter that you're carrying? You know—a small child that grows into a monster? Or the child you're trying to protect long after she can fly alone and take care of herself?" Sally hypothesized. "Is it Clea?"

I laughed. "Maybe it's her wedding. That started out small and is growing into a monster." Then I said seriously, "I don't know how I know, but somehow, I'm sure that's not it."

Becca put her arm around me and bumped her head against mine. "I know what it's like to worry about a daughter. To fear that you were not good enough, that you didn't have the time and energy to even think of her enough, and at the same time to be amazed at what you've done. Or what she's done. To realize that you share that life and agonize over her choices, not just because you are afraid for her, but because every time she chooses a different path, you question the one you chose, too. Were you wrong to make the choice you did? Is she going to be happier or not?"

"Yeah," I smiled at her. "You do know. It's not Clea."

"Then do you think it's possible this someone, or something, is forcing you to fight instead of flee?" Bobbie Jean proposed. "Maybe they don't want you to save them but to confront those forces on the ground, those horsemen that you say you hear sometimes?"

"That seems possible, but it just opens another question. Who am I suppose to fight and why?"

"Maybe we are concentrating too much on *who* and not enough on *what*," Becca suggested.

"Meaning?"

"Well, it seems to me that you are not really afraid of what is on the ground. It is dangerous, yes, but also sort of thrilling. You don't seem to really be trying to escape, only to find something or somewhere to land," she explained. "Maybe, if you knew *what* it was, then *who* it is would be obvious."

"And what do you think it is, Becca?" Bobbie Jean asked.

"I think Lucy will have to answer that, but I don't think it's something from the distant past."

"You think it's my job, don't you?" I asked her.

"I didn't say that."

"But that's what you think."

"If it were me, yeah. If I retired, I'm sure I'd be dreaming about it still. Wanting to catch one more ride."

"But I'm not you. And I don't think I was ever the success that you've been. I guess I really did think I could save the world…or at least the women of North America."

"You feel like a failure?" Bobbie Jean asked with surprise.

"Well, sometimes. Things don't seem any better, not really. Look how hard women have to work today and how much violence there is. There were plenty of times I felt like I was more a part of the problem than a part of the solution."

"Okay, Lucy, truth time," Bobbie Jean said. "What was it really like out there?"

And so I told them. I told them about the real world as I had seen it, the world that was even stranger than my dream. I told them about the young women who were afraid to marry or have children, who were afraid to invest in love only in careers. About the men and women who had made their jobs their families only to see them disappear like a coin in the magician's hand. About the Sophie's Choice and Saddam Maisun and the babe with balls and the Ladies Room scale of employee worth, and the women who judged themselves by that scale.

"Maybe I didn't make a very good angel or *hetaira*," I confessed. "Maybe I wasn't anything but the slick magician's smiling assistant fooling everyone including myself."

"You sweet idiot, you aren't an angel or a whore. Just a woman. If you helped anyone, that's more than most," Becca assured me. And I thought how much I'd missed her. We never make this kind of friend after a certain age. We become too cautious, too guarded, too afraid to let anyone see the real thing or walk around inside us.

"You don't have any other secrets you haven't told us, have you, Lucy?" Wallee asked.

"I wish. I'm getting too old for exciting secrets."

"Well, I have one more," Bobbie Jean confided.

"I knew it," Becca said triumphantly. "Let's go back in the house. It's getting too hot to sit out here."

26

Roberta

You opened your arm just so,
And let me crawl beside you there.
Then you would touch my head,
And push the hair from my eyes,
And say,
    Little girl, little girl,
    Where are you?
    Where are you now?
But I would never tell,
Because I was always where you were,
And I feared that
You would know I loved you too much.
                    Roberta Jean Harris

"I have never told anyone what happened to me after college. I wasn't going to tell you. But last night, I realized I may never have an opportunity like this again. And I need to tell it just like Lucy needed to tell us her dream," I started as soon as we were all settled in the welcome cool of the living room.

"What did happen between college and Jeffery?" Becca asked.

"After I graduated from Agnes Scott with a major in Art History, there wasn't much I could do. I tried it in New York for a while. I was almost willing to pay them to let me work in a gallery. I taught school in Atlanta for a year. Then an old friend from college got me the job at the gallery in Atlanta. And the rest is history."

"No other loves in all those years?" Becca anticipated.

"Yes," I heard myself whispering, "Yes, but he hurt me so."

It was as if the whole room was holding its breath. I could hear the clock's soft tick and the coffee maker perking in the kitchen and even the sound of gulls crying outside, but not one human sound.

Then Lucy said, "What happened Bobbie Jean?" And I saw the same look in her eyes that I'd seen there in seventh grade when Mrs. Hamilton tried to humiliate me by stripping off my petticoats. I almost laughed and thought, maybe I shouldn't tell this story because Lucy will summon her horsemen and try to slay him for me.

"We had an illegal loft in New York together," I began, remembering the wonderful feeling of being young and invincible, and of not just discovering love for the first time but inventing it. "We were in love. More in love than anyone, at anytime, any where. He was a painter, and I was his model, his canvas, and his muse. We were completely penniless, except for the small checks that Mama was able to send me now and then and what little I could make. I waited tables at night and tried to find a gallery that would hire me during the day. There is something about being hungry that makes love even more intense, don't you think? I lost weight because he could either buy paints or I could buy lunch. So, I only ate at night, what the restaurant would let me have. But I didn't care. He was going to be famous, the most glorious painter since Klimt. Finally, he sold three small canvases."

I stopped. I couldn't go on. I couldn't tell the rest.

"You don't have to finish, Bobbie Jean," Sally soothed.

"Yes, she does. She hasn't told anyone this in thirty years. Have you, Bobbie Jean?" Lucy prodded.

"You're right I need to say this. I feel like I need to reach down and pull it up. Spit it out and then just scream."

"Then let's do it. Let's all go out on the beach and just scream." Lucy proposed.

"Tell us what happened first," Becca pleaded. And she got up to draw the shades.

"Yes, Becca, close them please. It's easier if I can't see you too well." So in the half darkness of Becca's living room, I finally told someone. The only someone who I thought would understand.

"The three canvases were nudes of me. They were very beautiful. The man who bought them praised them extravagantly. Calling them *fascinating* and *beyond compare*. We were ecstatic, sure that this was only the beginning of a wonderful and famous life. We celebrated most of the night, smoking pot, making love, and making plans. Big plans. It was time to try a big canvas. Now that he had the money. But a week passed, and the canvas and paints didn't show up. When I asked him why, he told me that there hadn't been enough money after all. Then a few days later, the man who bought the three nudes came to the restaurant. He told me that he wanted to buy me. I was furious and told him that I'd never consider such a thing. I left the restaurant in a panic and ran all the way home.

"But when I got to the loft, a woman was there. She'd come to buy five more of the smaller works. We got the big canvas and the paints. And started the best work he'd ever done. I never knew I could look so translucent, so sensuous and at the same time ethereal, so naked and so close to holy. It was almost frighteningly good, like he was pouring our love across the canvas, exhausting the passion with each brush stroke." I stopped. Funny, I could barely recall a single detail of his face, but I could still see that painting as if it were yesterday. It was burned into my memory like a branding or stamped like a stigmata on my soul.

"Did he finish it?" Lucy whispered.

"Not as such," I sighed.

"Why?" Becca asked, "What happened to it?"

"I went home for a week at Christmas. I hated to leave, but I wanted to see my family. I hadn't been home for two years, and Gran Ma'am was ill. He assured me that the painting could wait, that he would wait. But when I returned, the painting was of another woman, the woman who had bought the smaller canvases, and he no longer needed me. She had a gallery and could get him patrons, he explained. I understood, didn't I? The art was the most important thing. I swallowed my pride and went to see her. Couldn't she help him without destroying what we had?"

"Oh, Bobbie Jean, how could you?" Sally's voice was so soft and sad, I thought she might be gently scolding one of her children.

"Because I thought she was destroying his talent, too. The painting of her was nowhere near as good as the one of me. I believed he had been able to achieve that special illumination only because he loved me. She laughed at me. He didn't love her, she said. But he didn't love me either. Hadn't I figured it out? Silly, little fool. He had tried to sell me to the other patron, the man who came to the restaurant. Only I was too proud. I wouldn't cooperate. So he had to turn to her."

"Did he ever become famous?" Sally asked.

"No. I never heard of him again after I left New York."

"Good," Wallee gloated. I looked at her dear face, wrinkling with a small smile of guilty satisfaction, and I remembered telling her once, a long time ago, how much I feared being just a pretty thing, some man's *objet d'art*. I could tell she remembered, too. She understood. I took a deep breath and then went on. It was time to drop the last veil.

"Last night, Lucy, you said that you thought it would be very easy to sell sex if you didn't love someone and very difficult if you did. I don't think it would be even possible if you loved someone. I think it would destroy all love. You see, I tried. I found the man who bought the three nudes, and I sold myself as well. I thought if I could just get the money and prove my love for him and for art, then I could fix things, put it all right again. I would be giving him what no one else could. My sacrifice would be a bond beyond anything else, something of supreme worth."

The room was dreadfully quiet. Then Lucy inferred, "But it didn't work, did it?"

"No, he took half the money and gave me back the rest and told me, 'Go home little girl, this is no place for you.' And I went, like someone whose soul had been ripped out of them through a great gaping wound of reality."

Sally gave a little sob and then a dismissive little wave of don't-mind-me. But I realized I was dry eyed, and finally, very, very light and unconstrained. I'd carried around this dead love for so long, that pruning it away now didn't hurt at all. I simply couldn't wait to fill the space it left with all the good things in my life and, for a moment, I longed to be home. To see my wild flower garden—the poppies, baby blue eyes, scarlet sage, and columbines—and watch the sun set over the Pacific at the end of another day. To smell rye bread baking and hear my dog, Maggie, barking. To taste the grapes and the new wine. To feel the excitement of looking at a new artist's work or the deep satisfaction of finding something in an old work that I'd never seen before. And probably most of all, to settle down at night and wrap my legs in Jeffery's, to feel the cool sheets against my skin and his warm breath in my hair. This was what I wanted, what I'd always wanted, just to be me, without my magic cloak to hide behind.

"If it hurts so dreadfully when love ends, I wonder why we keep falling in love if sex alone is enough to sustain the species?" Lucy pondered.

"Oh, Lucy, you never change. Always some esoteric question," Becca laughed.

"Maybe love is letting someone be who they are, and we can't do without it because then we'd simply cease to be."

"Let it go, Lucy. I say we all get out on the beach and scream," Wallee suggested, and I realized then that she'd been holding my hand the whole time, just as I'd once held hers while she poured out the worst of her pain.

"Yes, let's," I agreed. "Hot sunshine is just what I need right now."

We went to find our sun hats and lotion and were just about to go out when the phone rang. Our little group was waiting by the doors to the porch on the ocean side when Becca returned.

"That was the guard at the gate," Becca said. "Millie is here."

We all hurried to the windows by the door to the street, crowding around to watch. A few minutes later a well dressed matron stepped out of a white Lincoln Town Car. Her clothes were bright, yellow and green, but conservatively cut. Her hair and face were almost completely hidden behind sunglasses and an enormous blue hat. She carried a huge, yellow Coach handbag and a small paper bag of Mrs. Fields cookies.

Becca opened the door and she breezed in. The hat sailed across the room revealing a messy, platinum blond bob with dark roots showing. The sunglasses were dropped on the table by the door along with her car keys and the cookies. The enormous, yellow handbag was deposited on the coffee table, and then she turned to face us, arms outstretched. I'd have recognized her teasing eyes and smile anywhere. Since I was afraid no one else was going to hug her, I did.

27

Millie by Wallace Anne Mason

Your embrace releases murderous consorts,
Who slay the gentle graces,
And free the unbelled cat.
           Lucy Jones

I'd like to think that I was chosen to speak for Millie because I'd finally learned to keep my head when all about me were losing theirs. But I guess the real reason is that I was the closest thing we had to an objective witness to the hours Millie spent with us that afternoon. Just as I'd expected, no one knew what to say when Millie breezed in, not even Sally. We were all so uncomfortable, it was like some unpleasant itch had infected us. I don't think Millie had ever understood women much anyway. She never offered to do something, like straighten up or wash dishes. I don't know if it just never occurred to her to do these things or if she had a real disdain for those who did.

Sally and Bobbie Jean gave her a hug, and, I think, I gave her kiss on the cheek. She had always been a tease and I think that's all she meant for this to be. I don't think she ever meant for it to get so out of hand. But when I saw her standing there in Becca's living room, the first thing that popped into my head was how closely she matched the image I had conjured up when Lucy had described the babe with balls. A cat on the prowl.

When she dropped onto the sofa, the others joined her in the living room. "What's with the hats?" she asked and then she must have realized, we were all decked out for the beach. Skin conscious. She didn't look like she'd been on a beach in the daylight in ten or twenty years.

"We were just going out," Becca explained. "Care to join us?"

But she ignored the invitation, and instead ask, "Well, ladies, what have I missed so far?" Sally and I sat down. Then Bobbie Jean ease herself onto the arm of Sally's chair.

"Too much to go over again," Becca insisted. She and Lucy were still standing.

"Ah, that's okay. Let me guess. You're all moms. Becca, you're divorced. Wallee, you, Sally, and Bobbie Jean don't work. And Lucy, you're remarried," she pretended to conjecture, seeming to enjoy the look of surprise.

"That's almost right," Bobbie Jean said. "How did you know?"

"Ya got that look. But, maybe, you're not a mom, huh?" Millie asked her.

"I told her," Sally confessed. She was definitely not amused.

"And did you tell them about me, too?"

"Yes, I'm sorry, but I had to. You didn't give me any choice," Sally said looking her straight in the eye.

"Aay, that's okay. As long as you got it right. Did you tell 'em I got twenty-three girls now, two houses, and plenty of money?"

But Sally was not as easy to shock as she used to be. Instead she shot back, "No, you never gave me any of the details."

"Well, it's true. Pretty good for a little girl from Ashbeen, Georgia, and I've broken a few hearts in my day, too."

"What about the jail time?" Becca returned.

"Even that works out well. The local constables gotta make their public quotas. I like to take some time off every winter. So, they put me up and get their *Atta Boy*'s, and I get a vacation."

"It can't be that easy," I said doubtfully.

"You'd be surprised what having the right people in your obligation will do."

"How are you really, Millie?" Lucy wanted to know. "You've told us your business is good. But how about you?"

"I'm okay fine, Lucy. And I have you to thank."

"Me? What did I do?" she asked.

"Well, I figure y'all showed me my true calling that summer at Tybee Beach when you buried me in the sand and left me there. That's when I first discovered how powerful sex could be. All those guys hanging around with their tongues out. Just to see one even if it was made out of sand."

Becca and I laughed. Bobbie Jean and Sally exchanged looks. That should have been my first warning that things were not what they seemed to be, but I missed it.

"So, do you actually enjoy your work?" Lucy asked curiously.

"Yeah, what'd you think? That I had to do this cause I couldn't do nothing else? Cause Brinkley killed Allen and all my girlhood dreams." She laughed but made sure Lucy got the point.

"Brinkley didn't kill Allen," Becca said. "And Lucy didn't have anything to do with the wreck."

"Did I say she did? Lighten up, Becca, will ya. Is that your daughter?" She asked nodding in the direction of the pictures on the mantle.

"Yes, that's Shea," Becca answered stiffly.

"Pretty girl."

"Thank you, I'm very proud of her."

"I'll bet you are. Nice body."

"So, Millie. Have *you* never wanted any family?" I asked, hoping to deflect Millie's barbed comment before Becca really took offense.

"Are you kidding? Me want kids? Not a chance. I see one of my girls stop sometimes—thinks she's found Mr. Right—only to be fat and lonely a few years later, while her hubby either runs out on them or cares only about the kiddies." That was pretty much what happened to Millie's mama, I thought.

"Well, you certainly had us fooled thirty years ago," Sally said. "Why were you in Future Homemakers?"

"Oh, that was Mama. She had this other plan she'd hatched for me."

"And what was that?"

"Allen. She wanted me to hook Allen. 'Really good catch,' she'd say. 'Get safely married. Set for life.' "

"And did you fall for him, Millie? Were you in love? " Sally asked. "I thought you only dated him once or twice."

"Yeah, well, I tried. For a while there I was sort of planning to get pregnant and force him to marry me." She said this in an off-hand way like telling of a plan to invite him over to dinner.

"Millie, you can't mean that," Sally said in a tone that was truly stunned. So, she can still be shocked, I thought.

"Sure I do. What else did I have going for me? I wasn't pretty like Bobbie Jean or smart like Lucy. Or even witty like Becca. But I didn't need that. I had all I needed, right between my legs. Allen was crazy for me." Eyebrows went up all over that time.

"Did you love him?" I asked. I should have known better than to egg her on.

"What did it matter? He had the hots for me. He made me feel special. But Brinkley fixed that, didn't he Lucy?"

"What do you mean, Millie?" she asked rigidly. "That's twice you've mentioned Brinkley. Just exactly what do you mean? What are you getting at?" Lucy's hands were starting to clinch.

Maybe, Millie realized that was her signal to back off, to change the subject, because when she continued her tone was lighter, definitely more kidding. "Only that I never got my chance, that's all. Becca, y'all got anything to eat? It's about lunch time, and I'm starved."

This suggestion set us all rushing to put out plates and fix stuff for lunch. This was familiar territory, things that we could handle. Millie stopped me and got me to sit and talk while the others worked.

"Hey, Wallee, where's your brace?" she asked.

"I don't have to wear it all the time any more, just when I get tired," I explained. "I even got to dance at my daughter's wedding last year."

"Yeah, that's great. Why don't ya take a load off? Come sit by me and catch me up while lunch is fixing," she suggested patting the seat next to her. She pumped me for the details on the others. While they set out the salad, deviled eggs, sliced tomatoes, and bruschetta, I filled her in on their marriages, careers, and children. I thought she was genuinely interested in hearing about it. But maybe, while they were absorbed in details, she was working out her strategy.

"Got any wine or beer?" she hollered toward the kitchen. "They really need to loosen up a little," she whispered to me.

"Bobbie Jean brought the wine. I think it comes from her own vineyard," Sally said.

"No, from a neighbor's," Bobbie Jean corrected. "But it's one of the oldest wineries in California and so very Old World. I think you'll particularly like the Cabernet Sauvignon, I do," she said to everyone as she put two bottles on the table, one white and one red, and Becca set the wine glasses beside them.

"Come on everyone. Enjoy." Becca ordered. She turned her CD player on, and Percy Faith's orchestra spilled out the soft strains of *A Summer Place*.

"I never hear that that I don't think of Tybee Island," Bobbie Jean smiled.

Millie poured herself a glass of white wine and filled her plate from the picnic laid out on the kitchen counter. The others followed her lead. We crowded around the table by the windows overlooking the ocean, and started talking about crabbing and swimming and flirting at the Sugar Shack so many years before. Millie didn't say much, she just listened to us reminisce.

"Is that old place still there?" Becca asked me.

"Many of the old houses on Tybee Island have been leveled for condos in the last few years," I said sadly. "I think the place we stayed that summer is still there, though. It was last spring."

"The land must be worth a whale of a lot more than that old house," Millie offered. "I wonder if it's for sale."

"The Sugar Shack is still standing, but they don't carry that wonderful strawberry ice cream anymore," I added. "And the lighthouse is still there."

"What about that little lake in the mountains?" Sally asked.

"I don't think I could find it again if I had to," Lucy declared. "I have trouble just finding my reading glasses." We all laughed and agreed. We had glasses scattered all over our houses.

"Miss Jennings died last year," Becca told us. "I ran into her once in Atlanta at the airport. Do you know, she still remembered my name and that I'd married Richard. I think she was the best teacher I ever had."

I raised my glass in a little toast and said, "We were all so desperate not to be *just* teachers. Well, maybe we were wrong. She was a great lady. She really made a difference in my life."

"Do you remember the red stain she used to have in the hair near her temple sometimes?" Lucy laughed. "We could always tell when she'd been grading a bunch of really bad papers if that red was there. She must have run her finger through her hair while she was grading, and the worse the papers were the more red ink she used and the more she pulled at her hair."

"My spelling was so awful, it's a wonder the poor woman had any hair left."

The music and good food and wine were starting to work. We'd begun to relax again. To let down our guard.

"Can you stay 'til tomorrow?" Becca asked Millie as she cleared away her plate. I knew she was just being polite. Maybe she recognized something the rest of us had missed and really didn't want Millie around. It was like she was afraid she'd break something. Millie must have known it too, because she began to make her excuses.

"No, I gotta get back tonight. I've been away too long. Things get kind of out of hand when I'm gone for long."

I think she'd planned to just pull Sally aside and explain before she headed home, but then Bobbie asked, "What is it you do when you're there?" And it was like she couldn't resist one more game. Damn.

"Are you sure you want to know?" Millie replied, taking another glass of wine. Bobbie Jean always did blush easily with that fair skin, and she flushed crimson when she realized what she might have started.

"Why don't you tell us and let's see," Becca said.

"I interview the new girls, and if I like them and they wanna stay, I'll train them, teach them to take care of themselves, decide which clients would go for them, settle fights between girls, keep them from leaving.... Not too different from what your mamas did for you or you do for your daughters." As if she were hoping to find a nerve, Millie tossed out the bait.

Becca struck first, "I try to teach my daughter that she has unlimited opportunities, that she doesn't have to sell herself short."

"My mama never felt I needed to learn to pretend to love someone." Sally said, nibbling but not yet taking the hook.

"What do you teach your daughter about making it in the business world, Becca? Is selling your soul to some corporation better than selling your body?"

"I wouldn't know. I've never done either."

"And what about you, Lucy? You were the one who wanted to be a courtesan. Ever try it?"

"No, I guess I was lucky. I found a better way to get what I wanted."

"And what was that? What did you want?" Millie probed.

"A chance to get my ideas heard. A chance to do something that might make a difference."

"And have you?"

"I'd like to think so," she said, but her voice was even less certain than her words. Millie should have stopped then, but it was like she couldn't help herself.

"Maybe you just sold out. Married not once, but twice. Couldn't quite make it on your own, could you? Had to sell your freedom for security? I thought you'd like that feeling of really getting dirty playing with the boys." she said and jerked the hook.

"Why did you come here?" I interrupted, hoping I could stop this before any real harm was done. But maybe I was just playing into her hands.

"I don't know. Why did you?"

"Because these girls helped me, in ways big and small, to become who I am. Because we had some good times together, and we weathered some bad times, too. And I thought I'd like to see them again and remember some of those things," I answered.

"Well that goes for me, too. If Lucy had a hand in getting you dancing, why can't she be responsible for me as well? Or maybe she just didn't try hard enough to save me. Maybe I wasn't as worthy as you."

Lucy's face went white, but her voice was stronger as she asked, "Why do you blame me, Millie? What is it that you wanted from me?"

"Didn't Brinkley ever tell you Lucy? No, I guess not." I don't know why she did it, but she looked right at Lucy, nailing her to the spot with the worst thing I could imagine. "They were arguing over you, baby. I had told Allen about your little flying dream, the one you described to us that night at Wallee's. All of them knew, and they all wanted a crack at you. The dream fucker. The walking wet dream. That's what they called you."

"That's enough Millie," Sally shouted, jumping up from the table. Her chair turned over with a crash. "I think you should leave."

"I thought you knew," she laughed. "David told me. He was in the back seat that night and pretty drunk, but he said they were really going at it. Allen called Brinkley a homo. He claimed Brinkley just wasn't doing it right, that he probably didn't even know how. Allen wanted his turn. After all, anyone who could come just dreaming about stars should be an easy lay. You were, Lucy, weren't you?"

"Millie, shut up," Becca growled.

"See, Lucy, they all know, too. They just haven't told you. Everyone knew," she said quietly, her eyes narrowing but her lips still smiling. She was playing her trump card.

"Don't believe her, Lucy," Bobbie Jean said, "There was an inquest. Don't you remember? Brinkley fell asleep at the wheel. He said so. She's making this up."

"Why would I do that? I'm grateful to Lucy, she saved me from marriage, definitely a fate worse than death." She laughed, but I believe she meant every word of it, because she added, "Marriage is a terrible investment. If I had married Allen, we'd probably both be dead."

Lucy looked at the others. Was it true? Her eyes moved from face to face and stopped at Becca's. "Becca?" she pleaded.

"Richard would have told me. I would have told you, Lucy. I swear this isn't true," Becca vowed.

"Why are you doing this, Millie?" Sally demanded.

"Because it's time she knew. Don't you think?"

"Millie, I don't get it," Bobbie Jean countered, refusing to take the bait. "You weren't stupid. You could have worked as a secretary or gone to college and gotten a regular job. You didn't turn to prostitution for the money, regardless of what you say. You seem to enjoy playing with us and making yourself the victim. It's almost as if you want our disdain and disapproval. I wonder if you even are what you've told Sally and the rest of us you are."

None of us was prepared for her abrupt reply. She roared with laughter. "Couldn't fool you, could I? Well, Mrs. Roberta Jean Whatever, you are absolutely right. The only victim here is Sally."

"Me?" Sally gasped.

She looked at our bewildered faces and seemed to be enjoying a wonderful joke or savoring her revenge. And then she started to explain, "I was married...for awhile. I even finished UGA and got a Masters. But, I had this *little* problem."

"What problem? Or which problem, it sounds to me like you've had plenty," Becca said, her anger clearly showing as she balled up a paper napkin and threw it in the trash, then she slammed a plate against the counter so hard it cracked and splintered, causing us all to shift our focus momentarily from Millie to her. She turned her back to us and grabbed the edge of the sink, as if trying hard to regain her balance both physically and emotionally.

I guess it was then Millie realized that maybe she had gone too far. She tried to start over in a softer voice without all the earlier bravado, "I...I like to gamble...too much. I push everything to the edge. It gives me a thrill I can't quite describe...but it has also destroyed my marriage and nearly every friendship I've ever made. And it's kept me in debt most of the time. I was going to Gamblers Anonymous for awhile, really. I swear I was. I thought if I told Sally that I had a gambling problem, she'd never lend me one red cent...but if I told her I was a poor, tragic prostitute...well, she'd feel sorry for me and send me some cash. And she did."

We all just sat there, angry, dumbfounded, and incredulous. Like we couldn't believe this was all a ruse to get money from Sally.

"Is this some nasty little prank like something a bunch of fraternity boys would pull? Didn't you realize or care how much it would hurt?" Becca asked. "God, what were you thinking, Millie?"

She looked genuinely contrite for a moment, then the manic bounce returned, like she knew we'd all forgive her when we knew the rest. She went on in a rush, "When Mama died in '89 and I came into a little money...well guess what ladies, I finally found the right craps table—Wall Street. I've made a mint in the last ten years, y'all," She smiled, proudly waving her diamond bejeweled hand. But it wasn't enough, we weren't smiling with her. Shit, I thought, she's done it again.

"Why the charade today?" Becca asked. "Why didn't you just tell us?"

"Had you going, didn't I?"

Millie winked at Becca, still hoping we'd get her amazing joke, but when no one did, she spelled it out, "Because y'all had it coming for that time you buried me in the sand. Especially you, Lucy. I don't blame you or Brinkley for Allen's death. I never did. God, I barely knew him. But I've been pissed for almost forty years about that damned sand sculpture," she gloated gleefully until she realized she was still laughing alone.

"It really isn't funny, Millie," Sally said. "I don't like it that you took advantage of me."

"Oh God, Sally, please don't be so hard on me. I'll make it up to you. Really, I will. Next time I go to jail, I'll take you along."

"And where were you, if you weren't really in jail?"

"Shopping. In Hong Kong. And Singapore. For discount investments. They've had some really great deals this year. You just needed the balls to go after them. Want to go with me next time?" She cocked her head to one side and looked at us, and when no one answered, she continued, "I'll say one thing for you. You're pretty accepting. You really were ready to make a place for me here, whatever I was. I like that."

Sally finally gave in and gave her a hug. But the rest of us hung back. Only Becca would meet her eyes and Becca wasn't smiling.

Then, drawn like a moth to Millie's flame, Lucy asked, "You aren't day-trading, are you?"

"No, thank heavens. I refuse to learn anything about computers, even though my fingers are itching to play. I know I'd be addicted." She smiled at Lucy, and the tension between them eased a bit. "A good part of the money is in a trust, so I can't gamble it away. My lawyer insisted. Old fart thinks I'll lose his meal ticket." And she added, sincerely meaning it, "Thanks for asking, honey."

It wasn't enough though. She'd lost big this time, and I think she knew it. She started gathering up her hat and bag and began making her good-byes. As she bent over to give Lucy a hug, she kissed her on the cheek and whispered, "Do you still have that dream?" Then she secretly dropped something in her lap, and still laughing to herself, she left the house.

28

Lucy

Your kiss melts glacial kingdoms
  millenniums in suspension,
And with a boiling fury,
Floods all sensory orders,
Devastating, arcing,
Overloading in a heartbeat
Such ordinary paths.

Lucy Jones

"What was that?" Becca asked, letting out a deep breath like she'd been holding it forever.

"Talk about nightmares," Wallee whistled.

We sat hardly daring to move, Percy Faith still playing on the CD. The very walls even seemed to be catching their breath. I felt as though I'd been knocked down by a powerful wave and rolled along the bottom until I was not sure of any direction. I thought of Annie's frantic struggle to keep her head above the water at any cost. Had I turned my back on Millie like I had on the dog? Let it go, I told myself. Don't go there. But the horrible agony of the two little girl friends caught in that bloodthirsty death grip at the lake so long ago, flash before my eyes.

"What did she give you, Lucy?" I heard Bobbie Jean ask and saw her peering over my arm.

I blinked at her to try to focus, then looked at the package in my lap. Wrapped in red paper with black Chinese characters and fastened with tape, the small square was no more than three by three. I picked it up by one corner and dropped it on the table, then quickly pushed it away.

"You open it," I said.

Becca loosed the tape on one end and poured onto the table a small pair of highly stylized, golden wings on a delicate gold chain.

"What on earth?" Sally gasped.

"It must be symbolic." Bobby Jean said. "But is it a charm or a curse?"

"Maybe it's a threat…or an apology."

"How did she know that flying dreams are still important to me?" I asked.

"Perhaps she didn't know."

"I'll bet she is the one who told," Becca suggested.

"Told?" I left the question hanging in the air.

"Yes, Lucy, that night when you told us about your dream for the first time, I was afraid of the rumors that might get out. And although everyone promised not to, someone did tell," Wallee explained.

"Oh, I never knew."

For a moment no one said anything, then Bobbie Jean confessed. "No, y'all, it wasn't Millie who told. It was me," she sighed. "I'm so sorry, Lucy. But I thought it was a joke, that you were just making it up. I'll bet Millie didn't even know about the rumors. I don't think she meant for what just happened to get so out of control."

I couldn't count all the times Bobbie Jean had been there for me. I'd dropped a piece of chocolate pie on her mama's rug, and she had taken the blame for me. I'd tortured her with a June bug, and she'd never told. She'd been my bride's maid in the wedding from Hell. And I'd never kept my promise to her. How could I have been so careless with something so precious, I wondered.

"Forget it, Bobbie Jean," I assured her. "It was nothing. I never even knew." I could feel the fragile thread between us tremble, but it didn't break. I don't think I could have born that.

"What are you going to do with it?" Wallee asked pointing to Millie's gift.

"Bury it," Becca said. "You can't accept this. You've got to get rid of it."

"I agree," Sally said. "It's too spooky, even if it is a coincidence. The sooner that thing is out of here, the better I'll feel."

"You're right." I concurred. "I'd never be able to look at it without thinking that maybe I'd failed her in some way. Can we use your beach, Becca?"

"Yes and now, let's do it now," she insisted.

Bobbie Jean poured the last of the wine into her glass then slid the chain and wings into the empty wine bottle and plugged it with the cork. Becca selected the largest, silver serving spoon to use as a shovel, and we all headed out into the afternoon sun without stopping for our hats and sunscreen. Just inside the last line of dunes, Becca dropped to her knees and scooped out the hole in the soft, white sand. Bobbie Jean set the bottle in place, and we all helped Becca to her feet. Then we kicked the sand over the grave.

"Let us bury here all hopeless loves, both true and false," Wallee said.

"And all attempts to be other than what we are," said Sally.

"And any beliefs that still linger that we can save those who won't be saved," I said.

"Let's fill all that wasted space with peace and grace however small," Bobbie Jean added.

"And live the rest of our lives as they are." Becca shouted.

"To the rest of our lives!"

I'm glad our husbands and our daughters couldn't see us, because we acted like complete fools. We shouted and whooped. We were singing and hollering and cheering, until we gasped for breath. First we embraced and applauded each other, then we raised our arms to salute the heavens. We were dancing and prancing and stomping the sand, until the sweat poured down and mixed with the tears of joy and laughter already running down our necks. And when we couldn't say another word, we just leaned on each other and giggled.

Just as we were going back inside, Wallee's leg collapsed under her, and she would have fallen except for Becca's and Sally's quick move to catch her. "I'm quite exhausted," she said barely above a whisper. "I think I'd better go in and lie down. Sally, will you come sit with me a while?"

"Of course," she replied and squeezed Wallee's arm.

While Wallee rested, Bobbie Jean, Becca and I cleaned up the remains of lunch. We covered the leftovers and returned them to the refrigerator, started the dishwasher, and straightened up the living room, where Millie's presence still hung like a dusty web across an otherwise cheerful scene.

"Bobbie Jean, how did you know that she was faking?" I asked.

"When I told Jeffery that I wanted to work with AIDS patients in the 80's, he insisted I get some professional help first. You see, his first wife, Charlotte, had committed suicide. She had a fragile personality anyway, but the despair she saw while doing charity work with battered children was too much. She became entangled in a hopeless situation and could not rise above it. Jeffery didn't want to see that happen to me. I got help to please him, but I was glad I did."

"And do you really believe that she has never been a prostitute?" I asked.

"Yes. I've seen a good many hookers at the women's shelter. It just didn't ring true. It's much more likely she has a gambling problem. She may have been married though. Did you notice all the diamonds? I'm no expert, but they sure looked real to me. And she could just as well have been in Hong Kong as in jail."

"Then why was her phone discontented when I tried to call?" Becca asked.

"Well, she never could take care of herself. She probably just forgot to pay the bill."

Sally appeared in the doorway. "I think we should eat in tonight rather than going out. Wallee should rest up for the long drive home tomorrow."

"That will work," Becca concurred. "There's a seafood place with take out just up the road. Lucy and I can go get it."

"What time is your flight tomorrow, Bobbie Jean?" Sally asked.

"Around noon. I should leave by nine."

"Me too."

"Is Wallee all right? Can she make the drive to Savannah?" I asked.

"Yes, she'll be fine. She said she'd wear her brace tonight, just in case."

"What I want right now is a long, hot bath," Becca announced.

"That sounds like heaven to me, too." Bobbie Jean agreed. "Why don't we go first and use up all the hot water."

"What a plan! Last one in is a rotten egg."

The rest of the afternoon and evening passed without event. We were all tired and the excitement had caught up with us. We talked quietly, filling in the details of our lives and reviewing each other's snapshots. We laughed about the common little tricks we used to get through the day, the little deals we made with ourselves—like trading off an hour of reading for an hour of vacuuming. We discussed our favorite films and books. But wherever our conversation led, it always seemed to come back to Millie, like some sore spot you can not help touching.

"You don't suppose the figure in your dream is Millie, do you, Lucy?" Bobbie Jean asked.

"I don't see how that's possible. I had no idea where she was or what she was doing. Not that we know now for sure."

"It does bare a morbid similarity though, doesn't it?" Sally shuddered.

"What were you and Wallee talking about this afternoon?" I asked to change the subject. They exchanged a furtive glance. I was wondering why Wallee had sought out Sally rather than Bobbie Jean.

"I was asking Sally what it's like to know you may be dying," Wallee said.

"It's not what you think," Sally added hastily. "Wallee isn't dying."

"Not any faster than the rest of you anyway," Wallee drawled.

Sally patted her hand and said, "Do you remember that game we used to play at camp? I don't know what it was called, but the counselors would give us big paper bags with all kinds of ridiculous things inside: a hat, a spoon, a piece of gum, a plastic fish…"

"Yeah, I remember," Bobbie Jean said. "We were suppose to make up a skit using the things in the bag as props."

"Well, that's what I think life is like. You get this big bag full of all sorts of meaningless stuff. It's what you do with the stuff that gives life meaning."

"That and the friends you have to share it with."

The morning of our departure dawned bright and hot. I took my coffee cup out on the porch only to change my mind when the humid air washed over me. The heat was already creating those waving patterns in the air above the sand, like a miasma of torrid affliction. I was just turning to go back into the cool house when I saw the bottle lying by the path. Setting my cup down on the table, I walked down the steps and out to the spot where we had buried Millie's gift the afternoon before. The hole had been dug up, and the bottle lay open in the sand. Neither the cork nor the chain and wings were anywhere to be seen. I looked up and saw Becca on the porch and waved for her to join me.

"What is it? What's happened?" she asked as she walked toward me. When she saw the bottle and the hole, she added, "You didn't do this, did you?"

"Of course not. But who did?"

"Well, we weren't exactly quiet about it. Anyone could have seen the ruckus we were making and come to see what we were up to."

"Yes, I suppose so. Or a dog could have dug up the bottle."

"A dog wouldn't be able to open it. More likely my neighbor with the metal detector. He's out early most every morning, although he usually stays closer to the water."

"You're right. It's nothing too mysterious."

"I see no need to disturb the others, do you?"

"No, not now anyway."

So we kicked the bottle back in the hole and brushed the sand back over it.

A little before nine, with hugs and promises to keep in touch by email, we took our leave.

Epilogue

"What's this?" he asked.
"Just something. A little gift."
"And you're going to wear it all the time. Even to bed?"
"Yes, I don't have the nightmares when I wear it," she said.

Notes

This text refers to several children's games: Red Rover, Jack's Alive, and Strut Miss Lizzie.

Red Rover is a game familiar to most people raised in the US in the last eighty years. The game is played with two teams of equal number. Each team's members link arms and form a line with teams facing about twenty to thirty feet apart. Each team in alternate turn requests a member from the other team by calling, "Red Rover, Red Rover send (child's name) right over." The selected child runs at the opposing team's line attempting to break through. If he succeeds, he may select a player from the opposing team to return with him to his own team. If he fails, he is captured by the opposing team and joins its line. The objective is to completely win over all members of the opposing team.

Jack's Alive is an obscure campfire game. The starter for the game removes a stick about a foot long from the fire. The stick should have a glowing coal at the tip. Each player in turn blows gently on the tip, and if the coal glows, she says, "Jack's Alive." and passes the stick to the next person in the campfire circle. The objective is to never be the person holding the stick when the coal is no longer glowing. The loser is usually given a task to do, such as singing a song or telling a story, or she may have to be the one to cleanup the campsite or put out the trash.

Strut Miss Lizzie is purely a girls' game. The only objective is to be as silly and whimsical as possible. The players form two lines and clap and chant a little ditty: "Strut, strut, strut Miss Lizzie...Here comes another one just like the other one...." Each girl in turn walks between the lines strutting in her own style, this could include vamping, shimmying, wiggling, bumping, slinking, skipping, dancing, blowing kisses.... Occasionally the game may include props such as floppy hats, long strands of beads, feather boas. There was a ragtime song of the same name by J. Henry Creamer written in 1921, but I can find no direct link between the two.

The poem "If" by Rudyard Kipling was first published in 1910 as a pendant to the story "Brothers Square-Toe" in the book *Rewards and Fairies*. It now appears in over 150 sites on the World Wide Web. It was required memory work for many students of the 1950's and 1960's. Some critics believe that the single biggest weakness in the poem is the line: 'If neither foes nor loving friends can hurt you...," because it suggests that the real man will never let friends get so close to him that he could be hurt by them.

References

The poems "If" by Rudyard Kipling and "The Fool's Prayer" by Edward Rollin Sill appear here as memorized by the author.
All other poetry is the work of the author.